Burning the Map

LAURA CALDWELL

was born in Chicago and raised in suburban Crystal Lake, Illinois. She attended the University of Iowa, where she graduated Phi Beta Kappa.

Laura returned to Chicago and became the third generation of the Caldwell family to attend Loyola University School of Law. After graduation, she spent a month with two girlfriends in Italy and Greece, a trip that spurred the idea for *Burning the Map*.

Laura began her legal career at a large Chicago firm where she became a trial lawyer, specializing in medical malpractice defense. Later, she worked at smaller firms and eventually became a partner.

Despite juggling trial work and a relationship with an equity trader (who is now her husband), Laura began taking writing classes and weekly writing workshops in the mid-nineties. Her work has been published in *Woman's Own, The Young Lawyer, The Illinois Bar Journal* and many other magazines. *Burning the Map* is her first novel.

Laura has taken a sabbatical from her practice and is currently teaching legal writing at Loyola University School of Law.

Burning
the Map

Laura Caldwell

**RED
DRESS
INK** ™

First edition November 2002

BURNING THE MAP

A Red Dress Ink novel

ISBN 0-373-25021-5

Visit Red Dress Ink at www.reddressink.com

Printed in U.S.A.

ACKNOWLEDGMENTS

I lucked out by getting the most
wonderful editor, Margaret Marbury,
and the most amazing agent, Maureen Walters
of Curtis Brown, Ltd. A thousand thanks to both
of them, as well as everyone at Red Dress Ink.

Much admiration and appreciation to
my writing instructors and fellow workshop members,
especially Pam Sourelis of Green Door Studio
and Jerry Cleaver of The Loft.

I am eternally grateful for everyone who took
the time to read drafts of this novel and offer their
suggestions including: Beth Kaveny, Suzanne Burchill,
Katie Caldwell Kuhn, Christi Caldwell,
Rochelle Wasserberger, Ginger Heyman,
Ted McNabola, Kelly Harden, Kris Verdeck,
Trisha Woodson, Kelly Caldwell, Joan Posch,
Alisa Spiegel and Edward Worden.

Thanks also to everyone who offered moral support
and guidance, especially Margaret Caldwell,
William Caldwell, Kim Wilkins, Kevin Glenn,
Miguel Ruiz, Karen Billups, Beth Garner,
Dave Ellis and Mary Hoover.

Lastly, and most importantly, this book
is for Jason Billups, who makes everything possible.

PART I
ROME, ITALY

1

Our taxi bumps and jostles its way along Rome's cobbled streets, swerving around centuries-old buildings, narrowly missing women shopping at the outdoor markets. The scent that gusts through the open windows is old and heavy. Lindsey and Kat wrinkle their noses, but to me it's a sweet, familiar fragrance—bread and dust and wine and heat. The way Rome always smells in the summer.

I haven't been to Europe since my junior year in college, most of which I spent in Italy sodden with Chianti and wide-eyed over a bartender named Fernando, yet I've always considered Rome my second home after Chicago. It's a place that sticks with me, so that an image in a movie or a line in a song can immediately send me back here in my mind. Now I really am back, and I feel the first twinge of optimism I've had in months.

The taxi driver continues his Formula One maneuvers through the slim stone streets, winding toward Piazza Navona. The Colosseum appears before us, a towering, earthy structure with gaping holes like missing teeth. I raise my hand to point it out to the girls, but the driver accelerates and flies by it with all the reverence of passing a 7-Eleven store.

"We are definitely going to crash," Lindsey says through clenched teeth as a pack of mopeds streaks alongside and passes the taxi.

I laugh for what feels like the first time in a long time. "No, he won't. This is how they drive here. He knows what he's doing."

Lindsey gives me a long look, which was designed, I'm sure, to wither her underlings at the ad agency where she's been crawling up the ranks for the last four years. "What he's doing is trying to kill us. You know some Italian, Casey. Tell him to slow down."

Lindsey, or Sin, as we call her, has always been a pragmatic, cut-through-the-crap type of person, but all that cutting seems to have sharpened her edges. Lately, she often borders on a state of irritation, and I find myself holding my breath around her, afraid to piss her off. Her nickname is something of a misnomer, since she's the most straight-laced of all of us. The name should have been bestowed on Kat instead.

I lean forward in my seat. "My friends find you attractive," I say to the driver in rudimentary Italian. In fact, I think I may have referred to him in terms usually saved for food, but he seems to get the point.

The thirtyish, swarthy, perspiring man slows the cab considerably and gives Kat and Lindsey a meaningful look in the rearview mirror.

"*Grazie,*" Kat calls to the driver, trying out one of the Italian words I taught her on the plane.

I'd also told Kat and Sin that one of the most important Italian words they could learn was *basta,* which, loosely translated, means "get the fuck away from me." It would come in handy for some of the Italian men, I explained. Lindsey had nodded intently, mouthing the word, but Kat told me I was nuts. She wanted to *meet* Italian men, not tell them to take a hike.

You know that stereotype about how most men are like dogs, wanting to mate with hundreds of different women, while we gals pine away for the split-level suburban home, minivan and offspring? Well, Kat blows that one out of the water. She constantly has at least three guys on deck in case she gets bored with the current one, and I don't think she's been celibate for more than two weeks since I met her eight years ago.

By the time the car rolls down one of the side streets that lead to Piazza Navona, I'm sweating along with the driver and sticking to the cracked leather seats like gum. Yet when the taxi stops outside the courtyard for Pensione Fortuna, the sight of its burbling fountain and abundant flowers rejuvenates me.

"It's gorgeous," Kat says. She pushes open the door and practically skips down the path between the flowers, looking like Maria from *The Sound of Music.*

Sin and I follow her, Sin lugging Kat's suitcase along with her own. Lindsey can be like that—biting and impatient one minute, mothering the next.

The mothering is something I've looked forward to on this trip, since my own mother seems more like a teenage sister right now. For the last year, I've been trudging through my days trying to avoid lengthy, intimate discussions with her, while at the same time attempting to engage in them with my boyfriend, John, who's been practically living at his law firm, slaving over a huge M&A deal. Meanwhile, since I blew off my corporate law class, I can't even have an intelligent conversation with him about his work.

I'd found Pensione Fortuna when my parents came to visit me in Rome, and I'd hoped to bring John here this summer, figuring a few romantic weeks in Italy and Greece would be just what we needed. But he couldn't, or wouldn't, get away.

So I turned to Kat and Sin, knowing that both had always wanted to go to Europe and had lots of vacation time racked up. I hadn't seen much of them this summer, and to be truthful I'd been a little distant before then. I'd spent most of my last year of law school studying at John's condo on Lake Shore Drive, painting and repainting the walls of my own apartment in an attempt to find a color that would uplift me, or holing up in the school's library checking citations for obscure law review articles no one would ever read. Even though I've been out of circulation for a while, or maybe because of it, they quickly agreed to the trip: a few days in Rome and then a few weeks in the Greek islands.

I'm determined to make up for lost time with Kat and Sin. I don't want to fall into the same trap my mother has. My father's gradual withdrawal is destroying her, and *I'm* the one she talks to about her womanly needs and her upcoming face-lift, as if she can't trust her friends with that information. But isn't that what friends are for?

As we walk through the courtyard, I notice that it's changed little since I last saw it. A few wrought-iron tables with linen umbrellas still surround the fountain, and the carved oak door to the pensione still stands open.

For a second, I flash back to my parents sitting at one of those tables, sharing a bottle of wine, laughing as they play their hundred thousandth game of gin rummy, but I can't reconcile the image with the present.

"You coming, Casey?" Kat calls from the doorway.

I look at the table one more time, seeing my parents smile and raise their glasses, before I nod at Kat and shake off the memory.

Our room is sparse but cheerful, with three single beds covered in sunny-yellow spreads, the color reminding me of a recent paint I had on my apartment walls. It was cheerful all right, but I could never seem to match my mood to the color. I went next to an eggshell-blue that made me feel twelve years old, then to the current mossy-green. It gives the place a foresty feeling, which can be good or bad depending on whether I'm feeling lost at the moment.

The beds here are placed under huge French windows that open to the courtyard, while a bureau made of dark wood is pushed against one wall, a vase of fresh cut flowers on top. If they'd let me decorate, I'd put the beds on the other side of the room so you could lie down and see the flowering tree outside.

After a two-hour nap, it's eight o'clock at night, and our stomachs are beginning to rumble. We decide to get cleaned up and hit the town.

"What's with this dribbling?" Lindsey calls from the bathroom. "Is this really the shower?"

"Get used to it," I say. I don't know what it is about Europe, but as far as I can tell, the entire continent suffers from a lack of decent water pressure.

When I get my turn in the bathroom, I peer at myself in the mirror and sigh. I'd hoped that taking this trip, even just getting to Rome, would alter me, make me feel more alive, look more exotic. No such luck. Same old Casey.

I give myself a big smile in the mirror, thinking of those self-help books I've read that recommend acting happy as a means of transformation. The grin looks fake, though, almost lecherous under the fluorescent light, so I drop it.

As we get dressed for the night, we fall back into our old patterns—I can't decide what to wear, Lindsey is ready in two seconds and talks me through my outfit decision, and Kat dawdles. Finally, Lindsey and I sit on the bed, waiting for Kat to make her finishing touches—a dab of perfume between her breasts, the application of jewelry.

"Let's go," Kat says at last, but as she turns around from the mirror, something glints and sparkles from her ears.

"Are those diamond earrings?" Sin asks, leaning toward Kat. "Where did you get those?"

Kat fingers an ear, a self-conscious gesture, which is strange for her. "Hatter," she says.

"The Mad Hatter gave you diamonds?" I can't keep the surprise out of my voice. Phillip Hatter is Kat's stepfather, whom she'd nicknamed the Mad Hatter shortly after her mother's marriage to him when she was nine. He's one of those ridiculously wealthy Chicagoans who gets his money from a trust fund and whose name is always in the society pages followed by a phrase like "patron of the arts" or some other pompous description. His contact with Kat is usually limited to those occasions when his presence is absolutely required for a show of family unity. I do recall him being in Ann Arbor for our college graduation four years ago, seeming ill at ease and slightly mortified to have found himself in such a provincial setting. I don't think he's ever given Kat a gift on his own, so the diamond earrings seem a bit much.

Kat shrugs. "They were a present."

"When?" Lindsey asks, her voice hard. "When did he give them to you?"

Kat shoots Sin a look I can't read. "My birthday."

"Oh, shit. I'm sorry," I say. Kat's birthday was in June, and I'd totally forgotten it. For months, I'd been completely consumed with the bar exam and my too-frequent, too-revealing chats with my mom. Menopause, hidden insecurities, vaginal dryness—my Catholic mother who used to shield me from anything she considered unpleasant suddenly has no censor on her mouth. Last week, during one particularly illuminating conversation, I'd learned that my father never really knew how to give her an orgasm.

Kat waves a hand at me, as if to say *don't worry about it,* but she keeps her eyes on Lindsey. I begin to feel like I can't understand some significant undercurrent.

"I was with you on your birthday when we had dinner

with your mom and the Hatter. He didn't give you anything then." Lindsey stares at Kat.

I glance down at the floor for a second, thinking that I wasn't invited to that little dinner party. I can't blame them really, since I didn't even call Kat to wish her a happy birthday, but I've always been included before, and hearing about it now smarts a little.

"It was later," Kat says. "Now let's get out of here." She picks up her purse and heads to the door.

I look at Lindsey, who doesn't move, still watching Kat as if she's trying to decide if she should say something more. She gets up from the bed then, silently following Kat, and I trail behind, wondering what I missed this summer.

2

We purchase paper cups of beer from the McDonald's tucked in a corner of Piazza di Spagna. Beer at McDonald's—just another reason to love Italy. We carry them, looking for a seat on the Spanish Steps, a gorgeous run of wide stone stairs that's topped with a two-towered church and crowded with bushes and people.

"*Basta,*" Sin keeps saying to the young boy of about fourteen who's tailing her and mumbling declarations of love in Italian. "*Basta!*"

She loses him eventually, and we find an open spot on the steps. As I sit down behind Kat and Sin, I make sure to tuck my dress under my legs, but I know it makes little difference, since most of the men in the piazza are looking at us as if we're parading around naked. While this probably sounds unfeminist or downright sad, I rather like the ogling from the Italians, the crude sort of flattery that comes from their eyes so squarely on you that there's no hiding what they're thinking.

For the moment, Lindsey has dropped the diamond earring interrogation, but I know Sin. She won't let it go for long.

"Get a load of those pants," she says, jabbing Kat in the arm and gesturing to a woman in black leather pants and a flimsy camisole that shows off flawless breasts. "She'll sweat her ass off if she has one."

Kat laughs, and she and Sin start talking, quietly pointing out one woman's shoes, another's dress, the distinguished man in the suit smoking a cigar. Talking about someone else—it's the way they always smooth over a rough spot. But it's also the game everyone immediately learns to play in Rome—gawk and be gawked at. Do it too much and you'll convince yourself you're the most poorly dressed person in the city. I'm glad to see Kat and Sin getting along. It'll be a much better trip for all of us if they do, but watching Kat's long, amber locks mix with Sin's short, dark hair as they tilt heads together and laugh only reminds me of hearing about Kat's birthday dinner after the fact.

I lean back and make myself take a deep breath. Light sparkles from the stars and the apartment windows overlooking the piazza, making the place look like a glittering movie set. The Spanish Steps had been a favorite hangout of mine when I lived here, and for a second, being back makes me feel like I did then—fairly confident and actually anticipating the future. Well, the immediate future, anyway. I don't want to think about my parents or even John, who I miss a bit already. I certainly don't want to think about the job that awaits me at Billings Sherman & Lott, one of those oh-so-cool firms featured in a Grisham novel. My law-type friends are green that I landed the gig, but I've been working there for a few months part-time, and the thought of going full-time feels oddly like a prison sentence.

"Case, come down here," Sin says, reaching behind and grabbing my leg.

I scoot down the step as fast as if I'd been offered free shoes.

Once I'm level with them, the three of us huddle together, giggling like schoolgirls, talking about the cute guys and the great clothes until we're interrupted by a shout.

"Hey you! Americans?"

I glance down to see four men, all good-looking, who've just pulled up to the base of the steps. It was just a matter of time before this happened, especially since Kat is with us. All the guys are on very large, expensive-looking Vespa scooters, with the exception of one on a Pepto Bismol pink moped that's on its last legs. The leader of the pack, the one who called to us, is so gorgeous it's silly. He looks like an Italian poster boy—shiny black hair, deep-set liquid brown eyes, full pink lips, the works.

"Biscuit," Kat says.

Biscuit is Kat's irreverent word for a hot guy, or a hot boy for that matter, since she doesn't discriminate on the basis of age.

"How can you tell we're Americans?" Kat calls in her best come-hither voice, cupping a hand around her mouth.

"The most beautiful women are Americans."

"Oh puh-lease," Lindsey says, but Kat is sold.

"Come with me," she whispers as she stands and throws her hair over her shoulders.

I glance at Lindsey, ready to say, "It'll be fine," or some other platitude that she usually looks to me to provide when Kat is on the prowl and we're dragged along, but she doesn't turn to me this time. Instead, she mutters, "Jesus Christ," and heads down the stairs.

We learn that Alesandro, the poster boy, had attended boarding school in London, hence his perfect English. His friends, Massimo and Francesco (of the lame moped), have quite good English, too, making it easy enough to talk. The fourth, Paulo, speaks no *Inglese* whatsoever, and he stands there kicking a foot back and forth while he watches the group. I make an effort to have a brief conversation with him using the minimal Italian I've retained. Unfortunately I can't get past the, "How old are you?" "Where do you live?" stage.

"Why don't you ladies join us for a cappuccino? I know a very good coffee bar near the Pantheon," Poster Boy says.

"As long as we can get food and beer there," Kat says without a glance at Sin or me.

I smile at Sin, geared to reassure her, to tell her that they're just a bunch of harmless pretty boys as far as I can see, that we'll be perfectly safe. Again, her eyes don't seek mine. No conspiratorial grin comes my way.

Poster Boy makes room for Kat on his scooter, and Massimo, a tall, lean guy with an angular face who'd been making eyes at Sin, does the same for her. But she just stands there with a hand on her hip.

"Can we talk about this?" she asks Kat, who's already climbed behind Poster Boy. I take a step toward them, but neither seems to notice.

"Please," Kat says, practically bouncing up and down on the seat. "We need to eat, so we might as well have them take us somewhere."

"Any of them could be Italy's version of Ted Bundy," Sin says.

Kat responds with a shout of laughter.

"Oh, all right." Sin climbs cautiously on Massimo's scooter.

Poster Boy's machine roars to life, and he takes off with Kat, while Massimo and Sin follow closely behind. I watch them pull away, two trails of blue-gray smoke shooting from the scooters, Kat's hair flying in the wind.

I turn around and realize that I'm left there with Paulo and Francesco. I prefer to ride with Paulo, who has a state-of-the-art scooter that could fit a family of five, but he's facing in a different direction.

"He does not feel comfortable because of his English," Francesco explains to me. He's a shorter, solid guy with inky-black, wavy hair and kind eyes.

Paulo and Francesco exchange a few words, and then Paulo is off. Francesco straddles his tiny pink moped, gives me a smile and waves his hand toward the two inches of space behind him as if he's inviting me into a palatial villa. I suck in my stomach, perch on the minuscule seat and hang on like hell.

I've always been the sane middle between Kat's desires run amok and Sin's inability to let hers run enough. The first time I knew I'd found my place was freshman year in college. I hadn't known them long, so I was more the type of friend who passes you a beer rather than one who holds your hair back when you throw up after too many. But they were tight. They'd known each other only six months longer, yet they gave the impression of having been friends since biblical times.

One night, though, something was off-kilter. They'd brought me along to a party given by some senior guys I thought were godlike at the time. The apartment was chock-full of smoke and people and Zeppelin music so loud you could feel the bass in your stomach. I walked into the kitchen to find Kat sitting at the table with two guys, a bottle of Jaegermeister between them. Though easily fifty pounds lighter, Kat was matching both guys shot for shot in some kind of contest. About eight people hung around the table chanting and cheering with each drink. Sin was one of them, but she stood slightly apart, her arms clamped over her chest, her face tense, eyes staring.

"Don't," she said to Kat when another shot was poured, but Kat waved her away with a lazy arm that seemed to float.

I watched this for a minute. I don't know why Sin didn't speak up more, tell her to fucking knock it off, but that's how it is between those two. It's as if Sin can't comprehend Kat's behavior, or maybe she wishes she could be more like her.

Either way, at Kat's craziest moments, Sin seems to lose her usual strength and drop into the background.

I didn't know the whole pattern that night. I just saw one friend about to pass out on her face and another about to combust. So I leaned over Kat, poured a huge triple shot in the plastic cup she was using, and chugged it.

"There," I said, trying not to gag. "She won."

The guys protested, but the crowd around us burst into applause. I pulled Kat from the chair and out the door into a chilly Michigan night.

She slung her arms around my neck in a stumbling hug. "You're all right," she said, her words a little slurry.

"Thanks," Sin said, when she came out with our coats. She squeezed my hand and shot me an open, relieved kind of smile I'd never seen on her before.

I hadn't done much, at least I didn't think so at the time. But I had earned my role in our little group that night. I'd found my place.

The piazza surrounding the Pantheon is aglow in a warm, gold light that shines from the fountain in the middle. Francesco knows the owner of the bar and is able to get us a table just to the right of the fountain. Kat, Lindsey and I order Moretti beers, while Poster Boy orders cappuccinos for his crew.

Once we sit, Poster Boy places his arm around Kat in a way that strikes me as proprietary rather than friendly, but she doesn't seem bothered. She keeps touching him—her fingers grazing his hand, her head resting briefly on his shoulder—and even the way she gazes at him when he's talking seems more a stroke than a look. She's always been a flirt, but this is fast. Maybe it's the change of scenery, being on the other side of the pond for the first time.

I keep glancing at Sin to see if she's noticing this, but she seems more loosened up than usual, too. She asks the guys questions about living in Italy and kids them about their need to tie sweaters around their shoulders.

Meanwhile, Francesco pays little direct attention to me, which is slightly insulting, but just fine, since I'm not looking to hook up. I let the conversation swirl around me while I stare at the Pantheon, a huge circular temple made of stone and cement. The interior design classes I took in college taught me that it's an engineering marvel because of the massive domed ceiling that lets light onto the marble floors, but what really baffles me is that it was originally built in 27 B.C. Ironic, because it's now surrounded by cars and cell phones and platform sandals.

As a History Channel junkie, John would have loved it here if only he could have ripped himself away from the office for a few weeks. Lately, I've wondered if he enjoys his work more than he enjoys me. As I sip my beer, I start to review the moments we've spent together during the past few months, then going back further, to come up with the last time we'd had fun together, real fun, not just the getting-dressed-up-to-go-to-a-cousin's-wedding-and-drinking-bad-table-wine kind of fun. I want to remember the belly laughs, the accidental fun, the spontaneous good times at the end of an otherwise crappy day. We'd had those times at the beginning—the pub crawl we arranged with John's neighbors during a blizzard; the time John surprised me with a weekend trip to Manhattan because I was depressed about a bad grade; the New Year's Day that we drank every bit of leftover alcohol in his place and watched football and movies for fourteen hours. But where are those times lately? Absent, it seems, lost somewhere in the desire for career advancement and the late nights at the library.

"Casey," Lindsey says, bringing me back to Rome, back to the now. "Ready to order dinner?"

I nod.

She leans across the table. "Are you okay?"

I haven't told Kat or Sin about the distance I feel growing between John and me, probably because a different kind
of space has grown between them and myself as well. But
now with Sin looking at me, some concern in her eyes, I wish
that we were alone, just the three of us, so I could spill everything out—my parents' problems, this thing with John that
I can't put my finger on, the way I'm terrified to start working for a living. But Massimo and Francesco turn to me, too,
waiting for me to answer Lindsey's question, so I just nod
again and take the menu from her hand.

Kat orders spaghetti carbonara, a rich, egg-filled pasta.
She's one of those criminally thin people with a perpetually
high metabolism. I opt for a light caprese salad to try to whit-
tle away some of my post bar exam girth, and Lindsey orders the same. When the food comes, she offers bites to
everyone at the table, although only Kat accepts. The tomato
and mozzarella, dribbled with olive oil and sprinkled with
basil, taste ridiculously fresh and healthy, two foreign con-
cepts, since I subsisted the entire summer on various members of the Frito Lay family.

Once I'm finished, I notice that Francesco sits silently
while Kat is busy making faces at Poster Boy. Lindsey, surprisingly, appears to be enjoying her conversation with Massimo. My side of the table is overly quiet except for the
clinking of glasses from other diners and the lilting Italian
music wafting from the bar.

"Pretty hot, huh?" I say to Francesco.

His mouth turns up slightly at the corners, and his eyes
skate to our friends. "It seems to be getting that way."

I follow his glance to find that Poster Boy and Kat are now
kissing like they're alone on a couch somewhere. I wonder
if I should stop her, maybe reach an arm across the table or
toss some cold water like you do with unruly dogs, but I'm
suddenly unsure of myself, of my role. I try to meet Lind-

sey's eyes, but she's talking to Massimo, her back turned to Kat.

"So," I say, looking back at Francesco, who wears an amused expression.

"So," he says, mimicking me, and we both crack up.

Silence settles between us then, during which I try to focus on Sin's explanation of her job to Massimo and ignore the forms of Kat and Poster Boy, which have become a single, entwined mass across the table.

"You are going to be a lawyer?" Francesco finally asks. I'm startled for a second, but then I vaguely remember hearing Lindsey mention my new job to the guys while I was drifting off about John.

I only nod and sip my beer, not sure that he wants a real answer, and a little nervous that he might expect me to follow in Kat's footsteps and lock lips with him.

"What kind of lawyer will you be?" he says, without a trace a flirtation.

"A litigator," I say, thinking this sounds pretty interesting, even if the thought of doing it every day doesn't particularly interest me right now.

"What is 'litigator'?" He's apparently confused with the English and unaware of how cool I am.

"Trials. In front of a judge," I say.

Actually, what I've learned is that litigation really means taking a million depositions about car accidents and medical treatments, compiling page upon page of tedious written discovery, attempting for years to make a settlement, and then maybe, just maybe, eventually trying a case in defense of some company or some person lucky enough to have an insurance company behind them. But for some reason I want to impress Francesco—and maybe myself—about the job that's waiting for me, so I embellish my soon-to-be reality, prattling on and on about fascinating lawsuits and standing before a high-powered judge every day. Total crap. I'll probably see more of the library than I ever will the courtroom, and even if I do work on a big case, it'll be on the grunt end for a very long time.

"And this is what you love to do?" Francesco seems to be going deeper than the surface conversation, making me squirm a little. On the other hand, his question flatters me. John assumes I'll love the law as he does, so we've never truly discussed the subject of whether I'll actually like my chosen profession. I've never even told John that I always wanted to be an interior designer before I convinced myself that the law would bring money and a decent lifestyle easier and faster.

"I haven't started yet," I say to Francesco.

"But you believe you will love it?" He holds his head a little bit to one side and waits for me to speak, those nice brown eyes watching me.

"It's a job." I squirm again and glance away. Sin is still talking to Massimo, and luckily, Kat and Poster Boy are chatting again instead of giving each other tonsillectomies.

"How do you like Roma?"

This is a much less complicated topic, and I give Francesco a smile. "I love it. I went to college here for six months."

"Ah. So you know Roma?" He leans back in his chair and crosses his legs so that one ankle rests on his knee. He strikes me as someone who's completely comfortable with his body, a trait I envy.

"I do. I have such wonderful memories of this city."

"Why are the memories so good?"

I think about this for a second. "I was in school and in a new place. Everything was simple." I close my eyes for a moment, remembering how my life was then—sleeping in, going to a few classes and spending the rest of the day exploring Rome, drinking wine and mooning over my favorite bartender.

"Things are not simple now?"

I open my eyes and shift about in my seat. I'm out of practice talking about things like feelings and wants and desires and realities. Somewhere along the way John and I had stopped doing that, too.

"Life gets more complicated as you get older. There's more to worry about." In one swoop, my memories of Rome are replaced with the prospect of fourteen-hour workdays.

Francesco pauses a second, his eyes never leaving my face. "I think life is what you do with it. How you decide to live it. It can be simple or not."

I want to say, "Easy, Pollyanna" but instead I opt for, "It's not that easy."

"Why not?"

I look at his face. Can he really want to have this conversation with me, some American girl he just met? He leans toward me, and the humid air seems to lighten and swirl with his nearness. I guess he does.

"It's not that easy," I say, "because you have responsibilities as time goes on." Awaiting me when I get back are loans to pay, my family to deal with. Hell, I'm not even sure what to wear to work. I've perfected my student wardrobe—jeans, khakis, two pairs of leather boots (both black, one high-heeled, one low), and nearly every sweater put out by Banana Republic in the last three years. That's all I've really needed. But now, I'm entering the world of pinstripes, pumps and pearls, and I'm clueless. Petty, I know, but this is the stuff I think about.

"If you are happy and living how you want to live, responsibilities can be a joy, not a job," Francesco says.

"You're reading too much Deepak Chopra."

"Scusi?" Francesco cocks an ear toward me, and he looks adorable in that earnest, coffee-shop guy kind of way.

"Nothing." I start asking him about his family, his work, what he wants to do with his life. He tells me he's from a big family and works in his uncle's restaurant supply business, which is how he knew the café owner and could land us this table. His two best friends are his sisters, both of whom live in Milan and work in the fashion industry. I glance down at my cotton dress as he says this, wishing I'd worn something fantastically hip, but he doesn't seem to notice. He's going to school at night to get his college degree, he tells me, so that someday he can open his own business. He wants to have something to hand down to his kids.

Francesco smiles when he says "my children," as if he knows them already. It reminds me of the dinner I'd had with some high school girlfriends recently, when I'd felt left out listening to them talk about their babies and husbands. They seem to be adults already, worrying about adult things like preschools and mortgages and car seats, while I fret about whether to have another glass of wine and what to wear to John's holiday party.

Our conversation continues to flow. I try to seem disinterested so that I don't give Francesco the idea I'm as fun as Kat, but he intrigues me. He doesn't seem to have the quick temper of many Italian men, and he says he loves women. Of course, he could be lying through his perfect white teeth—lying being another characteristic Italian-male behavior.

"Casey," he says, briefly laying a hand over mine. "I think we could be friends."

"The way they're friends?" I jab a finger at Poster Boy and Kat, who've begun full-throttle kissing again.

He laughs. "Different than that. Better."

I'm not sure what he means, so I give sort of an embarrassed guffaw, yet I don't want to doubt him. I want to believe that this man finds me interesting and stimulating. Logically, I know I shouldn't need a man to make me feel good about myself, but lately being with John has made me feel like putting on a housedress and curlers and schlepping off to a Tupperware party.

I shove all thoughts of John out of my mind and try to concentrate on what Francesco is saying. Something about the differences between American and Italian women. There seem to be many.

At this point, Poster Boy announces that he's going to give Kat a tour of Vatican City at night.

Kat beams a smile at me as if this is the most exciting thing that's ever happened to her, when I know for a fact it's not. She has hundreds of crazy stories about getting it on with rock stars, sneaking into movie premieres and getting ludicrously expensive gifts from men of all ages. But I'm glad she's happy, and there's no denying how hot Poster Boy is.

"Would you like to come?" Poster Boy asks the rest of the group.

Francesco barely glances at me before he answers with a definitive, *"Sì."*

"No!" I say, more harshly than I intended. I'm not a big fan of people answering for me, and I'd suddenly envisioned myself in an Italian housedress (okay, it is cuter than the American version), beating out a rug on the side of a dirty pensione, while Francesco yells at me to cook his favorite fusilli arribiata. When I see everyone's surprised looks, I add in a nicer tone, "I need some sleep."

Francesco nods graciously. "I will take Casey to the hotel."

I give him a smile, not wanting to ruin his image of me, not wanting to erase the talk we had. I'd actually enjoyed the last hour more than any other in recent memory. Still, I do have a boyfriend at home. "That's all right. I'll walk back with Lindsey," I say.

"Actually, Case," Lindsey says, a sheepish grin playing on her mouth, "I think I'll go check out the Vatican, too."

"Oh," I say, stumped. Sin is usually not the type to follow in Kat's footsteps. She has little tolerance for men. She gives them a whirl now and again, but her hopes are always too high, or the guy's ambitions too low. Her one major boyfriend, a charming, curly haired guy named Pete who was as short as she, she'd dumped about two years ago.

"Sorry," Lindsey whispers, leaning across the table to squeeze my hand.

Kat sees the gesture and wakes up from the sexual stare she's exchanging with Poster Boy. "Are you cool with this, Case?"

"Sure, sure." I push back my chair, which makes a screeching sound on the pavement. I tell Francesco I'll take him up on the ride.

"We'll see you in a bit," Kat says, her hand on Sin's shoulder.

I nod, but I don't expect either of them until dawn.

On the ride home, I try to remain aloof. Well, as aloof as one can get while straddling the end of a battered moped designed for one, and clutching Francesco's midsection like a life preserver. He chatters over his shoulder, pointing out famous churches and hotels and mansions.

"You know, I've lived in Rome," I tell him when we stop at a light. "I know all these places."

"Oh," he says, a mocking tone in his voice. "You know them all? You have been everywhere?"

"Yep." I match his tone with a smug voice of my own. I was zealous about seeing everything when I lived here. I'd fallen in love with the sculpted fountains and the steeples shooting from the churches.

Francesco revs his sad little bike, which answers with a chug and a whine before it starts moving again. "Tomorrow night we will take you and your friends to a place maybe you have been, but you have never been there *a notte,* at night."

It sounds mysterious, but I refuse to take the bait. "Fine," I yell into the wind so he can hear. "Whatever you want."

I tell myself I'm not interested, that I'm only accepting because if I want to see my friends while in Rome, they're ob-viously going to be a package deal with Poster Boy and his crew.

Francesco pulls into the courtyard, and I climb off the scooter as elegantly as possible.

"I will call you early tomorrow evening," he says, "and we will make arrangements to pick up you and your friends, *sì?*"

"*Sì,*" I reply.

He moves toward me, and I panic for a second, thinking he's going to kiss me on the lips. Then I get a weird shot of hope that he *is* going to kiss me. Instead, he plants a soft, chaste kiss on each cheek, the Italian greeting, which is about as sexual to them as cleaning a closet. He smiles at me and gives the scooter another lame rev.

"Tomorrow," he says, and putters away into the night.

3

I'm surprised to hear Lindsey and Kat clomping into the room only an hour or so after I crash, but I'm too tired to find out what brought them home so soon. The next morning I wake them at eight o'clock, determined to show them all of Rome within the next two days, since we're planning on leaving tomorrow night for the Greek islands.

"It's too early," Kat moans, looking as stunning as the night before.

While my appearance always does a nosedive by the time I get up in the morning, Kat is blessed with long, black lashes and smooth skin that never blotches. Her perpetual good looks come in handy, especially on Sunday mornings at 7:00 a.m. when she starts a twelve-hour shift as an ICU nurse. She still goes out every Saturday night without fail, and she almost always picks someone up, but it never seems to affect her nursing. In fact, she's won awards. She even gets flowers and cards from her patients and their families.

"Too bad," I say to her now. "We've got lots to see."

Lindsey groans and props herself up on her elbows. "You are not going to believe the shit those guys pulled last night."

I immediately sit on the edge of her bed, ready for some of the good girl talk that's been missing from my life. I've certainly had no interesting stories of my own. "What happened?"

"Apparently—" she shoots a mean look at Kat "—the boys' idea of a Vatican tour was to drive by Saint Peter's from a mile away and point at it."

I cover my mouth, trying not to laugh.

"Don't even," she says, before she continues. "Then they just sped away, and when I asked Massimo where we're going he tells me Monte something."

"Monte Mario," I tell her. It's a nice neighborhood just outside the city limits. "And then what happened?"

"Well, it was obvious they were looking for an evening of Love American Style," Lindsey says, again glaring at Kat, "which I guess I should have expected the way those two were making out at the table—but I really did think we were going to the Vatican. One minute we're cruising along real slow, and Massimo's being nice, telling me things about Rome. Then we pull up to a light, the two guys talk in Italian, and the next minute they floor the scooters and start flying down the street away from the Vatican."

We both look at Kat, waiting for an explanation. The way she was tonguing Poster Boy at the table, I wouldn't be surprised if she was groping him on the scooter.

Kat gives a guilty shrug. "Alesandro asked me if we wanted to have a beer at their apartment, and I said 'sure,' assuming he meant *after* the tour. But before we got anywhere Sin started arguing with Massimo at a stoplight."

Lindsey snorts. "He made a comment about bringing me home the next day before work, and I didn't appreciate the assumption." She throws off her covers and starts going through her purse. "I thought those guys would be different, but they're the same as the ones back home. I don't have time to mother some post-college idiot into adulthood."

"Oh my." Kat rolls her eyes and waves off Lindsey's speech. "That's fine, but you jumped off the scooter and stalked away in the dark. I was worried about you."

Sin turns around with a serious look, but after a second she gives a bashful kind of half laugh. "I guess the seven beers I had helped a bit."

"We chased her," Kat explains, laughing now, too, "and we had to talk her back onto Massimo's scooter."

"Yeah. By that time they wanted nothing but to get the hell away from us." Sin slumps on Kat's bed.

"And I was none too happy about it," Kat says. "Alesandro was a hottie, and I came on this trip to have a good time, damn it."

They're giggling now, leaning against each other and looking like the best friends they are. I used to fit in that picture. "The Three Musketeers," we used to call ourselves unoriginally.

"What happened with you?" Kat says. "Did Francesco make a move?"

"No, no. Perfect gentleman." I tell them about his promise that the guys will pick us up that evening and take us somewhere off the beaten path. "So," I tell Kat, "if they still want to do it, you'll have another shot at Alesandro."

"I hope they don't," Lindsey says. "I want absolutely nothing to do with Massimo."

"Maybe they'll have more friends," I say, "or maybe they'll take us someplace where there's lots of people. It could be fun."

Sin narrows her eyes a little. "You're really selling tonight with these guys. You're sure nothing happened with you and Francesco?"

"Of course not."

"Don't hold out on us," Kat says.

"There's nothing to hold." I look at the two of them slumped on the bed, and I think, there's nothing to tell about Francesco, not really, but there's John, there's my parents, there's—

"All right. Well, I call the bathroom first." Lindsey heads for the shower.

Kat groans and rolls off the bed. She moves to her suitcase and starts sorting through her clothes.

I sit there for a second, thinking that at least they didn't refuse to go tonight. Because I want to see Francesco again more than I can admit.

All day we hike around Rome, making the requisite stops—Castel Sant'Angelo, Trevi Fountain, Piazza del Popolo, Sistine Chapel, and at least a dozen other churches. The majority of Rome's treasures are religious, whether the cathedrals themselves or the baubles and sculptures collected inside. Although I consider myself a lapsed Catholic, I still find the interior of a church soothing. It's like walking back into childhood, a world of orderly rules and schedules. I love the cool marble and the impossible, enormous quiet, despite the teeming city outside.

"Pete always wanted me to pretend I was a virgin," Lindsey says, as we stand in front of a portrait of the Virgin Mary just inside the entrance to one church.

Kat and I burst out in giggles at the thought of cute, little Pete making such a request. We get shushed by a passing couple who might as well have the word *tourist* plastered on their heads what with the rain slickers tied around their waists and the five guidebooks they're juggling.

"So why didn't you?" Kat says in a whisper.

"What was I supposed to do? Get drunk and pretend I was in a dorm room?" Sin shakes her head. "I told him he was an asshole, but I think he was just trying to mix it up a bit, have some fun." She shrugs and walks to a white marble sculpture of an angel.

They haven't dated for two years, but it doesn't stop Lindsey from bringing up Pete every so often. An open, vivacious guy, he was the one man Lindsey had seemed to care about. Everyone loved to have him around, until Lindsey decided he wasn't going anywhere in life. He was happy running the family business, a large fruit and vegetable market in Bucktown. Lindsey, on the other hand, wanted to run with the moneyed set, the kind of people who worked out at East Bank Club and owned second houses in Aspen. So it was so-long-Pete, although Lindsey doesn't seem able to say good-bye.

I follow Sin to the statue of the angel, whose placid face and soulful eyes make it look like it needs a break from centuries of standing in the same position. "You ever talk to Pete?"

She looks surprised at the thought, then turns away and walks down the marble aisle toward the altar. "Of course not," I hear her say.

The heat is unrelenting, but it gives us an excuse for frequent stops at neighborhood bars for *tè fredda*—sweet Italian iced tea—and snacks. About three in the afternoon, we're thirsty again, but because of the siesta, we trudge around forever looking for an open restaurant.

A few women pass us, walking arm in arm, then a few young girls holding hands.

"Lot of lesbians around here," Kat says.

"They're not lesbians," I say, laughing. "That's just what women do in Rome."

Kat stops and watches the girls enter a store. "I like that."

"Let's adopt that custom." She links her arms through Sin's and mine, pulling us forward until we all fall into step with each other, our hair flying behind us, and I feel like we're Charlie's Angels. Three good friends on the town.

It reminds me of a day we'd spent a few years ago, right after we'd graduated from college and moved to Chicago. A doctor Kat worked with had invited her to a party during Old Town Art Fair. The three of us hit a few other bashes first, making the rounds in khaki shorts and halter tops, drinking keg beer. When we stopped at Dr. Adler's, though, we knew we were out of our element. For one thing, the house was a stunning brownstone with a manicured front lawn and an interior so full of antiques that I held my breath as we made our way through the living room. For another thing, the women wore linen skirts and wide-brimmed straw hats, the men tailored pants and nice shirts. Conversation seemed to lull as we came in. Everyone was at least fifteen years older than we, and in comparison we looked like hoochy mamas with our tight little shirts, holding our plastic cups of beer.

"Stick with me," Kat said after Dr. Adler's wife gave us the once-over, her mouth curling in distaste as she pointed us toward the backyard.

"Like we're going to mingle," Sin said under her breath.

We made our way out back and stood, joined at the hip, while Kat made pleasantries with the doctors and we sipped wine that Dr. Adler described as "good, but not as superior as the '92." Finally, Kat was able to make an excuse for us to leave, and when we got outside the front door, we all burst out laughing.

We keep walking arm in arm now until we finally find an open bar called Mel's on a winding cobbled street off Piazza Cavour. It's small and quaint, with old posters of Italian movie stars plastered to the walls. We order our food and slide into a table under the front awning. When our teas and food arrive, we dig in as if we hadn't just eaten a few hours ago.

"Oh my God," Kat says. "Did you see the biscuit?"

I glimpse a guy walking through the door and get a glimpse of sandy-blond hair.

"Wish me luck," Kat says, pushing back her chair.

Neither Sin nor I say anything. We both know she doesn't need it.

Kat trots into the bar. Within seconds we hear the rumble of a man's voice, the peal of Kat's laughter.

"Great," Lindsey says. "We're going to be here forever."

"Yep," I say with a certain degree of resignation. Since Kat is widely known for her ability to meet men under any circumstances, Sin and I usually spend a lot of time standing around until Kat decides whether she wants to do something about it. Usually, we talk and make jabs about Kat's libido, but Sin says nothing this time, she just keeps eating her pizza, pulling off the whole slices of tomato, which seem to offend her.

Kat comes out of the bar in record time and introduces us to Guiseppe, who looks like he could be an underwear model. He's got a stunning body, a jaw so square you could use it as a ruler, and jade-green eyes under eyelashes that are longer than Kat's.

"Buona sera," Guiseppe says to us with a slight bow.

"He designs leather!" Kat gushes, with such wide-eyed enthusiasm you'd have thought he was next in line to be the pope.

Sin and I shake his hand and drag our chairs around the table to make room. When Guiseppe and Kat take their seats, there's a pregnant pause, as if we all know that someone should talk, but none of us can figure out whose turn it is. I keep expecting a look from Lindsey that says, *take over, please, and get us the hell out of here,* but she doesn't even glance at me.

Finally, Kat says, "Guiseppe wants to come sightseeing with us."

Sin and I are quiet, but our silence is probably for different reasons. For Sin, it's just another round of dealing with Kat's string of men. For me, though, it means an end to my role as the one who knows Rome, the keeper of the Italian knowledge. I'd enjoyed being teacher all day. It meant Kat and Sin needed me in some fashion. But now that there's a Roman onboard, it's over.

Guiseppe, it turns out, is a very pleasant, mild kind of guy who happens to know all sorts of Rome trivia. I find myself warming to him as he gives us informative tidbits at each stop.

"Did you know," he asks us in carefully pronounced English as we stand in front of the Vittorio Emmanuel Monument, a white marble monstrosity that looks like a wedding cake, "that this was built by the monarchy of Italy, whom the people hated?"

Actually, I did know this, but Guiseppe looks at each of us as if he's really trying to help, so I keep quiet.

"We do not like this," he continues. "It was built from marble stolen from the Colosseum and the Forum, and it is ugly."

"That's terrible," Kat says.

Guiseppe looks down at Kat, pulling her close to him. "But you are not like this monument," he says. "You are beautiful."

"All righty," I say in a loud voice. "It's time we got back to the hotel."

Sin turns to me. "Which way is home, Case?"

I point to the street behind us, happy to be needed again, and Lindsey and I set off toward the pensione, Guiseppe and Kat trailing behind us. By the time we make it back to Pensione Fortuna, my feet are killing me, and I'm dying for a nap.

"I'll join you," Lindsey says, yawning as we stand outside the pensione door.

"Well, it was nice to meet you," I say, holding out a hand to Guiseppe.

He shakes it, but a perplexed look crosses his face.

"We're going to take a nap, too," Kat says, putting her arm around Guiseppe's back.

His face rights itself, as if everything's been cleared up.

I stifle the desire to roll my eyes, less than thrilled that I won't be able to walk around our room in my underwear and grungy but comfortable Chicago Bears T-shirt. Still, I'm too tired to take Kat aside and protest, and since Lindsey only lets out a small groan and heads in the door, I assume she is, too.

Once in the room, I change into a clingy white T-shirt and some cute running shorts. Guiseppe may be Kat's guy, but he's still a guy. I get more time with him than I ever wanted, though, when Kat and Sin huddle in the bathroom. I figure Kat is probably primping while they analyze Guiseppe's potential.

"Kat is very beautiful," Guiseppe says. He sits on her bed, across from me.

"Yes, she is."

"Very beautiful," he says again, nodding.

"Yep." I pray they'll get out of the bathroom soon so I can take out my contacts.

Kat bursts into the bedroom then, her hair piled up casually on her head. I dive into the bathroom before Lindsey can shut the door.

"What are the odds that they'll actually nap?" I ask Sin as I peel off my contacts.

"Slim," she says through a mouthful of toothpaste, "but I could sleep through a train wreck right now. This jet lag is killing me." She spits, rinses and leaves the bathroom.

After she's gone, I close the door and stare at myself in the mirror. Without my contacts, I look hazy and ill defined, but it feels familiar.

When my head hits the pillow, I fall asleep immediately, only to be awakened a half hour later by muffled smooching sounds coming from Kat and Guiseppe. I glance to my left at Lindsey, who's snoring, blissfully unaware. I turn back to my right and my worst fears are realized. The sounds aren't coming from lips on lips, but rather Guiseppe's lips on Kat's perky breasts. Kat's head is thrown back, her mouth open, her face holding a look of pure rapture. Guiseppe is bent over her, working with all the fervor of a newborn infant.

I close my eyes again, not entirely surprised. I'd expected some activity, and it's certainly not the first time Kat has fooled around within spitting distance of me. It's just that she usually confined the contact to kissing, and it usually occurred after bar-hopping during our undergrad days, when I was too loaded to give a rat's ass. But this? This seems too nuts even for Kat.

I steal another glance in their direction, hoping that it was just a momentary lapse of discretion. Instead, I find Guiseppe's form hidden entirely by the blanket and way below Kat's gravity-defying boobs.

"Kat," I say in an exasperated whisper. "For Christ's sake!"

"What? What's wrong?" As if a complete stranger wasn't performing oral sex on her in the company of her two friends.

"Give it a rest, will you? I've got to get some sleep."

Kat lugs Guiseppe up by his shoulders. When he emerges from the sheets, his golden hair is tousled, his pouty lips decidedly glistening.

"Sorry," Kat says to me, but when she looks at Guiseppe, she starts giggling.

I feel like a second-grade teacher, yet I can't help barking, "Quiet. *Please.*"

Kat and Guiseppe try to feign seriousness, but it's hard to quell their delight.

I pull the covers over my head and squeeze my eyes shut.

Francesco has not called.

I began watching the clock at approximately 7:30, when Guiseppe exited, amid a flurry of kisses from Kat. Since that time, Lindsey and I have listened to Kat's play-by-play of every word or action spoken or performed by Guiseppe since their chance meeting at the coffee bar.

Kat has already forgotten about Poster Boy Alesandro, and has plans to meet Guiseppe tonight at a disco in Trastevere. Wanting nothing to do with Massimo, Sin has also opted for the Trastevere plan.

"Come with us," Sin says as she lounges on her bed. Naturally, she's already dressed for the night, looking cute in trim black pants and a fitted blue halter top. Outside the open French windows, I can hear the low roll of conversation, an occasional burst of laughter, a few lines from a song—Piazza Navona heating up for a Friday night.

"But I promised Francesco." I realize how pathetic it sounds. I came on this trip for some girl time, which at least one of my friends is trying to give me. Why am I making such an effort to see some guy I just met, especially when I have a nice enough boyfriend at home?

No answer comes to mind. To keep myself busy, I refold the clothes in my backpack while I try to decide what to wear. It's easier than looking at Sin, who is way too good at reading faces, mine in particular.

"So what if you promised him?" Kat says, coming out of the bathroom in a lacy bra and thong. "Nothing happened last night, right?"

"No, of course not, but you guys should come with me. What if Alesandro and Massimo are there and expecting you?" Meanwhile, I keep looking at the phone, wondering if Francesco will even want to hang with me after his friends got the cold shoulder last night.

"I really don't think they're dying to see us, and if they do..." Lindsey shrugs "...they won't find us."

I have nothing to say in return. I can't explain this desire of mine, not even to myself.

"Go with Francesco if you really want to," Kat says.

Sudden panic at the thought. I make my fingers continue folding socks into little balls, but what I'm thinking is that I can't be alone with Francesco, not without chaperones. For the last two years, the only man I've been alone with, other than John, is my dentist.

I turn and face them. "Come on, you guys. Just come with me for an hour or two. I really want to do this."

"Why?" Sin says.

Great question.

"Let's stick together," Kat says. "This is supposed to be a girls' vacation, after all."

"No shit, Kat. I'm surprised you remembered that." It flies out of my mouth before I can stop it.

She freezes, looking like I slapped her.

Lindsey doesn't say anything, but she's watching me.

"I'm sorry, it's just that you guys had no problems leaving me last night," I say.

"You were going to sleep," Lindsey says.

"It's not like you thought twice about me." I try to keep my voice light, wondering why I'm arguing, since I may never hear from Francesco again. I'm ready to retreat when I see Lindsey's face harden.

"Well," she says, "you haven't been setting much of an example lately."

"What's that supposed to mean?" But I know. Some sick part of me wants to hear her say it, though, because in some fucked-up way it'll mean she missed me as much as I've missed them.

"Hey," Kat says, walking toward us. "Let's not get into this. Not now. Casey, if you want to go with Francesco, do it. Let's just make it an early one so we can get up tomorrow and do some more sightseeing before we leave for Greece tomorrow night."

Neither Sin nor I answer for some time.

"Yeah," Sin says, finally breaking the silence. "Just go." She gives me a lopsided smile with one corner of her mouth, which means she's trying to be nice.

"Okay," I say. "What time should we meet back here?"

"Midnight," Kat says. "Will that work?"

"Sure," I say, and I give Lindsey a small smile in return. Just then the phone rings. I lunge at it.

"Pronto," I say.

"Casey." Francesco's voice is so soft that he breathes my name more than he speaks it. "How are you?"

4

"I will pick you up at 9:00," Francesco says, "and we will have a special dinner, as I told you."

I push down the flicker of excitement that rises in me, trying not to notice how odd it is, how long it's been since I'd felt that particular rush. "What about Alesandro and Massimo?"

"They will not be joining us," he says, without explanation.

"Where? I mean, what kind of place are we going? What should I wear?" Something similar to terror replaces my excitement as I realize that this sounds more and more like a date. I know I should protest, explain that I have a boyfriend, and traipse off to Trastevere with my friends, but I can't. I just can't get those words out of my mouth.

"Wear whatever you like," Francesco says in his liquid-honey voice. "It does not matter."

Easy for him to say.

I immediately begin trying on every article of clothing packed by myself, Kat or Lindsey. They both attempt to offer advice, neither commenting on my obvious anxiety, but their pearls of fashion wisdom do little to calm me. To make matters worse, because of the weight I've put on this summer, I can't wear the majority of their clothes for fear that the seams will explode and take out everyone within a mile radius. This leaves me alone with my meager wardrobe. I can think of fifty outfits in my closet back home that would be perfect for tonight, while I cringe at everything I packed.

I finally decide on my most slimming skirt and a sleeveless white top with a loose, semi-sheer black shirt over it.

"Are you nuts?" Kat says. "You can't wear that black thing. It's one hundred fucking degrees out." She gives me a disgusted look while she fastens the diamond studs into her ears.

I glance at Sin, still on the bed, who notices the same thing and scowls at Kat. Those diamond earrings again.

"I'm trying to hide my arms," I say, mumbling as I climb on a spindly wooden chair, where I attempt, unsuccessfully, to get a full-length glimpse of myself in the foot-long mirror above the dresser.

"Oh, please," Sin says. "Your arms look fine. What's gotten into you?"

"About ten pounds," I say.

She sighs. "I remember at Michigan when we used to have to beg you to wear a coat over your little outfits, even in the dead of winter."

This is true. I dressed like a slut in college, most of my clothes more suited for a provocative music video. I always groan and roll my eyes when I look back on pictures of myself in those getups, but the sad thing is that I was happy and completely confident in them.

"Oh God," Kat says, brushing out her long chestnut hair, a grin taking over her face. "Remember that blue dress that

was up to your crotch and showed every bit of your tits except the nipples?"

Lindsey gives a shout of laughter. "And what about that
silver bustier she used to wear with the black pants?"

"Times change," I say, smiling despite myself. This, I like.
This reminiscing about how we used to be, even if it is at my
expense.

"So," Sin says, and I can hear the shift in her voice from
lighthearted to something more serious. "Did you call John
yet?"

"Not yet." I get down from my chair, having decided to
go for beauty over comfort and stick with the outfit. I don't
mention that my plan is to not call anyone for at least a week
or two. Not John, not Gordon Baker Brickton, Jr., my newly
assigned partner and boss at the firm, and certainly not my
mother. This trip is intended to be an escape. Avoiding phone
calls with anyone from my real life is a means to that much-
needed end.

"Why not?" Sin says, refusing to give up.

"I think he's out of town this weekend." This is a total lie.
He's in Chicago, and I know exactly what he's doing right
now. He's in his apartment, puttering around the kitchen,
making chicken Alfredo. He'll work on a file while he eats
at the kitchen table, and then he'll head to Stanley's to meet
his buddies for one or two beers—at the most. He'll be missing me by now. I'm sure of that. Despite his crazy schedule
lately, he turned all moony and sad when he realized I was
leaving for three weeks.

"The place won't be the same without you," he'd said a
few nights ago as we stood in his living room, his pale green
eyes big and turned down at the corners.

I get a sick flash of guilt, but I'm not sure if it's caused by
my memory of John that night or the way I'm now trying
to push it out of my head.

★ ★ ★

"*Signorina,* Francesco...here...for you," the hotel concierge says in halting English, with a heavy Italian accent.

"Yes...*sì...grazie,*" I mumble into the phone, knocking over the bottle of my Fendi perfume in my nervous state.

"You smell fine," Lindsey says from the bed, where she has patiently counseled me through the difficult decision of whether to apply more perfume. I love her for this and for dropping the topic of John. "You look fine, too."

I fuss with my hair in the mirror. "Are you sure?"

"Positive. Do you have MILK?"

I check my purse—Money, ID, Lipstick, Keys. "Yep."

"So, go already." She rises from the bed and, collecting her purse, yells, "Kat, let's go!" in the direction of the bathroom.

"Two minutes," Kat says, and Lindsey sits back down. We both know that Kat's two minutes are more like twenty.

I inhale deeply, as I'd been taught to do in one of my self-help books. I imagine that these inhalations bring the desired calming effect. "Here I go."

I take only three steps before it hits me.

"What am I doing?" I ask Lindsey. "What am I doing to John?"

She gives me a very long, very pointed look, during which I regret the question and fear she's going to set me straight. So straight that I won't be able to live with myself if I go out with Francesco. A moment goes by, then another.

Finally, she says, "You're not doing anything to John. You're going out for a drink with a nice Italian boy, which was what you wanted to do so desperately an hour ago."

Neither of us acknowledges the cutting side to her supposedly light remark. Another silence. The phone rings again. Saved, I think, snatching it.

"Francesco...here...for you," the concierge repeats.

"I'll be right there." I enunciate the words for fear Francesco will leave, yet I don't move for the door.

"Go," Lindsey says, and she actually gives me a wink.

The tiny elevator, which usually takes an eternity to run from the third floor to the first, brings me to the lobby in record time. I'm trying to catch a glimpse of my hair in the reflection of the metal doors when they open. Francesco, dressed in tan pants and a silky white shirt that probably came from his fashionable sisters in Milan, is conversing with the concierge in what appears to be rapid, raucous Italian. They gesticulate, shrug and nod all at once, as only Italians can do. Their conversation comes to an abrupt halt as I approach the desk with what I hope is a nonchalant, I-do-this-all-the-time look on my face.

Francesco turns to me. His hair is still wet, the black waves shiny, lying close to his head. "You look beautiful," he says, drawing out the last word so that it sounds like "bee-yoo-tee-ful."

"Thank you. *Grazie,*" I say, surprised to hear my own voice coming out demure, even more surprised to find myself dipping my head in sort of a bow. I'm not usually a demure woman. This is some redheaded-stepchild part of myself I have yet to meet. It makes me wonder if she has other relatives that are usually kept in the basement, away from the guests.

If Francesco drove his scooter in a meandering way yesterday, tonight he's in a full-steam-ahead race. I clutch him around his middle as we speed along the cobblestone streets of Rome. Charming enough to stroll down, but hell on the ass if you're the second person on a one-man moped. I'd tried not to touch him. I tried to simply place my palms on some Switzerland-like neutral area of his body, but the dangerous speed and the bumpy effect of the cobblestones made this full-body grip from behind a requirement. So now, my breasts lie on his back, my hands hold tight to his waist. He feels so different from John who is softer and certainly not as reckless.

As the scooter hugs a particularly curved street, both of us leaning to one side, I'm sure we're about to crash. One part of me wants to yell at Francesco to slow down, and either take it easy or take me back to the hotel and forget he ever met me. At the same time, I'm exhilarated to the point of wanting to throw my head back, like some sappy character in a romantic comedy.

I can feel Francesco's taut, lean stomach muscles under my fingers. I clasp my hands together, one over the other, to stop the sudden, random urge to let them migrate lower. The scooter jostles over a pothole and the side of my hand nicks Francesco's belt buckle.

"Okay?" Francesco shouts over his shoulder. "You okay?"

"Fine. *Bene,*" I yell into the wind.

We speed down the Corso, past grand hotels and designer boutiques. The city isn't as crowded as it normally is because some of its residents have left on holiday already. Still, the sidewalks are relatively packed with couples, families out for a stroll, and bunches of tourists.

Francesco stops for a light. "You see there? You see this bank?" he says, pointing to a solid, stone building with an ATM machine outside. "This is where Mussolini was hung."

"Oh." I'm imagining Mussolini dangling from a rope, his bald head at a sharp angle, when Francesco guns the bike. I seize him around the waist again.

After a minute, we putter to a stop at a neighborhood grocer. *"Un momento,"* Francesco says, untangling himself from my limbs.

He disappears into the shop. I attempt to lean against the parked scooter in a feminine James Dean kind of slouch, but the damn thing starts to tip over. I scramble to upright it, grabbing the handlebars and pulling with all my strength, which, admittedly, isn't what it used to be. I finally succeed in straightening the thing, and I'm searching for the kick-stand when Francesco returns, brown bag in hand, a bottle of wine peeking out.

"Trouble?" he asks, dark eyes laughing.

He relieves me of the handlebars and adjusts the kickstand without looking down.

"You are perspiring," he says in a matter-of-fact voice.

Mortification makes me mute. Of course I'm perspiring. Between the ninety-degree heat, the damned black shirt, Francesco's proximity and my grapple with the bike, I'm a sweating mess.

"I will be back." He places the bag on the street and returns to the store.

I stand by the scooter, mopping my forehead with my hand. *Breathe,* I tell myself. *Breathe.*

Francesco returns with a fistful of napkins.

"Let us see what we can do." He says this in a low voice as he gently starts dabbing at my cheeks, temples and collar-bone with the napkins. I am paralyzed with embarrassment, my arms hanging limp at my sides. I feel my face become a deeper shade of fuchsia, and my heart beats like a rabbit's, making me sweat all the more. Francesco doesn't seem to notice. He keeps dabbing me with a light touch, like an artist sponge painting.

"Now," he says after a minute. "You have to remove this. It is too warm." With slow hands he slips my camouflage shirt from my shoulders.

Francesco's face is only inches from mine, and when I look, he's staring directly into my eyes. I return his gaze, unable to turn away.

I am undeniably cooler without the shirt, but I feel bare in more ways than one. John and I don't really baby each other, at least not lately. We take care of ourselves—we go to school or work, we pay our own rents, buy our own groceries and clothes—and when it's all done, we spend time together. Being pampered like this leaves me exposed, my nerve endings jangling.

Francesco takes a step back and looks me up and down with a quick, appraising glance. "Now," he says with a nod, "you are better."

And he's right.

Francesco and I are on the road again, and this stretch seems more comfortable. I feel lighter now that my black shirt is tied around my waist. My mind seems lighter, too, though I still have my arms wrapped around Francesco, anticipating a possible collision. I'm all too aware of my breasts pushing against his back as the scooter stops briefly at a corner.

I turn my head to the side, and without letting myself think about it, I rest it against his shoulder. The scooter starts to fly again, and Rome whizzes by—myriad fountains, marble statues, larger-than-life doors with gigantic handles, streets that look like alleys. Neon lights blaze from the trattorias and bars, illuminating the history of the place.

The rigidity that has settled in my bones and head over the last year seems to thaw a bit. Yet with the thaw comes an army of questions from some unused corner of my brain. What about John? Will you tell him about this little excursion, this man you are hugging? What happens when you get back, when you have to start work, when you can no longer escape the world? I lift my head and let the wind snarl my hair around my face, trying to forget these questions, the ones with rifles in hand that are waiting to fire holes in my flimsy curtain of contentment.

It pisses me off that my good feelings are so fleeting, so damned hard to hold on to. Like so many of the other uncontrollable parts of my life, I have little mastery over my emotions. Lately, it's been even worse than usual. I'll find myself in a situation where I should be ecstatically happy—my law school graduation, for example—and yet, inexplicably, I can't match my mood to the circumstances.

My parents threw a party for me after the ceremony at the apartment of one of their friends, a place with a rooftop deck and a view of Wrigley Field. My family was there—my little brother, Danny, who as a college sophomore is not so little anymore, and a handful of cousins and aunts and uncles. Kat and Sin were there for a while, too, spending most of their time fending off Danny and one of his friends, both of whom had made too many visits to the beer cooler. I was touched that my girlfriends had made it, especially Kat, who normally worked Sundays.

The sun was out. There was a game at Wrigley, so we could hear occasional surges in the noise of the crowd. It was hypothetically perfect, but the tension between my parents was thick as they circled the party like planets at opposite ends of the solar system. John hadn't shown up yet. He'd already missed the graduation ceremony because of some technology merger he was working on, yet he'd assured me over the phone that he'd be there for the party. "Right there at your side," was how he put it. But he wasn't. As the party swirled around me, I felt incredibly alone. I drank more champagne, but couldn't get a buzz. I tried listening to my uncle's advice about office politics, but it just depressed me further. I wanted nothing more than to flee. Instead, I resigned myself to sitting at a table piled with gifts and plates of food.

"We are almost there," Francesco says now, as he slows for a stop sign. He throws me a smile over his shoulder, and I notice how white his teeth are against the improbable pink of his lips.

"Great," I say, pushing away all the memories and squeezing him tighter because I've suddenly discovered a day, or at least a night, that I want to stick around for.

I feel a flash of wariness as we slow down again and pull into the circular drive surrounding the Colosseum. The actual Colosseum. This massive, ancient auditorium, a popular tourist destination by day, is now completely deserted and locked up for the night.

Gravel crunches as Francesco maneuvers around the back of the place. He stops, and an eerie quiet descends as the chugging of the bike dies. The only sounds I hear are the revs of the spitfire Italian cars hundreds of yards away. Francesco busies himself, gathering random items from the basket on the front of his scooter. I see a blanket, the wine and bread he recently purchased, another bag.

"Come," he says, gesturing.

"Come where?" A nervous giggle escapes my mouth.

"Come," he repeats with a grin. He turns away, walking with his arms full.

"Francesco," I call after him. "What are we doing?"

He gives me an exasperated look. "We are having a picnic," he says, as if this were the most normal thing in the world.

"Um...okay, but where? It's almost ten o'clock at night."

"Inside."

He turns again and keeps moving until he reaches an arched entrance protected by medieval-looking prison-style bars that are driven into the ground.

I follow with tentative steps, feeling as if I should tiptoe. Is this legal?

Francesco drops to his knees, the blanket and bags at his side. He grasps two of the bars, shakes and jiggles them with practiced movements of his arms, and miraculously slides them upward. He stands, holding the bars up about four feet.

"This way." He gestures with his head toward the opening he's created.

I do as he says, and duck under the bars. Francesco kicks the blanket and the two bags in after me, then scoots inside with one graceful movement. The bars make a violent clang as he lets them fall.

I jump. "Will we be able to get out?"

"Of course." He gathers the bags, hands me the sack with the wine and takes my elbow. "It is okay."

I glance around. We're in some sort of anteroom, a dank place with a trodden dirt floor. Across the way, a long, dark hallway stretches into the building. I look back at Francesco, ready to ask him exactly where we're going to have this picnic, but he leans in and kisses me. Not on the lips or even on my cheek, but on my forehead. The gesture is simple, tender. I close my eyes and breathe in his scent from the crook of his neck, a woodsy, chocolatey smell.

He takes my hand, leading me down the hallway in silence.

The hall opens up, and as we keep walking, the sky seems to open above us. I realize we're at the edge of a round pit, the very center of the Colosseum. Francesco stops, drops my hand and spreads the blanket on the ground. He kneels on it and starts to lift things out of the sacks—wine, bread, a tomato, a chunk of hard white cheese and two squat glasses— the kind that Americans use to rinse their mouths after brushing and Italians use for wine. He uncorks the bottle and pours a dark maroon wine into the glasses. Out of his pocket, he withdraws a small knife and cuts off neat triangles of cheese, using one of the brown paper bags as a plate.

He sets the knife down and raises both of the half-full glasses, holding one of them out to me. *"Salute,"* he says, the customary Italian toast. "To tonight."

I sink to my knees and, taking the glass, I touch it to his, making a pleasant clink. I take a sip and feel the wine warming my insides, loosening me again. He offers a piece of cheese, and I take it because although I'm not hungry, I want something else to do with my hands.

"How did you know how to get in here?" I ask.

Francesco shrugs. He keeps cutting the cheese and tomato, breaking off chunks of bread, offering them to me.

I rest one hand behind me on the blanket, sipping the warm, spicy wine. The only light in the place is from the stars and the streetlights peeking through the stone arches. As I look around, it strikes me that thousands of people have died here. Thousands more have enjoyed themselves, watching the festivities, reveling in the prime of their lives. And they're all long gone.

I suppose that this is the prime of my own life, although until tonight it hasn't felt like the prime of anything. The days and months have raced by me like a high-speed train, making everything vague and fuzzy.

Until tonight.

Francesco moves behind me. I can sense him coming closer, and I lose the air in my lungs.

He spreads his legs around me, sheltering me, and I feel the gentle weight of his breath as he speaks into my ear. "Lean back."

I allow my rigid back to decline like a beach chair a few degrees, but I land in an awkward position, my head against his chest, my legs too far forward. He touches my hips, urging me back until I fold into him, nearly cheek to cheek now, with the back of my head resting on his shoulder. He keeps his hands on my hips. I feel my blood pulsing there.

Francesco's earlier reluctance to tell me how he knows the way in here makes me suspect that this scene is from a well-worn bag of tricks, and I wonder what's next. I remind myself that this is probably where he takes all the foreign girls he picks up, but my warning does no good. I'm still enthralled with this place, with his breath in my ear.

We sit like that awhile, Francesco doing nothing except supporting my body. My lungs start working again. I relax, but I'm intensely conscious of his arms around me, his chin grazing my ear.

Then he tightens his arms and I think, here it is, the come-on from Francesco I've been expecting since last night. His breath grows even heavier in my ear. I can't decide whether to run or return the gesture, lost somewhere in the purgatory between sheer panic and complete acceptance.

I don't consciously decide to do anything, but then I'm turning my head toward Francesco's so my ear pushes against his mouth. I hear him whisper Italian phrases I can't understand.

I feel my own breath catching in my throat, and then I feel a kind of melting. My uptight, button-up, worry-about-everything persona that I've been wearing like a cloak dissolves, and for a moment, I feel like someone I barely recall, someone I desperately want back.

Francesco nuzzles my cheek, my ears, my neck. My awareness has grown so acute now that I imagine I can feel my lashes resting on the soft skin under my eyes. My mouth opens in an O. I arch back into his hips, his mouth. I haven't felt like this in so, so, so long. When was the last time? I hazily search my memory in that small cabinet of my mind where this feeling was filed away years ago. Did I ever feel this way with John? John is like a comfortable old flannel shirt that you love to put on in the winter. But this—this is a black silk shawl, clinging to my bare shoulders.

I hear a moan escape my lips, and it startles me. Some force flows out of me, turning my body over, pushing Francesco's shoulders until he lies flat on the ground. Our tongues and lips clash, soft groans from both of us, low gasps of Italian words from him, hands searching. Our bodies roll on the thin blanket that covers the hard ground.

I lose my sense of time, and it's bliss. Sharp and clear, as if everything in my life has stopped and focused on this instant.

After what may have been twenty minutes, or two hours, our faces separate, our eyes lock.

"Thank you," I say, because even if this was part of Francesco's frequently utilized seduction repertoire, he's given me a momentary peace, a sliver of life.

"*Bella, bella,*" Francesco says, holding my eyes. "You are beautiful, but you do not know." He laughs. "And you make me tired."

He falls back on the blanket. I lean over him, turning my head and placing my temple on his chest where his shirt has become unbuttoned. The tawny, tanned skin of his stomach rises and falls, trying to catch up.

I fall asleep with his shirt clenched in my fist.

5

I feel simmering heat and roll over to escape it. So hard. The bed is so hard.

"John," I murmur, reaching for his hair, which I always tousle in the morning. But I'm greeted by thick waves, not John's smooth, thinning locks.

As I sit up, my back screams in pain. Everything is foggy. I awaken a little more, realizing that my contacts are gripping my eyeballs like hubcaps on tires. I blink rapidly to dispel the haze...and it all comes back in a sharp second. Italy, Rome, Francesco, who is still in the throes of sleep, limbs outstretched, face turned to one side, mouth partly open. To me, there's nothing more adorable than a sleeping man, stripped of all the society-taught, sports-induced toughness.

I study him, comparing Francesco's posture to the way John sleeps, always on his side in a tight fetal-like ball. John never moves, with the exception of one hand that always seeks me out, no matter where my erratic positioning takes me.

The irony of it hits me then. I'm thinking of John while

I'm sitting here, clothes askew, gazing at a near stranger who I spent the night with. I remind myself that I didn't "spend the night" with him as in a euphemism for sex. There was no intercourse, nothing even close, really. It was more of a combination roll and grope, but my memories of it make me blush.

It's not that John isn't tender or considerate. He's both of those things. He's even quite well-endowed. It's just that sex has become, for lack of a better word, routine. It's like watching a favorite movie over and over. The first few times, you think, Oh! Here comes the good part! I *love* this part. After a while, though, you know exactly what's about to happen down to the minute details, and it doesn't particularly excite you anymore, but you watch anyway because there's nothing better on. I'm sure that I'm as much to blame as John is. Lately, I just haven't felt sexual enough to try and break out of it. Yet now I have these feelings from last night. I'd almost forgotten it could be like that.

I stretch and look around me. Sun streams through the eastern arches of the Colosseum and over the raw, broken pieces of the upper rim. Our blanket is twisted beneath us, the cheese congealing, the disks of bread hard.

I glance at my watch. Christ, it's 5:40 in the morning, and I was supposed to be at the room by midnight. Kat and Sin will be asleep, but still, I need to get back.

I nudge Francesco, clearing my throat to make some sound. What if he's one of those people who wakes with a start—confused and angry? But no. He brings his hand to his head and groans. His eyes open slowly, like a man with nowhere to be and no commitments.

"Buon giorno, bella," he says, fixing his lazy, lidded eyes on me with the look of a cat who's gotten in the bird cage and plans to stay.

He pulls me to him and into another kiss. My instincts are to fight it, because John and I have an agreement to always brush our teeth before an a.m. kiss, but Francesco seems to have no such requirement. His tongue seeks mine again, his hands roam, but I keep seeing John curled in his bed.

"Francesco," I say, gently pushing his chest with an open hand. "I can't."

"Okay. It's okay." He moves a strand of hair that's hiding my eyes. He gazes at me, and I feel myself being drawn, pulled back to him. I want to be all over him, but my thoughts of John are stubborn in the harsh light of day.

I don't explain this to Francesco. How can I?

"I've got to get back," I say.

A sharp clang comes from our left, followed by muffled Italian. Our heads jerk in the direction of the sound. About three hundred feet away guards in navy-blue are opening the largest gated entrance.

Francesco jumps to a crouch, shoving the corked wine bottle, his knife and the errant bread and cheese in the center of the blanket. He gathers the edges and swings the package over his shoulder like a hobo. I'm frantic, tucking my shirt in, smoothing my hair, retrieving my purse.

Francesco grabs my hand. Bending over like soldiers avoiding an attack, we creep away from the guards and toward the gate we entered the night before. As he rattles and raises the bars for our escape, I take one last glance around, and it dawns on me. I finally have a story for the girls.

I slip onto the back of Francesco's scooter with much more ease than the night before. I rest my head on his back as he darts through early-morning traffic. The city is quieter now than it was in the night, the antiquity more evident as the new sun spotlights the dirt, the film that covers everything, except those pieces lucky enough to be deemed landmarks and restored. Most of the businesses are still shuttered, but we pass a bakery with an open door, and the scent of baking bread wafts into the street.

I squeeze Francesco around the waist. He strokes my hand with his fingers. At a light, he glances over his shoulder with a quick smile, making my stomach bounce like a tennis ball. We take a sharp turn and he grabs my thigh, as if to hold me on the bike. His touch makes me flush again. I adore this part. The part where everything is new and electric, where every syllable, gesture and glance count.

It was that way once with John, wasn't it? Our meeting two years ago in a smoky bar, packed to the gills, both of us standing directly in front of a band. They were called Beef Express or something like that. One of those names picked at random from the Yellow Pages or the side of a truck. I was watching the band and, at the same time, keeping an eye on the TV airing a college basketball tournament. It was the one sporting event I got enthusiastic about because my alma mater usually kicked ass. Kat was there, too, but she couldn't have cared less about the game. She'd already met someone.

"Who're you rooting for?" John asked with a crooked smile that I would later become intimately familiar with. He was cute in a bookish sort of way—cropped light brown hair, washed-out, greenish eyes, a preppy shirt with every button fastened except the very top.

"Indiana. Have to root for the Big Ten."

"The Big Ten." He groaned. "You know they'll choke. They always do."

"Fuck off," I said, but with a light, funny tone and a coy smile. I was a great flirt back then. John and I started talking, going head to head on Big Ten basketball versus other conferences, but after a while there was a pause in the conversation. I acted like I didn't notice and filled the space with an intent look at the game. The band screeched on about bodies burning in a field.

"I'm John," I heard him say when the song ended with a cymbal's crash.

I turned to find him stretching out a hand, his crisp blue,

button-down shirt turned up at the cuffs. His arm was tan, which surprised me, the hair there golden.

"Casey," I said, meeting his hand, trying to make sure my handshake was firm, rather than one of those lame, fingers-only shakes.

"What do you do for a living?"

"Northwestern Law School."

"You're a law student, huh?"

"Yeah," I said. He moved closer as a waitress jostled him from behind, and he smelled clean, fresh, as if he'd just showered. "What about you?"

"Lawyer." He made an embarrassed sort of laugh. "M&A." And then, as if I might not understand, he added, "Mergers and acquisitions."

"I know what M&A means," I said, sounding a little huffy. In reality, I was trying to cover up how daunted I felt to meet someone roughly my age who actually made a living practicing law.

"Sure," he said, coloring a little. "Sorry."

"No problem." I graced him with my best smile. I liked his blushing.

I heard my name being called and turned to see my friend, P.J., another law student, pointing toward the door. "We're out of here," he yelled.

"Where's Kat?"

P.J., who'd been hanging out with Kat and me for a year by then, gave an exaggerated shrug, as if to say, "Who knows? Who cares?"

I glanced at John. "I guess I'm going."

"Are you sure? Why don't you stay for the rest of the game?" He smiled at me, his lips slightly parted, and for some reason, I wanted to lean into them. "I'll take care of you," he said in a joking tone.

But I sensed he was serious, and I stayed.

★ ★ ★

Thinking back on that now, that somewhat self-conscious meeting that led to a smooth transition straight into a relationship, makes it seem even more alien for me to roll into my pensione at 6:00 a.m., all hot and bothered and mascara stained. Yet in a strange way, I'm proud of my current state, because this sordidness smells of sex and lust, and I haven't had that particular scent for as long as I can remember.

Francesco drops me off in front as the early-morning commuters begin to surface. Their presence doesn't prevent him from snaking an arm around my waist and drawing me into an extended kiss while he still straddles his bike.

When I finally pull myself away, he says, "I want to show you more special places of Roma. I will come back in a few hours."

"I can't." My voice sounds unconvincing. "I'm sightseeing with my friends."

"Tomorrow then."

"No," I say, although right now I want nothing more than to spend my last hours in Rome with him.

His brow furrows as if we're experiencing a language problem.

"I'm taking a train to the coast tonight," I say, feeling the need to explain. "To Brindisi. And then a boat to Greece."

"But then you must spend today with me." He puts a hand to my cheek, a feather touch, and kisses me again.

When I open my eyes, I find myself shrugging and agreeing. The girls will kill me, but I'll have to kill myself if I don't see him one more time.

"Eleven o'clock," Francesco says. "I will be back." He kisses me once more before he sputters off into the day.

The concierge, a different one from the night before, raises his eyebrows as I burst into the lobby. I give him a quick half smile, feeling undressed and dirty from his leer. Rather than wait for the elevator under his scrutiny, I take the stairs two at a time.

When I open the door, the room feels dark and cool. Kat is sleeping in a little pink T-shirt on top of her sheets. She seems to be without Guiseppe, but one can never be sure where guys are lurking when Kat's around. Lindsey, though, is wide-awake. She's sitting on her bed, headphones stuck in her ears, a Scott Turow novel resting on her knees. She's studying it with intense concentration, as if she's reading an ancient scroll depicting the hidden tomb of a pharaoh.

"Hi," I whisper, waving my arms, trying to catch her attention and avoid waking Kat, although the fact is that Kat could sleep through an avalanche.

"Sin," I say a little louder. "Sorry I'm late."

I cross the room and stand right next to her, but she won't look up from her book. She's ignoring me. I feel my stomach drop.

I despise fights. I suppose it has something to do with the utter lack of conflict in my family. Even now, in the midst of their problems, my parents rarely duke it out. Instead, they stifle, pout, avoid and cry a lot. I guess I just never learned to do confrontation well, which is one of the reasons why I'm so nervous about practicing law. Litigation is inherently confrontational, a world of egos and bullshit and fighting for fighting's sake. I didn't really choose to go into it. Instead, it seemed to choose me during my summer associate position, when the firm kept pairing me with the trial group, telling me that my outgoing personality was perfect for it. Maybe, but I'm not well-suited for clashes with friends.

I nudge Lindsey with my knee, and she finally looks up at me, clicking off her Walkman with a punch of her finger.

"Where were you?" she says, her voice hard and demanding, and it hits me that Sin should be the trial lawyer, not me. She's much better at intimidation and interrogation.

I try to ignore her tone. "I'm so sorry I'm late, but you won't believe it. It's the best story. We—"

"You were supposed to meet us here at midnight," she says, interrupting me. *"Last night."*

"I'm really, really sorry."

She gives a short, bitter laugh that sounds like gunfire.

"We fell asleep," I say, wanting to make this better, to tell her all about my night, but she shoots me a look that could wither roses.

All at once, my natural inclination to avoid conflict dissipates. She had reason to be worried when I didn't come home last night, maybe even to be annoyed, but she's ruining the first honestly good mood I've had in months.

"What?" I say, my voice a fierce whisper. "How come Kat gets to pick up every guy from here to Munich, but when I meet one person, you act like the Gestapo?"

Our voices have roused Kat, who sits up on her cot, watching us in silence. I wonder for a second if she heard my comment and is pissed off, but I dismiss the thought. If there's anyone who hates confrontation more than me, it's Kat. Like me, she probably gets this trait from her parents. After they divorced, they both kept a room in each of their homes for her, but they were more interested in dating and their careers than they were in Kat. She'd tried to scream and yell, she'd told me. She'd thrown some fantastic tantrums, but the parent of the moment would simply ship her back to the other like a UPS package. Kat doesn't scream or yell much anymore.

Now she sits on her bed, biting a thumbnail, and I can almost imagine her as a little kid with her thumb in her pretty mouth.

"Well, for one thing," Sin says, "you have a boyfriend."

"I'm well aware of that," I say in a haughty tone. How dare she remind me?

"And for another thing, Kat always comes home when she says she will. She's around when you need her. She's a *friend*."

"What's that supposed to mean?"

"It's just that..." Lindsey stops, pursing her lips as if trying to gather the right words in her mouth. This makes her look like my mother right before she's about to lay some doozy of a revelation on me, like how she's started masturbating again after a twenty-year hiatus.

"It's just that what you did last night," Sin says, "blowing us off—it's basically what you've been doing for the last two years."

Her words hit me like a slap. I sense some shred of reality there, but it seems like an overstatement, a gross generalization.

"I've never said I'd be somewhere and didn't show up."

"No, maybe not like that, but you've been avoiding us since you started dating John. You never call. You never have time to go out with us anymore. And when we finally do get together, once in a great while, it's like you're not really there. You're just different. You're not like you used to be."

I can't believe she's saying this. Maybe I've been a little detached lately, but I've been studying for a goddamned living. My life hasn't exactly been a Martha Stewart picnic.

I turn to Kat. "Is that what you think, too?"

"Oh, honey." She rises to come to me, putting her arm around my shoulders. "It's just that we wish you were around more. We wish it was like the old days."

"That's not fair," I say, jabbing a finger at Lindsey. "You haven't been around all that much either, you know." Lindsey's been putting in ten- to twelve-hour days and lots of weekends at her ad agency. She wants to make vice president within the next year and be the youngest VP ever.

"That's true," she says, "but I'm going to change that. I have to."

"Well, things will never be exactly like they were in college, and you can't expect them to be."

"Maybe it's not fair, sweetie," Kat says, "but what Sin's talking about is true. You're not the same person we used to know. I mean, I know you're in there somewhere." She squeezes my shoulders. "I just haven't seen you in so long, and when I do get to actually go out with you, it doesn't seem like you're having much fun."

"I had fun last night." I shake her arms off me.

"It's okay," Kat says. "We just miss you."

I know what she means. I miss me, too, sometimes. I drop my head in my hands.

But as I sit there, some realization dawns. I raise my face. "Wait a minute. You've felt like this for two years, and you've never said a word?" I'd been a tad mopey for a while, particularly this summer, but they're talking about *two years*. The whole time I've been dating John.

I leave Kat's side and walk across the room to the window. Across the way, I see a couple on their terrace reading papers, eating grapefruit.

I turn back to Kat and Sin, sitting side by side. It's me against them right now, and I hate it.

Kat looks down, then back up at me. Sin shrugs. "We knew you were in love with him."

"You're supposed to be my best friends. How can you be pissed off at me for years and not say a word?"

Kat blinks a few times like a stumped contestant on *Jeopardy.*

"We were just hoping it would go away," Sin says.

Her words feel like a betrayal. *All this time,* I keep thinking. *All this time they've been holding it back.* We used to be the kind of friends who said anything and everything to each other, the minute the thought occurred to us.

"Hideous," Kat would say when I came down the stairs

of the sorority house in one of my slutty outfits. "At least take off the fuck-me pumps."

And Sin didn't know the meaning of holding back, which was something I'd come to love about her. It was Sin who helped me decide on what law school to attend. I'd narrowed it down to Northwestern or Harvard. I was enamored by the thought of Harvard Law School. I liked simply saying those words, and I imagined the tingle I'd get every time I told someone, "Yes, I attend Harvard. Harvard Law School." I'd only gotten in because my father's boss was an alum who happened to donate hundreds of thousands of dollars a year, but that didn't bother me. I just wasn't sure I wanted to move to Boston.

I was debating the subject one night about a month before our college graduation. Sin listened to my list of pros and cons for about ten seconds before she held up her hand and said, "You're not the Harvard Law type."

"What's *that* supposed to mean?" I sat back and crossed my arms.

"C'mon," she said. "Harvard Law is Birkenstocks and environmental activism and people whose ancestors went there before them. You're not about that. You're..." She threw her hands up. "You're Steve Maddens and aerosol hair spray, and you're the first person in your family to go to law school."

I kept my arms crossed over my chest, trying to look insulted, but she was right. She usually was. The next day, I sent my acceptance form to Northwestern.

Now I turn back to the window again. The couple on the terrace is discussing something, grapefruit dishes pushed aside, their heads close together.

All the confidence and allure I fleetingly gained with Francesco drains away. I feel like a day-old balloon. My friends don't feel like friends, and this hurts more than anything in recent memory. I've always had this innate sense that while schools and boys and jobs might pass through my life as if on a high-speed conveyor belt, my friends will be the one steady force. I should be looking for a way to smooth things over, but I feel attacked and vulnerable.

"Come on, Case. Let's get an early start and head to the catacombs," Kat says, trying to make nice. "We can talk more about this later."

"I'm meeting Francesco, and I need to get some sleep first." My voice is stiff, flat, and even as I say it, I know I should call and cancel. There are two problems with this potential cancellation, though. One, I don't have his phone number. Two, although it's juvenile, I want them to hurt as much as I do.

The room is so quiet it feels like it's made of glass and the slightest movement will shatter us all into pieces.

"Un-fucking-believable." Lindsey's loud voice breaks the silence, the volume something I haven't heard often. She pauses, but gets no response from me. I stand with my back to her, still staring out the window. "Jesus. You're acting like a fucking child!"

I'm vaguely aware that she has a point, but I'm too stung by their criticism to be mature about it. I go into the bathroom and splash water on my face, feeling jumbled and confused. I can hear them whispering, moving about the room. I brush my teeth and, for lack of something better to do, rearrange the toiletries on the counter, putting the moisturizers and hair products and eye creams in a height line like a row of marionettes.

About ten minutes later, I hear Kat say in an imploring tone, "Leave her alone."

Footsteps approach the bathroom, then I hear Lindsey's sarcastic voice. "Have fun with your new *friend*."

6

After they leave, I lie on the bed with my eyes closed for two hours, although I catch only brief moments of sleep. I can't seem to stop reviewing the argument, re-running each of Kat's and Lindsey's words in my head. My feelings bounce back and forth between furious and betrayed, then skid to the unrealistic hope that they'll walk in the door with doughnuts and cappuccinos.

When I get up, I see a note on the bureau from Kat, ever the peacemaker. "Casey," it says, "I hope you're okay. Lindsey and I went to the catacombs. We'll meet you back here at four o'clock so we can check out and get to the train station. You are coming with us, right?" I know she probably meant to be humorous, but the question cuts me. As if they don't know me anymore. But isn't that their point?

My fight with Kat and Sin seems to dull everything. The tree outside our window is lackluster now, some of its blooms fading and drooping. Even the thought of being back in Rome doesn't seem as exciting. Yet when I step outside the pensione and hear the anemic chug of Francesco's scooter rounding the corner, adrenaline shoots back through my veins. I tug my shirt down so that it shows a little more cleavage. I try for an alluring pose on the stoop.

He's wearing sunglasses and a light blue shirt that billows around him as he pulls into the courtyard, slows in front of me and turns off the engine.

"Ciao," he says, giving me a grin, a flash of white teeth.

Unfortunately, no witty greeting comes to mind. "Morning," I say.

"You are ready?"

I nod.

He holds out his hand, and I take it.

The bulk of my day with Francesco is a blur of cathedrals, museums, monuments, all amazing in their historical significance, yet rarely included in the standard tours for one reason or another—their disrepair, their locations in crappy or out of the way areas. Francesco gives me morsels of information at each stop, making me momentarily forget this morning's argument, yet it always comes back.

"Look at his beard from this angle," Francesco says.

We're standing in front of Michelangelo's sculpture of Moses, located in an unassuming, rather hidden church reached only by climbing high stone steps and walking through a tunnel. The gray sculpture is life-size, and strangely, Moses has two horns like the devil.

Francesco takes my elbow and guides me to the right. "It is Michelangelo's own profile cut into the beard," he says.

I move my head this way and that, squinting my eyes, striving to make out the sculptor's face in the long tangle of stone. I wonder, for a nanosecond, how long it took him to carve this hulking thing, before my mind shifts back into the worn ruts, and instead I start wondering if Michelangelo ever felt unclear, unsure of himself, or if he always knew he was creating a masterpiece. Was his identity ever vague? Did he ever cheat on a lover and feel guilty for not feeling guiltier? Did he ever argue with his friends and not be able to erase the scene from his head? I keep hearing Kat's and Lindsey's accusations, seeing Lindsey's face frozen in a sneer.

I try to regain the dreamlike reverie I had last night. I grab Francesco's hand, planting a quick, wet kiss on his lips, but daylight and guilt keep fighting against me.

We have lunch during the siesta at a small café near Piazza di Spagna. We sit in a corner by a vine-covered wall, ivory linens on the table.

The place reminds me of a trattoria in Piazza del Popolo where my parents often ate when they visited me. I told them over and over to try other places, other neighborhoods, but they were happy there, they said. They'd gotten to know the menu and the owners. Why try anything new? They seemed perfectly happy with each other then, too. Whatever had transpired over the course of five years to put them where they are now—two tense strangers who happen to share a home—is a mystery to me.

I've received my mother's version, of course, during our way too-frequent telephone conversations.

"You know, Casey," she'd said. "It's the sex. All of a sudden, he wants nighties and negligees, and I'm in sweatpants and T-shirts."

"So put on a teddy, Mom," I'd said, exasperated again, trying very hard not to imagine my father having sexual desires of any kind or picture my mother in a butt-thonged, demi-cup teddy.

My father, on the other hand, is so closemouthed about the subject of their marital discord, he almost convinces me there's nothing wrong.

But there is. Something is terribly wrong, and it can't simply be about sleepwear.

Francesco brings me back to the present, to Rome, by waving a menu in front of my face. I take it, realizing I'm starving, since I've eaten little since yesterday. It takes a glass of Pinot Grigio and a huge plate of spaghetti to satiate my appetite, but then I'm ready to move again. Sitting still lets too many thoughts surface.

"What's next?" I ask Francesco.

"It is siesta," Francesco says. "Nothing is next. Only another glass of wine."

"There are places open," I say, putting on my Jackie-O sunglasses that I bought for the trip, deciding they were rather international and cosmopolitan even though they're way too large for my face. "We could go to the catacombs," I say, collecting my purse, putting some lira on the table. "We could go—"

Francesco cuts me off. "Slow, *bella,* slow," he says. Gentle words.

I sit back in my chair again. We can't go to the catacombs, anyway. We might run into the girls, and Lindsey might cause Francesco to disappear in a cloud of smoke with one of her nasty stares. She probably scares the shit out of everyone at work.

I sip the cool, tart wine, trying to let myself get drawn back into a lazy conversation with Francesco, the way the Italian siesta was intended to be spent. I know I should enjoy this time, this day, but I'm struck by the fact that in a few weeks, there will be no more siestas for me. Instead, I'll make a haggard run for fast food or a salad and then eat at my desk without breathing. I take another sip of wine to drown the thought.

After siesta, Francesco leads me to a small, graceful fountain in a corner of the Borghese garden, which is situated at the top of the Spanish Steps. I study the curved nymphs of the fountain, attempting to enjoy it along with the surrounding purple blooms, but I'm not really seeing, because the more I think about the situation with Kat and Sin, the more I know they have a point. Sure, we haven't seen each other as much as we used to, but more importantly, somewhere along the way I stopped being there mentally. I'd still meet them on occasion at some of our regular spots—the River Shannon Pub for Thursday night drafts, Gamekeepers for burgers and the Bulls games—but I hung on the fringes, listening to the conversation rather than taking an active part. I'd opt out of late-night festivities to run to John's condo, where he'd already be sleeping, barely cognizant of my arrival.

Maybe it was because I was overloaded with law school and eventually the bar exam. Or maybe it was my desire to spend more time with John while he just spent an increasing amount of time at work. It could also have been my struggle to hold my family together, which has been like trying to support a stumbling drunk from under the arms. Whatever the reason, it seems that this morning's argument and the absence from home invites a certain self-awareness that lets me see myself more objectively than when I was mired in it all. Unfortunately, I'm not so thrilled with what I've uncovered. I'm still hurt that Sin and Kat felt the way they did for so long, that they couldn't trust me enough to tell me, but I'm as much to blame as they are. I hadn't really told them about my parents, after all. I hadn't confided much in them over the last few years. Somehow we'd gotten away from each other, from the way our friendship used to be.

I'd first learned that my parents were having problems about a year and a half ago, when I went home early on Thanksgiving morning. Our suburban stucco house on Orchard Lane was surprisingly quiet that day, and I walked through the place, past photos of graduations and Little League and a very odd one showing me in a nun's costume and my brother, Danny, dressed like a priest for Halloween. No one was in the sunny kitchen with the brown tile floor, or the family room with its overstuffed couches and clutter of antique lanterns my dad collected. My parents' bedroom door was open. I walked in and peeked my head in the master bath.

"Happy Thanksgiving," I called out, giddy at the reprieve from studying and the prospect of eating my own body weight in mashed potatoes.

"Casey!" my mom said, a hand flying to her heart. "You scared me."

It was then I noticed that her blond hair, which was dyed to look like mine—and like hers used to look—was severely pulled back from her face with a thick black headband that I used to wear to high school cheerleading practice.

"What's going on?" I said.

"Okay." She took a deep breath. "I have a question, and this is serious, so I need you to really give this some thought."

"All right," I said, leaning on the lime-green countertop, wondering what this was all about and when she would start making the rice casserole with the chunks of sausage.

"Okay," she said again. "It's either this—" she put both hands to the sides of her face and dragged the skin upward so that she looked like a cat "—or this." She shifted her hands so that the skin around her eyes was pulled straight back, giving her a rather Asian appearance. She dropped her hands and turned to me. "What do you think?"

"What do I think? What are you talking about?"

She blew out a quick blast of air like she did when dealing with a daft store clerk. "I'm getting a little work done, and Dr. Stangey says I need to decide *exactly* what I want."

"Work done," I repeated.

"Yes, you know—face-lift, eye-lift, laser resurfacing, Botox, cheekbone implants." She cocked her head at me. "I have to decide."

"Why would you do any of that?" This was a truly shocking turn of events. Not only was my mother an attractive fifty-two-year-old who was always being mistaken for forty, but she didn't care about these things. She was the mom at the public pool who jumped in with the kids, not minding that her hair got wet, and she'd always spent more on our wardrobes than she did her own.

"It's time," she said, yanking off the headband, stowing it away in a drawer. "It's time I started paying attention to my appearance. Some men might still find me appealing."

At the mention of men, I realized the absence of my father and brother. "Where's Dad?" I said.

My mother picked at her hair with a comb, sucking in her cheeks in the mirror. "Working out."

"On Thanksgiving?"

"Um-hmm."

And then a better question occurred to me. "Does he know how?" My father didn't belong to a gym that I knew of, but I'd hadn't lived on Orchard Lane for a long time.

"Apparently," my mother said in a particularly cryptic voice, straightening the lime-green towels on the rack, then moving back to the mirror and yanking at her face again. "So which do you think?" she said, shifting her skin up and down, up and down, until I started to wonder whether I was having a flashback from the ecstasy I did once.

"Have you talked to Danny about this?"

"Ha!" she said, and I couldn't blame her. My brother was a bit of a shit at that point, nearing the end of his adolescence. Still, he lived here, not me, a fact I pointed out to her.

"This is a woman's issue," she said. "You're the only one I have."

When my dad didn't come home that day until almost five o'clock, right when my mom was about to serve the pared down Thanksgiving feast she'd prepared—a Butterball turkey from a neighborhood store and Spuds potatoes—it was then I knew that something was truly off. Usually, my dad was in the kitchen right along with my mother, peeling the potatoes and generally poking his fingers into things that weren't ready.

I pulled Danny aside, asking him what in the hell was going on. But he was a senior in high school, and his vocabulary consisted mainly of two words—*dude* and *whatever*—which is verbatim what he said to me that night. "Dude...*whatever.*"

After I left that weekend, I thought about talking to Kat and Sin about it. I really did. But I knew that it sounded lame—my mom wants to get a face-lift and my dad was late for dinner. It was nothing, nothing at all, certainly not compared to Kat's complete lack of stable family life. And besides, I wasn't seeing my girlfriends quite as much as I usually had. I wasn't sure whose fault it was, but I blamed it on growing up, on having more to do than practice keg stands and beer bongs. When we did see each other, we just didn't have the same conversations that we used to—the ones that involved the minutiae of our lives. Instead, we got to the big points. We summarized.

And so I didn't mention that Thanksgiving scene with my mom, nor did I talk about that first scary phone call a few weeks later when she'd confided a sexual fantasy about Antonio Banderas. The barrage of alarming maternal confidences grew from there, one on top of the other, and I got used to internalizing them. Danny wasn't any help. College just made it easier for him to get pot, easier for him to avoid home and anything associated with it. I generally mentioned to Kat and Sin that my parents were having issues, but I never elaborated. I never told them how it kept me up nights, how I'd come to fear the ring of the phone. By the time I finally realized I should speak about it, that I *needed* to talk about it, John seemed the only good candidate. I'd slipped away from Kat and Sin, or they from me, and we all seemed too busy for the kind of analysis the conversation required.

"I have to get back to the hotel," I say now, interrupting something Francesco is telling me about the fountain.

"It is early, *bella,*" he says, looking at his watch again and raising his perfectly arched eyebrows.

His bedroom eyes turn back on like floodlights, and he lightly touches my collarbone, as if we'd been together a long time, and this is a familiar gesture.

"I really have to get back," I say.

Ten minutes later, I stand on the stairs leading to the pensione. With Francesco on the ground, we're at eye level, his face an inch from mine.

"I will miss you, *bella.*" He breathes the sentence. Despite the warring thoughts in my head about John, Kat and Lindsey, I'm stirred again.

He leans forward, his kiss infinitesimally slow. I feel the sun on his face as he moves from my mouth and kisses my eyelids, my forehead.

"Why don't you stay a few more days? You could meet your friends later."

I laugh. Kat and Sin would love that.

But I don't answer right away. His suggestion makes me think about a woman I knew during my semester in Rome. She met a metal worker in Cannes while we were there for a weekend trip, and she never came back. She dropped out of school, out of sight, out of the U.S.A. She was ridiculed by all the women in my school for selling herself short and giving it all up for a man. Secretly, I thought her brave.

Maybe I could do that, too. Sure, Francesco is only asking for a few days, but couldn't I stretch it out and never go back? I wouldn't have to start my job at the law firm. Instead, I'd find something wonderfully exciting to do here, like work for a fashion magazine or become a painter. I wouldn't have to deal with my family, or anything else, for that matter.

Yet as quickly as I conjure up these possibilities, I know

my answer is no. I'm too much of a planner. Danny is the spontaneous one, the appointed nutball of the family, not me. I've always valued responsibility over spontaneity, strategy over impulsiveness.

"Sorry, Francesco," I say. "I have to go."

I put my hand on the back of his head, feeling his curly hair, damp from the heat. I pull his face to me. Soon, both of my hands run through his hair. He holds my face while he kisses me as if he won't let me go. He ducks and kisses my neck, my collarbone where he had touched earlier. It's only when I hear myself moan that I come to. I snap my head around, embarrassed. The only person in the vicinity is an older, well-dressed shopkeeper, sweeping his sidewalk across the street. He studies his work intently, but a quick smirk over the top of his broom tells me he's enjoyed our little public display.

"I have to go," I say again. I push Francesco gently away from me.

"Okay, *bella,*" he says, his chocolate eyes on mine. "You will write me, yes?"

He hands me a white card with neat handprinting that says, "Francesco Giacobbe, Via Majorana 122, Roma, Italy, (06) 59 88 299." Funny, I never asked him his last name before.

I can't stop looking at the card. The fact that he has printed it out ahead of time touches me, and I don't want him to leave. A few seconds go by.

"*Bella?*" he says.

"Of course. I'll write you." I look up and smile. "Thank you, Francesco."

He shrugs, a nonchalant movement, as if to say there's nothing to thank him for. I open my mouth to tell him otherwise, but I can't find the words.

I kiss him one last time, a chaste kiss really, compared to our prior rumbles.

"*Ciao, bella,*" Francesco says, and starts his scooter. I watch him as he pulls away, his light blue shirt flapping behind him, his quick wave to someone he recognizes in the street. A moment later, he turns the corner, and I can't see him anymore.

7

Once in the room, I open the windows to let in some air and start repacking my stuff in the massive backpack I borrowed from my brother. Most of my clothes are scattered around the room from my "dress" rehearsals before going out with Francesco last night. It seems so long ago.

I fold my clothes quickly, nervous about seeing Kat and Sin again but looking forward to the rest of our trip. They were right about me changing. We've all changed, actually, but it doesn't mean we can't be close like we used to. I'm still a tad annoyed that they laid out their gripes now, after two years, but I'm willing to let it go.

I hook up my CD player to two tiny speakers and crank up a Grateful Dead album. Sometimes I use music like a drug to elevate my mood, and I decide that after the last few months, I could use some drugs. Jerry Garcia sings, "What a long strange trip it's been." Like a drug, the effect isn't immediate. It takes a while to settle into my brain and my limbs, but soon I'm snapping my fingers. I have my hair dryer in my hand, and I'm dancing around, coiling the cord, when Kat and Lindsey fall into the room laughing, juggling packages. I freeze like I've been caught doing crack cocaine. Silence greets me.

"Hey, guys," I say, my anxiety returning. "How's your day?"

"Fine," Lindsey says, her eyes wary. She stands hesitantly in the doorway.

"Are you all right?" Kat says.

"Yeah. I'm great." I walk to them and try to grab them both in a bear hug, envisioning a tearful reunion in a made-for–TV movie, but neither returns my enthusiasm.

"Listen," I say, taking a deep breath and a step back. "I realize that I've been out of it lately. I can't explain it, but you're right. I have no excuses, no reasons, but I think I'm shaking it off. I'm starting to feel like my old self again."

"Well, well," Lindsey says, dropping a Versace bag from her hand. It lands with a soft thud on the tile floor.

Kat says nothing but looks hopeful.

"I know I shouldn't have gone off with Francesco today, not after what happened this morning, but I was so shocked and hurt about everything you said. I was upset that you dropped it on me now—on vacation."

"There was no time before," Lindsey says. "You were always with John, or there were other people around. You never seemed like you wanted to talk about anything."

"Well, I think you could have found a minute or two to try." This comes out sounding snotty. I shake my head, as if I can erase it. "The bottom line is that I want us to get back to how we used to be."

Lindsey stands with her arms crossed. "That's great, Case. Me too, but it's not going to happen overnight."

This throws me a little. I'd imagined apologizing and then everything returning to some semblance of normality.

"All right," I say, "but I'm ready to have the best trip of

our lives. I really want to do anything I can to make it better."

"Sounds good to me," Kat says. "We all have to try, right?" We both look at Lindsey.

"I don't think it'll be that easy," she says.

Kat gives Sin a poke in the ribs.

Sin glares at her. "I guess we can all give it a shot," she says, nodding as if to convince herself.

I exhale a short burst of relief.

We get on the Rome subway, our backpacks knocking into the poles and other passengers. The subway will take us to the Termini, where a train will take us to Brindisi, at which point we'll hop a taxi to the port and board an overnight ferry to Corfu. I'd never even consider traveling like this in the States. If any destination requires more than three hours of auto travel, I fly, or I skip it altogether. But there's something that sounds authentic and wonderful about sitting in the cabin of a train as it chugs past the European landscape. And while I've heard that the boat to Corfu is much like those carrying immigrants to the U.S., I'm looking forward to it. To Greece. To patching things up with Kat and Sin.

As I stand in the subway car, separated from them by the crowd, I stare at the profile of a guy a few persons ahead of me. I take in the sensuous curve of the corner of his mouth, the dark hair curling slightly over his collar. The time that I spent with Francesco seems to have awakened a new crop of sexual feelings in me. I see and feel sex everywhere. Although I can't see the guy's eyes, or most of his face, I picture those lips on mine, whispering in my ear the things he wants to do with me, to me. I envision him taking me to his family's house in Capri, making love to me on the patio overlooking the water.

He shifts his body so that I glimpse his face, and I'm surprised to see that he's nothing like what I'd thought. His nose is crooked, eyes too deep set. Certainly not unattractive, but not my type, either. Shit. Now he's noticed me critiquing him, and he's obviously mistaken my surprise as interest. He smiles a slow, and what he must believe to be sexy, smile and gives me a meaningful look. Strangely, I feel trapped, as if he might come over to me at any minute and act on my earlier thoughts. I look around for somewhere to move, but with my pack strapped on I'm like a turtle, and abrupt movements don't work well.

Suddenly, I'm yanked toward the closing doors of the subway train.

"Let's go!" Kat yells. "We're here!"

I tumble out of the doors of the train, struggling to keep the backpack on.

"God, Casey, you are so out of it sometimes," Lindsey says.

I feel like setting her hair afire, but I just mumble, "Sorry."

"Shit," Lindsey says, looking at her watch. "We've got about a minute till the train leaves."

We run up the steps and into the station, our heads swiveling wildly, looking for the right track.

"There!" I say, pointing to a track a few hundred yards away. "Number 6!"

We all break into another run, Kat in front. She gets no farther than ten feet, though, when the large plastic bag she's clutching gives way, spilling its contents—Vatican souvenirs wrapped in green paper, a paperback copy of *Story of O,* a black leather makeup bag, an errant shoe, even a pair of tired-looking Victoria's Secrets.

"Jesus, Kat," Lindsey says as we bend to help her pick up the collection. "Why couldn't you pack this crap?"

"It wouldn't fit!" she says, scrambling to gather it all in her arms.

As I lean over to help the cause, the force of my overloaded backpack and the extra weight I'd acquired over the summer send me sprawling.

"Shit!" Lindsey says. "The train's leaving!"

Grabbing Kat's rank-looking undies, I push myself to my feet, and we all sprint toward Track 6, where the mustard-colored passenger train is beginning to slowly move away.

Lindsey manages to grab the handle on the last car, pulling her tiny self onto the platform. Once inside, she yanks in Kat and her armload of junk. A few of Kat's Vatican trinkets flit away.

"Come on!" Lindsey yells at me, holding out her hand.

Fuck, fuck, fuck, I think, as I waddle after the train. I'm never going to make it. I'm going to be left here all alone.

"Let's go!" Sin yells, shaking her arm at me.

Finally, I muster every shred of energy and heave myself upward, grabbing Sin's hand with one of mine. She drags me in, both of us falling to the floor in a jumble of luggage and limbs. I open my eyes. Sin's face is right below mine, so close we could kiss. I cross my eyes at her, and we burst into laughter.

8

The train is packed tight with other tourists, families traveling in bunches and Italian students who look bored with the whole scene. We wander from car to car like mules, carrying all of our belongings on our backs. The people who can't find a seat have set up camp in the aisles, and we have to step over mounds of luggage, sleeping backpackers and even mothers with children.

We're almost to the front of the train when I spot an oasis—a car with empty spaces.

"*Scusi,*" I say, sliding open the car door and smiling at an older Italian couple dressed all in black despite the heat. What is it about most Italians and their fear of cool, accommodating clothing? They refuse to wear shorts, shrugging them off as an ugly American thing.

"No! No!" The man gestures with his hands and unleashes a torrent of rapid Italian. Using my minimal skills, I'm able to understand that they paid for the entire car ahead of time and refuse to let us share.

"Please," I say, assuming a beggar's pose, my hands clasped in front of me. *"Per favore."*

"Please! Please!" echo Kat and Lindsey from behind me.

The man continues to hold out his hands as if to block us, speaking even faster now, so that I can't make out a word. I'm about to give up when the man's wife nudges him aside with a sharp elbow and gestures us into the car.

Kat sprawls on the seat across from me, her eyes shut, legs apart, her head propped up against the window. I can't imagine how she can sleep like that, but she's shown time and again that she can doze through just about anything. In college, when she wasn't with a guy, she was always the one who passed out on the couch while the party raged around her.

Lindsey sits next to Kat, apparently absorbed in her novel.

"Good book?" I say. I've already exhausted my conversational possibilities with the Italian couple, asking where they're from and explaining that we're from Chicago. The woman looks at me every so often, and we both smile as if not sure what else to do.

"Um-hmm." Lindsey nods, not lifting her eyes.

"It's so hot in here, isn't it?" I ask, fanning my face with my hand.

"Yeah." She continues reading.

"Sì, sì!" the woman says, catching my drift, fanning her face as well. We smile again, and another uncomfortable silence follows.

I want desperately to tell Sin about Francesco, to relive every moment. To me, an amazing experience doesn't seem like it really happened until I can tell one of my friends. Yet at the same time, I don't want to be the only one making the effort here.

I turn and stare out the window. The countryside whizzes

by, a blur of rolling burnt-yellow hills, vineyards with criss-crossed rows of vines, quaint stucco cottages.

In my mind, I go over and over the details of my time with Francesco—the feel of his waist in my hands as I sat behind him on the scooter, the way he patted my neck with the napkins. I could live for years on these memories alone.

We've only been gone four days, but it seems more like four weeks. Mostly, I feel far away from John. And with that reminder, the guilt comes rushing in. How can I be so cruel? John does nothing but love me, and I run off to Italy and roll around with the first guy on a scooter. What in the hell is wrong with me? Or maybe a better question is, what is wrong with us? It's too unfair a thought, though, one he's not here to defend against. I decide that I'll swear Kat and Sin to secrecy and do my best to forget Francesco. It was just a small blip, nothing else.

Think only of John, only of John, I tell myself. I squint at my watch and figure that with the time change, it's early in the morning in Chicago. He's probably just waking up. He'll mix together Grape Nuts and Raisin Bran, then add banana. He'll put on his olive suit but dress it up with one of his three hundred ties. He'll take the 7:04 El train into the Loop, and he'll go to work. Again.

The problem is this—there isn't anything particularly exciting to think about in terms of John. I try focusing out the window. We slow as we pass a small town, one with only a few dusty roads and three square buildings. A little girl of about seven stands in the doorway of one of the buildings, watching the train. She's wearing a brown dress and has long, dark hair in a messy ponytail. It seems like she catches my eyes as the train moves past, and I imagine that we hold each other's gaze until she fades to a tiny brown speck.

The Italian couple prepares to leave at the next train stop, which is about an hour outside of Brindisi. They don't speak, but while they gather their bags and suitcases, they seem to communicate by gestures and looks. It makes me think of John and me in twenty years, and I find the thought both sweet and terrifying.

At their stop, the man glares in our direction, but the woman smiles and nods her head.

"Grazie," I say, thanking her again. *"Grazie."*

One of the three guys who've been stuck standing in the aisle for the last few hours holds the door open for the couple then sticks his face in the car. He has shocking orange hair and freckles covering every visible surface of his wiry body.

"Hey, girls," he says in a thick Irish brogue. "Mind if we share the car with you?" He gives us a crooked smile.

"Of course not," Lindsey says, deciding to speak for the first time in at least an hour. She waves at the spaces vacated by the couple.

"Excellent, excellent. Come on, lads." He gestures to his friends in the hall before he carries in a battered, army-green canvas bag and tosses it onto the overhead rack.

"Johnny," he says, extending a hand to Lindsey and me. "And this is Noel and Billy."

"I'm Kat," Kat says, awakening at the sound of young males.

Kat is generous enough to introduce Sin and me, and we all shake hands.

Noel is a short, stout guy with shiny blue eyes and colicky brown hair that stands out at all angles. Billy is tall and sinewy with black curly hair.

"Hey, girls," they both say.

"Much thanks for the accommodations," Billy adds. "It was a feckin' mess out there."

His hair reminds me of Francesco's, but Billy is less mysterious, all grins and quick nods of his head.

"Where are you girls heading?" Noel asks, taking a seat

and leaning forward, his short muscular forearms resting on his knees.

"Corfu," Kat says. "We've heard about someplace there called the Pink Palace."

All three of the Irish guys snort, making sounds of disgust.

"Ah, the Pink Palace," Johnny says with a dismissive wave. "It's bloody awful. We've been to Greece three times before, and believe us, you don't need to go to Corfu. The place to go is Ios."

"We might stop at Ios, too," I say, "but Corfu is closer, and the Pink Palace sounds nice." I don't mention that we got our information from a guidebook used by Lindsey's cousin a decade ago.

"Nice? Nice?" Johnny, Noel and Billy are laughing now.

"All they do is break plates off your head and feed you ouzo for breakfast. You don't need that," Billy says. "Come to Ios with us, girls, and we'll show you what Greece is all about."

"I'm sure," Lindsey says, mimicking his brogue. "Guinness for breakfast and shagging, right?"

They all laugh again at her imitation, while I sit there astounded at her suddenly warm and witty personality shift.

"Anything for you, love." Billy holds Lindsey's eyes a bit long, it seems.

Lindsey's eyes sparkle like they do on the rare occasion she's interested in someone.

Their intimate little moment passes as the guys describe Ios in more detail.

"It's a little island that has billions of pubs and clubs packed onto it, and there's a great beach," Noel says.

"And we know a place to stay," Johnny says. "It's on a cliff overlooking the beach. And the best part is it's cheap."

I don't hear the rest of their enthusiastic description. For some reason, I've let Francesco out of the basement room in my head and started thinking about him again. I reach in the pocket of my shorts and pull out the card he gave me with his address on it. I wonder how many other women have the same card pasted in their scrapbooks next to his picture.

"What do you think, Case?" Lindsey says. "Should we go to Ios with these guys?"

Oh, *now* she's speaking to me again.

I think about it a moment. The truth is that the thought of deviating from our plan makes me anxious. These guys seem nice enough, but with them around I wonder if we'll get the time Sin says we need to make things better between us. Still, Sin's face is lit up like a neon beer sign. She's so rarely hot for anyone. I suppose if she's happy, it'll make everything easier.

I look at Kat. "What do you think?"

"I'm game for anything," she says. No surprise, really.

"All right," I say. "Let's do it."

PART II
IOS, GREECE

9

The ferry in Brindisi is monstrous, and yet they've managed to stuff in more passengers than there is space. We've already been laughed at when we asked for a sleeper cabin and learned that the rooms with cots were sold out weeks ago. Find a chair or someplace on the deck, we're told. The Irish guys were smart enough to book ahead, and they offer to share their bunks, but the other people in their cabin refuse to let us stay, assuming, apparently, that the six of us would be having raucous sex all night if we did. We say a temporary goodbye to the guys, promising to meet them at the Ios port.

Kat, Sin and I schlep from one level of the ship to another, struggling with our overstuffed backpacks. The inside of the ferry has a few lounge areas furnished with hideous, char- treuse-colored, faux-suede chairs. These, too, are completely occupied with travelers, most of them young, most of them sleeping, chatting or drinking beers, giving the boat the feel of an international floating college town. A bit stupid of us to choose the month of August to travel, when nearly every

European citizen is off for "holiday," but it was August or never for me because of the bar exam.

We eventually resign ourselves to sleeping on the deck, but even that is a struggle. The floor is littered with sleeping bags and makeshift campsites. We finally locate a small patch of open space near three large metal cylinders. We look longingly at those people with plush sleeping bags while we spread out our pathetic little beach towels.

Despite the paltry accommodations, I know I'll have no trouble falling asleep, due to the minimal hours I logged last night. I prop a sweatshirt under my head, happy to be horizontal. The last thing I hear is Kat striking up a conversation with some German boys who look about fifteen.

"Where you boys heading?" she asks.

"Crete," one replies.

"Really?" She sounds disappointed.

At 5:00 a.m., we find out the purpose of the metal cylinders we've curled up next to when these cylinders, otherwise known as steamer horns, sound off in three long, rumbling blasts, louder than anything I've ever heard. When they first start to boom, I have no idea what they are. I can barely remember where I am. All I know is that I'm being terrorized out of a wonderful dream where Francesco and I are kissing on a hardwood bench in one of the ubiquitous Roman churches. I bolt upright, terrified, my heart pounding almost as loudly as the horns. Lindsey sits up, too, and we stare at each other, our hands slapped over our ears, our mouths open in surprise. Kat is trying to untangle herself from the German boy who's sharing her meager towel.

Other than messing with the poor peasants on the deck, there seems to be no reason for the horns. We don't dock anywhere. There's no announcement of any kind. When the blasts are over, Kat and Lindsey slump back on their towels, but I'm entirely too awake.

I walk to the side of the deck, picking my way over the multitude of bodies. When I reach the railing, the sight of the sea overwhelms me. Last night, we'd boarded in darkness, and I'd almost forgotten that we were on the Adriatic. Now the sun creeps its way from the east, infusing the teal-blue water with a golden-white sheen. The water is peaceful, only a sailboat or two in the distance, no land in sight. The air smells of salt, and it's cool with an early-morning chill.

Kat joins me in hanging over the railing. The wind whips her chestnut hair and tangles it around her face, but this only makes her look like a model in front of a fan.

"So," she says, "are you going to give me the play by play?"

"What do you mean?" But I know exactly what she means, and I'm thrilled that someone finally wants to hear about Francesco.

She gives me a little push.

"How's your boy?" I say, gesturing toward the towels and her German friend.

She shrugs. "Just some eighteen-year-old."

"Right in your price range, huh?"

"Absolutely. Now tell me."

"Where do I start?"

"Just tell me, damn it."

"You know where he took me to dinner?"

Kat shakes her head.

"The Colosseum." My voice carries a pride I barely recognize.

"What?" Her mouth drops open.

I fill her in on the details, polishing the extraordinary ones, sanding off the more mundane, going on and on about sneaking into the Colosseum and the picnic Francesco had planned.

"Oh, this guy is good." Kat rubs her hands together. "Did you get any?"

I scuff a shoe on the deck, feeling my face getting warm.

"You did!" Kat says with a healthy amount of glee in her voice. "What happened?"

"Not much," I say, but I can't stop a broad smile from moving onto my face.

"C'mon," Kat says. She's practically jumping up and down now.

"No, I didn't sleep with him."

She raises one eyebrow, a patented facial expression of hers.

"I didn't!" I say. "I mean, we did fool around, and then we did fall asleep, but we did *not* have sex." I'm not sure this distinction would hold much weight with John, but I feel compelled to make it.

"Well, what then?" Kat says.

I give her the rest of the story, and as I do, I think, there's nothing better than this—hashing it out and reliving it with a friend, especially when that friend is Kat or Sin. During our senior year, we had a standing rule at our apartment that if you came home from a particularly good date—or a particularly good pickup, in Kat's case—you were allowed to wake the other two and bore them to death with all the gory details.

"It sounds magical," Kat says when I finally stop for a breath, "like something you've been needing."

I nod. "Exactly."

"But what about John?"

I stop my head in mid-nod. "It had nothing to do with him."

She raises one eyebrow again.

"Seriously, Kat. I know how shitty it was, being with Francesco, but it honestly had nothing to do with John. I still love him. I still want to be with him. This thing in the Colosseum, it was about me. A part of me that…I don't know, that I forgot about. Does that make sense?"

She falls silent for a moment. "It does, but what happens

when you get home? Are you going to pretend it never happened? Will you just forget about this, or did it really mean something? Are you going to tell John?"

In ten seconds, she has effectively cut through the jungle of excuses I have created for how I can keep this situation simple. Francesco and John swirl around in my head like a tornado.

I say nothing. Behind us, the sounds of conversation begin to grow as more and more people get up with the sun. It's becoming hotter, and I'm starting to feel a little rank and in need of a shower. Or maybe it's the conversation that's making me uncomfortable. Finally, I turn to Kat and give her a pathetic look.

She pulls me into a hug, laughing at my expression. "You'll figure it out, sweetie."

I hold her tight before we pull away. "Do you think Sin will come around?"

"Sure. Give her a little time."

I sigh. "And what's up with you?"

"What do you mean?"

"Well, for starters, what's the deal with the diamond earrings?"

Her full pink mouth opens and closes. She throws a hand in the air. "They were a gift."

"And that's it?"

"Yeah. That's it."

She seems irritated, but I'm not giving up on this. "If it's that simple then why is Lindsey ready to rip them out of your head every time she sees them?"

"Sin is overprotective."

"I'm confused. What does she think she's protecting you from?"

"The Mad Hatter." Saying her stepfather's nickname usually makes Kat laugh, but her voice is flat. "She doesn't like him."

"Does anyone like the Hatter other than Patty?" Patty is Patricia Reynolds-Hatter, Kat's mom. A high-powered publicist for the arts, she met the Mad Hatter when he donated a million dollars to some play she was working on. I've always called her Patty because Kat has always called her Patty. In fact, Kat has addressed both her parents by their first names since she was twelve, something I thought very cool when I first heard of it. Over the years, though, I've come to see that this habit shows a certain lack of feeling, a certain sterility in their family.

"Sin thinks he's...well..." she trails off, finally adding, "dangerous."

I scoff. "The Hatter? Please." Phillip Hatter is a pompous, overeducated man with too much money and too much time on his hands, but he's soft and harmless as a basset hound, as far as I can tell.

Kat shoots me a look.

"What? What happened?"

She brings a fist to her face, lightly tapping her mouth with it. All at once, I get a sinking feeling in my chest.

"What is it?" I say, more demanding now.

Still she won't speak.

I take her hand, moving it away from her face. "Kat, what's wrong?"

"He hit on me. Sort of."

I blink a few times, caught surprised. "What does 'sort of' mean?"

Another shrug. "He kind of attacked me."

"Kat! My God!" I say, completely shocked now.

"It's no big deal." She gives a mini shrug of her shoulders.

"No big deal? Are you kidding? He's known you since you were a little girl." Then a worse thought hits me. "Has this happened before?"

"No," she says, her voice firm.

"So what exactly happened?"

She leans lower over the railing, staring at the water that's churning against the side of the boat. "I stayed with them one night. We'd gone out for Patty's birthday."

"It was your mom's birthday? His wife's birthday, and he hit on you? The sick fucking bastard!"

She sends me a look to shut up.

"Okay," I say. "Keep going."

"I stayed because Patty and I were going shopping in the morning. I was asleep for an hour at least when I felt the covers being pulled back. I opened my eyes, and there was the Hatter." She laughs, but it sounds brittle. "He had a robe on, this ugly silk thing he calls a 'dressing gown,' but it was open and…" Her voice dies way.

"He had nothing else on?"

"Nope."

"And was he…?"

She nods.

"Oh, God." The thought of the Hatter naked with an erection is not a pleasant one. Under different circumstances, it might even be funny.

"Yeah, I got to see the *real* Hatter." Kat laughs that dry laugh again. "And then he lunged and grabbed me."

I gasp. "Jesus. What then?"

"He was putting his hands all over me." She shivers. "I was so surprised, it took me a minute to react, but then I kneed him, and that took care of the hard-on."

"He left?"

She nods. "He ran out of the room holding his balls."

She hunches over the railing, like she's trying to protect her body from assault, or the memory of his, I suppose.

I reach out my hand and rub her back, not knowing what else to do. I can feel her ribs through her thin T-shirt. "So the earrings were a peace offering?"

She turns her face to me and nods.

"Why would you wear them, though, if they're from the Hatter?"

"Well, they're gorgeous for one thing, but mostly because I want to turn it around. I want to feel like I got the good end of that experience. And I did, don't you think?"

"Not really, Kat. It's fucked up, and it probably messed with you." The Hatter has never been the epitome of good step-parenting, but he has held a fatherlike role for over a decade.

"Oh, hell no." She wriggles away from my arm. "Like I said, no big deal."

"It's a very big deal." I begin to wonder if this has something to do with the overly affectionate kissing of Poster Boy at the table or fooling around with Guiseppe in front of me. Neither of those incidents were completely uncharacteristic of Kat, but they seemed a bit irrational, a bit over the top even for her.

"It's really nothing," Kat says.

"Well, you told your mom, didn't you?"

Her body tenses. She shakes her head.

"Kat!"

I wonder for a second if she's going to tear up, but she only shakes her hair away from her face and over one shoulder, a five-star, supermodel hair flip if I ever saw one, but these things come naturally to Kat. "I really don't want to talk about this anymore," she says.

"I think you need to." This is true. I can't believe the Hatter attack wouldn't have completely freaked her out.

"No," she says, and I can tell by the set of her mouth that she won't go further down this road. "Not right now."

Still I try one more time. "You're sure?"

"Discussion over," she says.

Waving to the German kid, who's waiting for her like a forlorn kitten, she swivels around and walks away from me.

10

"Ios!" calls a heavily accented voice over a static-filled intercom. "Next port—Ios! All out for Ios!" A jumble of incomprehensible Greek follows.

With this, more than half of the ship's travelers sling bags over their shoulders, roll up their sleeping bags, and gather their friends. With the combination of sun, humidity and the ship's engine exhaust, the heat is oppressive. My arms are heavy and lethargic as I stow away my towel and sweatshirt.

Lindsey and I join the crowd shuffling to the exit, like cows being herded out to pasture. Behind us, Kat says goodbye to the German boy, who she'd flirted with the rest of the morning, avoiding my looks, making it clear that she wouldn't discuss the Hatter business anymore.

"Did you get some rest?" I ask Lindsey. She'd spent the entire journey lying on her towel, either sleeping or reading her book.

"Yeah," she says, smoothing her disheveled hair with her hand. "I needed it."

She doesn't attempt more conversation, so we fall silent. I

want to be annoyed with her, but I'm stuck on the image of the Mad Hatter in all his glory, pouncing on poor Kat. It's got to be eating at her. I mean, men of all ages and walks of life have always hit on Kat. That, I'm sure, she's used to. But her stepfather? How can she even think of wearing those earrings? And how could she not tell her mom? It's not that Patty and Kat are particularly tight. They've always been more like occasional girlfriends than mother and daughter, but certainly Patty should know the man she's living with. I want to get Sin's take on it, but whether she'll ever talk to me again is a whole other issue.

As we step off the ferry and onto the cement dock, I squint into the sunlight. Brown-skinned families rush forward to meet passengers. A gorgeous blonde in a sarong and pink bikini pushes through the crowd, throwing herself into the arms of a tall man, wrapping her legs around his waist.

At the end of the dock, people are lunching and lounging under umbrellas in a handful of unassuming cafés. Above them, the island is dirt-brown and mountainous, a sprinkling of pristine white buildings and a few broccoli-like clumps of green trees thrown in for good measure. One road winds up the island's craggy terrain, making S curves until it disappears without a hint of what's over the edge.

"Hey, girls!" we hear. "Over here!"

A few hundred feet away, the Irish boys are waving furiously, looking much more rested than we.

As we make our way over to them, we're accosted by hostel and hotel owners. They grab our arms and shove placards in front of our faces, showing shellacked photos of their establishments.

"Stay here, ladies!"

"Best place on the island."

"Free breakfast every day!"

Kat stops to view a brochure being held by a tiny, deeply tanned woman of about forty. The woman sends a gloating look at the other hotel people, who hesitate only a second before rushing off to tackle other hopefuls exiting the ship.

"Look how beautiful," the little woman purrs to Kat, wielding tantalizing pictures of sand and surf. "We only one kilometer from beach." She begins to run down the prices for the different rooms she has available, waxing poetic about how *clean,* how *beautiful* her place is compared to the other hotels in town, which she calls "slums."

"You understand?" she says. "We best on island."

Kat points to a picture of a lovely room with French doors and a woman sitting on a balcony, a dreamy look on her face. I'm sure this photo bears little resemblance to the actual rooms they're selling, and I'm about to say so, when we hear the Irish guys calling us.

"No, no," Billy says, jogging to meet us. "We told you— we've got a place for you girls."

"Okay," Lindsey chirps and, without a moment's hesitation, lets him lead her away. I notice how good-looking Billy is, his lean legs stretching out of khaki shorts. Maybe Lindsey will lighten up if they get together. A little action might put her in a good mood for a change. Better than Prozac, Kat always says.

"I'm sorry," Kat says to the woman, who looks dejected. "I guess we already have somewhere to stay."

"Thanks," I mumble to the lady, wondering if I should tip her or something.

Kat moves toward the Irish guys, and the woman sends me a nasty look before she sprints toward some new prospects, leaving me standing alone. What are we getting ourselves into? I wonder. Do these guys expect us to make like couples? Three of them, three of us. How convenient. They seem innocuous enough, but our trip has taken such a sharp turn at their direction, something that makes me very nervous. Billy is the only one who I find attractive, but I can tell Lindsey likes him. Johnny and Noel are both cute enough in their own way. Johnny with his shocking red hair and impish grin. Noel looks like a stocky rugby player, all muscles and brief limbs. Certainly none of them measures up to Francesco's smoldering grace. And what do I care, anyway? I had my little fling in Rome, my little indiscretion. Now I'm done with foreign boys. The rest of my trip is devoted solely to relaxation. I vow to be chaste until I get back to John.

I trudge over to the group, feeling my back grow wet with sweat where the pack rests against it. Kat and Sin are talking and laughing with the Irish boys as if they've all known each other for years. No one takes notice of my arrival, and I have a flicker of that picked-last-in-gym-class feeling.

"Spiros should be here any minute," Noel says. "We called weeks ago and told him when we'd arrive."

"Exactly who is Spiros?" I ask, trying to sound nonchalant and join in the conversation, but the question comes off snippy. The heat is getting to me.

"Oh, he's great!" says Johnny Red, as I've decided to call him. "You'll love him. He runs the Sunset—the place we're staying at."

I look at the girls. Kat is glancing around at the cafés, no doubt doing reconnaissance, searching for her next victim. Lindsey lets Billy slide her backpack off her shoulders. She smoothes her hair again, flashing him a smile that must feel alien to her mouth. I'm obviously not going to get any help from them in finding out about this Sunset place. Before I can press for details, a robust bearded man in shorts, thong sandals and a purple T-shirt pads up to us.

"Spiros!" the Irish boys cry out, clapping him on the back like a soldier returned from war.

We're introduced to Spiros, who doesn't say much other than, "Welcome to the island, friends."

Noel asks if he can spare a room for us, and Spiros beams a large smile, nodding magnanimously.

"Sixteen thousand drachmas," Spiros says. "We give you

breakfast and dinner. Beers you pay for." He chuckles, point-ing to the Irish guys, who all guffaw and start the backslap-ping again. "Four hundred drachmas for the beers."

I do the math in my head to figure that the room is the equivalent of $40.00 American, and each beer will run us an inexpensive $1.00. My concern about the Irish guys and this new place called the Sunset is replaced by a reminder of the thirty thousand dollars in student loans I have to pay off. It doesn't take me long to decide that cheap is better.

"Sounds good," I say to Spiros.

He holds out his large, tanned mitt of a hand, and I shake it.

Spiros leads us to a shabby looking pickup truck and tosses all of our luggage in the back, motioning for us to climb in. The pickup speeds up the road I'd seen from the port. I clutch the metal frame of the truck's sides, willing myself not to be catapulted out as Spiros screeches around hairpin turns, rais-ing a veil of dust around us. He reduces his speed as we reach the top of the hill and what is, apparently, the main village of the island. Little trinket stores, pubs and souvlaki stands dot the small space. They're separated only by tiny, twisting sidewalks cutting up another hillside to our left, leading past white, flat-roofed houses and ending at a domed church on what looks to be the island's highest peak. Spiros continues on the road, skirting the village, and then begins a steady drop past scrubby brush, the occasional rounded cement house, and a few campsites littered with worn tents. I see the water again as we make a steep decline to the other side of the is-land, a sparkling expanse of luminescent blue.

"Sin," Kat says when the truck slows around a particularly harrowing turn. "Doesn't this remind you of Monterey a bit?"

Lindsey nods, holding on to a stack of bags for support. "It looks like that hill by that bar with the great margaritas."

"Exactly!" Kat says.

"When were you guys in Monterey?" I ask, trying to keep the gym-class disappointment out of my voice.

Their smiles subside.

"A few months ago," Kat says. "Steve took us for my birthday."

"Oh," I say. Steve is Dr. Steven Monahan, Kat's orthopedic surgeon father, a superfit, supersuccessful guy who likes to think he's still twenty-one. In my opinion, this doesn't make for a good dad, what with the heavy drinking and the late nights at the bars, but it can be a hell of a lot of fun when it's a friend's dad. I can't help but think of all the events I used to be invited to with Steve and Khaki, his outgoing, outrageous third wife, who's much closer to our age than his.

"It was the weekend you had to go to that wedding in Cleveland," Kat says with a shrug.

"Oh, right," I say, struck by opposing images in my head. On one hand, Sin and Kat sip huge margaritas at a chic outdoor bar, warm coastal winds blowing through their hair. At the other end of the spectrum, John and I sit at a round folding table in a VFW hall while the deejay leads the crowd through a frantic version of the chicken dance. It was the first weekend in forever that we'd been able to get away together. Sure it was Cleveland, not Monterey, but I'd envisioned long walks, three-hour lunches with numerous bottles of wine, and John sweeping me around a candlelit dance floor. It hadn't quite worked out that way. We had long walks, but only to and from the VFW hall, since John had booked late and the main hotel was already full. And we'd had an extended lunch that Saturday, yet it was due to the piles of work John had brought with him. So I'd forgotten the wine, pulled out my civil procedure notes for the bar exam and studied. There were no heartfelt talks, only the sound of pages being turned, the occasional cough.

Of course, the whole weekend wasn't a total loss. John

sensed I was unhappy, and when we got home, he made me a meal of grilled chicken with angel-hair pasta and poured me a glass of chardonnay. We made love that night, and I got lost in it, forgetting myself and my life for as long as possible, which was all I wanted to do that weekend, anyway.

A pothole in the road rattles the pickup truck, wrenching me away from my thoughts.

Kat catches my eye and mouths the word, "Sorry."

I wave a hand, shake my head and say, "Don't worry about it," and I mean it. Kat probably had enough on her mind at the time. She'd just been pounced on by the Hatter.

The road turns dusty again, and after a few more turns, the truck lurches to a stop in front of a large cement building, very blocky in appearance. It's painted white, like all the others on the island, but it has a wooden door that's fire-engine red. Spiros gets out and yells something in Greek. Immediately, the red door opens and six children, ranging in age from about four to thirteen, race outside. They remind me of the Von Trapp family, although not as well dressed. The kids smile at us shyly, open the back of the pickup and pull our bags out. I want to stop them, thinking that there's no way some child can carry my massive pack. But they've obviously done this before, the smaller ones sharing a load, each taking one end, the older ones dragging two bags at a time.

"We're here!" Johnny Red says, launching himself over the side of the truck in one fluid motion. "I wonder how CeCe is."

CeCe, it turns out, is Spiros's wife. They both run the Sunset along with their kids.

Spiros gives us the grand tour, which takes about two minutes. The white building we'd parked near is the main unit of the place. In back, it houses a kitchen and a bar that's covered with a red-and-white-striped awning. In front of the bar, a stone terrace topped with tables widens to the very edge of a cliff, overlooking a stunning white sand beach that runs along the sea. It's one-thirty in the afternoon, the sun is high and relentless, and from what I can tell the beach is filled to capacity with people, many of whom appear to be naked or topless.

"What do you think, girls?" Noel says, bouncing around in front of us. "Didn't we tell ya?"

"It's great," I say, already in love with the terrace view, relieved that the place looks immaculately clean.

Spiros shows us to our room, which, rather than being attached to the main building, is its own freestanding hut. It contains a few beds, a bureau and a bathroom, and like the other areas of the Sunset, it's spotless. Stark white sheets are stretched tight across the beds. Cheerful white-and-blue curtains dance in front of the open windows.

Kat and Lindsey are already tearing off their clothes and rifling in their packs for their bathing suits.

"This place is perfect," Kat says, pasting on an obscenely skimpy white bikini. "Cheap and close to the beach."

"Amazing," Sin says, tucking her hair under a blue baseball cap and stepping into a two-piece bathing suit, much more tasteful than Kat's.

"Coming with us, Case?" Kat asks, but she's collecting her towel, her beach bag, not really looking at me.

Sin stays quiet, throwing her book and a bottle of SPF 15 in a straw bag.

"Nah, I'm just going to unpack," I say. The need to be alone overwhelms me, and I get the distinct feeling that neither Kat nor Sin will be crushed if I don't join them.

As they head to the door, Lindsey turns and looks over her shoulder. "We're meeting the Irish guys at the bottom of the hill," she says. "Come find us if you want."

Not exactly the warmest invitation, but at least she made it.

"Thanks," I say, giving her a polite smile. I feel like she's someone I just met on the ferry, not the person who's been a sister to me for most of the last decade. Between Kat's revelation about the Hatter attack and the still cool relations with my friends, I'm left a little bewildered. It's not an emotion I'd expected on this trip, and I'm not sure where to file it in my head.

I move most of my clothes from my backpack into the small, unfinished wood bureau. I usually don't unpack, since living out of a suitcase doesn't bother me in the slightest, but I need to kill some time. A whole sunny day stretches out before me, and I can't think of a thing to do besides join the throngs at the beach.

It's been so long since I've had any time to relax that I find it difficult to remember how. I struggle to recall how I've unwound over the last few years. I know that I've pored over old legal texts and memorized thousands of notes. I've logged countless hours on John's couch, my head in his lap, watching random TV. But was any of that relaxing? Did I actually like all that? I used to play tennis, yet that has fallen by the wayside. Why? I stand there, in the middle of our little hut, trying to remember. There seems to be no good explanation except that over the last few years my physical activity had been limited to raising Doritos to my mouth.

I get my PalmPilot out of the front pocket of my backpack. It's the first time I've pulled it out since we got on the plane, and for a second, the sight of its shape—its little black squareness—makes me think of school and work, and I nearly break out in hives. I make myself ignore the feeling, and after powering it up, I scroll through my calendar until I reach the Saturday morning after my first week of work.

"Play tennis," I write in the slot for ten o'clock. I try not to think about the fact that Gordon Baker Brickton, Jr., my new boss, may want me in the office slaving over a five-hundred-dred-page deposition abstract. I'd been warned that first year associates at my firm are often ordered into the office on the weekends, especially at the beginning, the thought being, apparently, that we can be broken in like house pets.

I've already seen a change in the way the firm treats me and the other soon-to-be attorneys. When we were summer associates, we were the star rookie recruits of the firm, stars that needed lots of attention if they were going to join the team full-time. There were lavish dinners on yachts, skyboxes for the Cubs games and nightly martinis at one hot spot or another. But when we signed up for good and started *really* working, it all changed. Partners who'd bent over backward to get to know you during the summer suddenly couldn't remember your name. The projects we were given were no longer interesting, but rather, grunt work that could have been assigned to a paralegal. It wasn't that I minded grunt work, or any kind of hard work, for that matter, but when all the hoopla died away and I took a look at what the work was really like, what the cases were really about, I found I couldn't muster up any enthusiasm. The thought of never being excited by my work scared the hell out of me.

I start playing with my PalmPilot now, not letting myself go any further down that road. Instead, I try to remember what else used to make me happy. I used to love seeing bands, I think. It was how I met John, even, but when John started working hard and said he couldn't stay up late, I didn't, either.

I lift the Pilot again, and under the Saturday night slot, I write, "See live music!"

The rest of my unpacking takes all of ten minutes. I get in the shower, but the plumbing at the Sunset makes the trickle in our Rome hotel seem like a gushing geyser, so bathing takes only a few minutes, too. I change into a fresh pair of shorts, delighted that they seem slightly baggier than before. I put on a light shirt and then consider rearranging the room, which is something that I *do* like, something that relaxes me.

I survey the room, figuring that at the minimum, I could move the bureau, the tallest piece of furniture, away from the door and put it against the far wall. I'm sure it would really open up the place, but I'm not so sure Spiros and CeCe would appreciate my efforts.

Instead, I head to the terrace for something cool to drink. CeCe is hard at work behind the counter of the bar, chopping vegetables and yelling playfully at one of the kids, a girl of about ten.

She looks surprised to see me. "You go to beach now," she says, pointing to a set of rock stairs that lead along the side of the terrace and down the cliff to the sand.

"No, not yet," I say. "Something to drink?" I pantomime a drinking motion.

CeCe places an icy bottle of Amstel in front of me. I'd been thinking more along the lines of a Diet Coke, but what the hell. I pull a rumpled traveler's check from my pocket and smooth it on the counter.

CeCe shoos it away. "You go. You go." She gestures toward the tables on the terrace.

"*Efcharisto,*" I say hesitantly, trying out the Greek word of thanks.

CeCe nods and turns back to her vegetables.

I have the terrace to myself. I choose the table at the very edge, liking that the sight of the sheer drop makes me woozy. I must be a few hundred feet above the beach, high enough that I can't make out Kat or Sin or the Irish guys, but I'm glad for the solitude. I need a little space in my head, a little silence. I follow the white swatch of beach with my eyes, noticing how it ends when it runs into a tall hill of brown brush and a few weatherbeaten houses whose white paint is starting to flake. I stare out at the sea, trying to forget myself in the aquamarine blue, trying to think clean, wholesome thoughts about John, but thickets of images keep growing in my mind—Francesco leaning over me on the blanket, the feel of his lips on my collarbone, the way he kissed me that last time on the step of the pensione. I chug my beer ambitiously, willing myself to enjoy the scenery and forget Francesco, but I can't seem to get any peace.

The first Amstel leads to another, and another. Pathetic really, drinking by myself, but each one makes me feel lighter and strangely carefree. Maybe this is why people become alcoholics. CeCe finally has to start charging me for the beers, and when I order my sixth, she looks at me with concerned eyes.

"You sure you want?" she asks.

The lack of food and quantity of beer has rendered me slightly stupid, and all I can do is give her an emphatic nod. She shrugs and places another dripping bottle before me. I traipse back to my seat on the edge of the cliff, taking another swig of the cold beer, and as I rerun the Francesco movie in my head again, I start to believe my own press. I *am* beautiful like Francesco said. I'm probably the sexiest woman on the planet. I try out Kat's hair flip to solidify the image, and I'm rewarded by a grin and a once-over from a blond kid hoofing it up the stairs and onto the terrace. He can't be more than twenty, but the body is all man—tanned, honey-brown chest, no shirt covering the six-pack of his stomach.

He raises his chin toward me in a cocky kind of greeting. "Hey," he says, and I can tell he's American. Los Angeles, I'd guess, from the witty banter and soap opera good looks.

"Hey," I say back, dredging my old flirty smile out of the attic and throwing it his way. He keeps giving me appraising glances as he makes his way to the bar and orders a beer.

It dawns on me that he's probably going to come over and sit with me, a thought that gives me an eruption of excitement and makes me grab for my bottle again. I'd forgotten how nerve-wrackingly fabulous flirting can be.

The soap opera blonde gets his beer from CeCe, and just as I thought, he starts sauntering among the tables toward me, one hand holding the bottle, the other rubbing itself over his chest and stomach, a motion that nearly mesmerizes me. I lean back in my chair so that I'm balancing on the two rear legs, an action that I imagine is sexy and confident. I perform the hair flip again in order to drag my eyes off his abs, but I overaccentuate the toss of my head and suddenly, my whole body is wobbling. I look into the blonde's eyes and see them go wide. He rushes at me, taking his hand away from his chest and holding it out toward me. I get a flash of blue sky, followed by a glimpse of the red-and-white awning. *I'm falling,* I comprehend, entirely too late. I hear the crash of my beer bottle, and then everything goes dark.

II

Something is jabbing into my back, something hard, about the size of a fist. I slip one hand under myself and grab the thing, raising it to my face, my eyes squinting in the sun, which seems to be shining its rays right into my brain. I blink over and over until the object comes into focus. A green-handled screwdriver. What in the hell?

I hear the yelp of a child, and I look over to see Spiros's daughter, the one who'd been helping her mother today.

"You awake!" she says, crawling over to me, her hair flapping around her face, and it's then I realize that I'm lying in the back of the pickup, being driven to God-knows-where.

"What are we doing?" I ask, trying to sit up, but the girl pushes me back down and scoots to the front of the cab, pounding on the window that looks onto the driver's seat. Almost immediately, the truck screeches to a halt on the side of the road, and Spiros's concerned face appears over the edge of the truck.

"Okay?" he says. "You feel okay? You can see me? You can hear me?"

I almost laugh, but the instinct brings on a raging pain in my temples, and I grab my forehead. "I'm fine." The fall comes back to me, or at least the beginning of it, and I wonder if maybe I really am hurt and I just can't appreciate it yet. "Did I fall down the cliff?"

Spiros cocks his head. "You fall off chair onto floor."

"Oh." Not as interesting an incident as I thought. I get a wave of embarrassment then, thinking of the soap opera blonde watching me wobble and sprawl across the terrace. "I'm sure I'll be fine," I say, trying to sit again, but the pain elevates, and I lie back.

"Hospital," Spiros says. "I take you to hospital."

I start to protest, but the girl puts her hands on my shoulder, and I close my eyes again, letting the rocking of the truck lull me.

Three hours later, after being prodded by a bored physician who looked like he'd seen more than his share of drunks, Spiros drives me back to the Sunset. This time I sit in the front with him and his daughter, whose name is Samantha. The truck jostles along the road, jolting every few seconds, since Spiros doesn't even attempt to avoid potholes.

"I'm so sorry," I tell him for the tenth time. The bored doc had determined that I'd passed out from the alcohol and heat, not from a head injury as I'd hoped. I'd actually have preferred some kind of real wound that would elicit sympathy, rather than snickers about my poor balance and inability to hold my alcohol.

"No problem," Spiros says. "I glad you okay." And in all honesty, he seems pleasant, not at all put out, as if this three-hour detour in his day was just what he'd been looking forward to.

Samantha, sitting between us in yellow shorts and a pink top, starts giggling, lifting her hand to her mouth. She says a few sentences in Greek to Spiros, who chuckles along with her.

"What?" I ask, smiling, too. "What is it?"

"She says you funny when you fall," Spiros says. "Your legs in the air." He flails his arms, mimicking my legs, and they both laugh harder.

When we get back to the Sunset, I stumble to our hut. It's only six o'clock and still sunny. Sin and Kat aren't even back from the beach yet. I get a wave of fatigue, and I crash like a cut tree on top of my bed.

When I awake, it's nine o'clock at night. Kat and Lindsey are showering, whispering about something.

"What's up?" I mumble through the sweaters someone has knitted on my teeth.

Kat hands me a bottle of water. "CeCe told us you got plastered this afternoon and took a tumble. How're you feeling?"

"Like shit." I gulp half the bottle and fall back on my cot, clutching my head.

"Are you sure you're all right?" Sin says, sitting next to me.

"I'm fine. The diagnosis at the hospital was too much beer."

She leans forward and starts patting my head. I close my eyes, loving her mothering touch. "No bumps," she says, pulling her hands away. "You think you'll live?"

"Oh, I'm sure," I say. "What are you guys doing?"

"There's a group going to town," Kat says, "but we'll stay with you."

"No. Go out. I feel stupid enough already. You guys don't need to baby-sit me."

"You sure you don't want to come?" Kat asks as she goes about trying and retrying two different shirts, both of which look adorable. "You could just drink water, and we can make it an early night."

"Can't do it," I say. Just the thought of being around alcohol triggers my gag reflex.

Kat and Lindsey don't seem particularly heartbroken that I won't be joining them, and neither tries to talk me into it as they normally would. But then I suppose that taking a drunken header will do that.

I managed to outrun my hangover while Kat and Sin were out chasing theirs. They both rolled in at 5:00 a.m., and now they're moving a little slowly.

"How was it?" I ask them, as we all climb out of bed at the crack of noon. "What are the bars like?"

"Fucking nuts," Kat says, yawning and stretching as she gets off her cot.

"Well, tell me," I say.

"You really have to see it to get it," Sin says, effectively cutting off a laundry list of questions I had about the bar scene.

Kat nods in agreement. "Are you feeling okay?"

"Fine," I say, and surprisingly, besides being famished, this is true. I just hope I don't run into the soap opera blonde again.

"So," I say, shifting topics, "did anybody hook up?" This is a fairly common question between the three of us, usually intended to elicit Kat's crazy stories. This time, though, I'm angling it toward Sin, wanting to know if anything happened with Billy.

They both shake their heads.

"I had this little Austrian man for a while," Kat says, "but I lost him somewhere."

"Were you with the Irish boys all night?" I ask.

"Most of the time," Kat says. "They're sweeties."

Sin stays quiet, pulling a new bathing suit out of her bag, and I wonder why she wasn't able to make a love connection with Billy.

A few minutes later, Sin sees me trying on different bathing suits in a one-piece versus two-piece kind of battle. She's already packed and ready to go to the beach, of course.

"Coming with us this time?" she says. I pick up a faintly sardonic tone.

"I'll meet you there."

But Sin stays and watches me. As I yank up the top of my black one-piece, I feel her eyes on me like glue. It's not a mothering kind of stare, though, not a relative to the head patting she gave me last night. Instead, it's more like she's studying me. It makes me nervous, but I won't give her the satisfaction of snapping at her.

Luckily, Kat is ready in record-setting time. Once they're gone, I rush to the mirror on the back of the door and model the bathing suits, turning myself this way and that, sucking in my stomach, sticking my chest out. I decide to go with the bikini, since wearing a one-piece to this beach seems a little like wearing a snowsuit to play golf, yet I keep trying to adjust the bikini in an effort at transformation. I pull the bottoms up high on my hips, making my legs look thinner but pinching my waist. I slide them a little lower. Next, I put my hands in the cups, scooping up my breasts, hoping to make them appear fuller. None of these things does anything to change the Casper's-ass-whiteness of my skin or the extra flesh, and sadly, I can't think of anything else that might.

I pull my hair up in a ponytail, noticing that it looks rather brassy blond from the sun I got in Rome and on the ferry. For a minute, I wonder if it makes me look like a tart. Then I remind myself that this would be fitting, since I acted rather tartlike with Francesco. I stick a floppy hat over my head, pulling it low, and I head outside.

I forget my self-consciousness for a moment when I see the beach. Pure heaven. Hundreds of yards of fine white sand that stretches from the base of the Sunset's jagged steps to where the blue water laps and rolls.

I spot Noel, Johnny Red and Billy spread out on a blanket, their bare chests glistening. Johnny is covered in freckles, but the other two are pretty brown for Irish boys. Must have spent some time in the tanning beds back home.

"Morning," I say when I reach them.

They wave and ask whether I'm feeling okay, Billy kidding me about getting too "pissed" for my own good.

Finally I manage to reassure them that I'm fine and get them off the subject of my bender. "Have you seen Kat and Lindsey?" I say.

Billy smiles a slow smile. "They're getting something to drink. Have a seat." Damn that boy is cute.

I drop my shorts quickly and glance at them. No one flinches at the sight of my flesh, and I take this as a good sign. I walk to the water, moving around the sunbathers, holding my body as firm as possible with the hope that nothing is jiggling out of control.

The water is cool despite the heat of the day, sending tingles through me. It's so clear that even when I wade to chest level, I can still see the "Not in Kansas Anymore Red" polish I've painted on my toes for the first time in over a year. I wiggle them as I look down, and just seeing my scarlet toes through the watery blue makes me feel glamorous.

Our days in Ios stretch into a pattern of sorts. An idyllic pattern, if it weren't for the weird tension that still hovers between Lindsey and me. Aside from her concern about my fall, she's been aloof with me, and Kat, while perfectly nice, seems to be joined at Sin's hip.

It's not that I don't spend time with them. Most days we sleep until at least eleven o'clock, then make our way to the terrace, where CeCe and the kids serve made-to-order eggs and toast. I always ask for egg whites only, as I've been trying, with some success, to knock off a bit more of my girth. After the food fills our bellies and clears some of the cobwebs from our heads, we stake out a spot at the beach, usually next to the Irish boys. Inevitably, Lindsey hurries to place her towel near Billy.

"Hello, boys," she'll say (as she had that first day I was on the beach with her) and as she speaks, she'll reach behind, unceremoniously unclasping her top, her breasts bouncing loose.

Kat does the same, asking Noel something benign like, "What time did you guys get in last night?"

The first time I saw this, I'd glanced at the faces of the Irish guys. Their eyes were hidden behind sunglasses, but none of them appeared particularly flustered. Either they had fabulous poker faces, or they were simply used to topless women. I chalked it up to a European thing, since well over fifty percent of the beach's female population is sans tops. There's even a core contingent of naked people, both men and women, who have nearly every inch of exposed skin tanned to perfection.

One guy we meet, a Frenchman named Richard, wears nothing at all except a thick coat of white zinc oxide on his nose and penis.

"So that was Richard, huh?" Kat says as he walks away, his white pecker bobbing against his leg. "I guess we can officially call him Dick."

We all laugh, the Irish guys hooting. Still, it amazes me that without batting an eye or clapping a hand over their browning breasts, Sin and Kat will engage in the most casual conversations as if they weren't half-nude. Sin, especially, shocks me. I'd expect her to go bungee jumping over Niagara Falls before I'd expect toplessness.

"Come on!" Kat cajoled me that first day on the beach. "Just take it off, Casey. It's no big deal."

"I have a fair complexion. I don't want to get third-degree burns," I said, using my light hair and peachy skin as an excuse. Actually, I can tan pretty well if I go about it slowly. I was just hoping that the lack of time I'd spent with Kat and Sin lately would play into my hands and neither would remember this. I'm disappointed when that wish actually comes true.

In reality, I'm simply mortified at the thought of going

topless. Not for any moral reasons, just physical ones. Flashing my overly white orbs wouldn't have thrown me for a loop a few years ago, but now, the thought of being available for public viewing by the hundreds of people on the beach makes me cringe. Francesco had made me remember how my body used to feel, but it seems I've forgotten again.

One day, I corner Kat while Sin is in the sea with the Irish guys, splashing water and generally trying to look as if she's frolicking, when the fact is she doesn't do frolic well.

"Hey," I say, plopping myself down on a towel next to Kat.

"Hey, sweetie," she says back in a lazy voice. She's on her stomach, her head on her arm, her hair splayed over most of her face like a hood. She opens one eye and gives me an equally lazy smile.

"How's it going?" I ask, feeling odd to be exchanging pleasantries with one of my best friends as if she were someone I'd run into at the dry cleaners.

"Too much ouzo last night, but I'm good. You?"

"Great." Well there you have it. Another illuminating heart-to-heart between friends.

When she closes the one eye, I move in with my real question. "You think Sin will ever give me a break?"

Kat sighs. "You know how she is. She doesn't shift gears very well."

"No kidding."

"Just give her some time," she says. "It'll get better."

"You think?" I hear a plaintive note in my voice.

"Sure," Kat says. It's not exactly the flag-waving reassurance I was hoping for, but it's better than nothing.

Another silence follows, so I decide to ask her something else that's been on my mind. "How are you feeling about the Hatter thing?" She's been wearing the diamond earrings almost every night.

Both of her eyes shoot open now, and Kat raises herself onto her elbows. As she does so, she bares her breasts, and I can hear a groan of longing from one of the British teenagers behind us.

"Case, I told you. I don't want to talk about that," she says.

"I know, but don't you think you should? I mean, it's just going to sit in your brain, corrupting your thoughts. You have to get it out." I'm thinking of the way I haven't talked about my parents for so long, how the issue is camping out in my own mind.

"No, I don't. I really feel fine. I got a pair of great earrings out of the whole thing, and now I just want to forget about it."

I mull this over for a second. I could certainly understand the need to forget. Wasn't that what I was doing on this vacation?

"You're sure?" I ask, thinking that while I might need to pretend certain things in my life didn't exist right now, Kat seems like she needs to remember this one thing.

"I'm sure," she says, her voice bordering on exasperation.

I give up, slumping back on the towel and throwing an arm over my head.

Most days, I drift away in the afternoons to a spot I found under a large overhanging rock. There, in the shade, I escape the crowd and the heat and write aimlessly in my journal.

One day, I find myself making lists of John's attributes versus Francesco's, in sort of a battle between them. Under John's name I write, "Sweet. Stable. Smart. Loves me. Great parents. Good cook. Good kisser." Below Francesco's I scribble, "Kind. Wavy hair. White teeth. Wants me. Sexy. Exciting. Hot. Amazing kisser." The lists don't help. I alternately crave Francesco's hands on my hips, his mouth on my breasts, and then squeeze my eyes shut, trying to drown out John's sweet smile, which keeps lingering, unaware I've betrayed him.

As I sit staring at my journal, Sin actually comes to me.

"Hi," she says, ducking under the rock and sinking down

next to me, wrapping her tiny arms around her knees. With her deep tan and no makeup on, wearing only her bikini bottoms, she looks like a small Peruvian child.

"Hey there," I say.

"Whatcha doing?" She leans over, peering at the scribblings in my journal.

I fight the desire to slam it shut, an odd inclination, since I used to tell Sin nearly everything. "Just writing about the trip."

"Franco?"

"Francesco," I say, knowing she massacred his name on purpose.

"And John," she says, glancing down at my page again.

"Yep."

"Who's winning?"

I laugh, an odd, coarse laugh that seems to scratch my throat on the way out. "It's not a contest."

"No, of course not." She puts her chin on her knees. "You can't have Francesco, can you? You don't live in Rome. Which means it's John by default."

I debate whether I should smack her with the journal or maybe just pull a handful of Peruvian hair out of her head. "Is that what you came over here to say?"

She laughs then. "Sorry," she says. "That was shitty."

"Yes." I close the journal, setting it on my thighs.

"So," she says, turning her head and resting it on her knees, her eyes on me.

"So," I say, all topics for easy banter escaping me. "Are you having fun?" The question rings lame, like the opening question on a blind date.

"Of course," she says. "How can you not have fun? We've got the sunshine, the beach. What more do you need?"

Good question, I think. A fucking great question. But the answer keeps eluding me.

"All is good with John then?" she says. "I mean, excluding Franco, Francesco, whatever?"

"Uh…well…" Here's my opportunity, the time I can dump out how much I miss the way John and I used to be even though we're together all the time, how I don't feel as connected to him as I once had. But that's the problem. I really don't feel connected to *anybody* lately, certainly not Sin, and the thought of bad-mouthing John to her seems a grave betrayal.

"Yes?" Sin blinks in a way that makes it seem like she's batting her eyes. "You were saying?"

"Everything's fine with John."

"Hmm." She stops the blinking and looks at me with eyes that seem sharp now, that seem to dig. "I don't think you know what makes you happy anymore."

She stands up, stretching her arms, then letting them fall to her sides. "See you later?"

"Sure," I say.

When she's gone, I open my journal and write the heading, "Things that Make Me Happy." I underline it and poise my pen beneath it, readying myself to write the millions of things that give me pleasure, but I can't think of any. *Think, think, think,* I command myself, determined not to let Sin be right. Finally I jot, "Ben & Jerry's Chubby Hubby ice cream. Repainting my walls. Buying a comfortable pair of shoes that still look hot. A brick of good Brie. Great music. Flourless chocolate cake." I put my pen aside, relatively pleased with myself. The list had come quite easily once I started. But I read it over, and it hits me. Fifty percent of my happy list is food.

12

Around six o'clock each day, the majority of the Sunset's patrons, full of sand and sunburn, climb the rock steps back to the huts. Nearly everyone spends the next few hours napping, preparing themselves for another night's festivities. Dinner isn't served until ten o'clock, but I've developed a habit of rising early for the night, leaving Kat and Sin tucked in their beds, each day making them look darker against the white backdrop of their sheets. After a quick shower, I head out to the deserted terrace, catching a glimpse of Spiros, CeCe and their family through the open door of their hut. The kids laugh and talk over each other in Greek, Spiros and CeCe passing food and smacking the hands that try to take a plate out of turn. It often strikes me that they don't have lots of money, nor do they live an elaborate lifestyle, but Spiros and CeCe seem like two of the most content people I've ever met.

While they're feeding their family, the bar operates on an honor system. I'll pluck down a few drachmas on the counter and help myself to an Amstel from the industrial fridge. Despite my fall that first day, I'm still attached to my table, the one closest to the edge of the cliff, and I'll sit there, careful not to rock back on the hind legs of the chair. I never saw the soap opera blonde again, thank God, and I've started to wonder if maybe I conjured him up in my drunken imagination.

Sitting at my table, sipping my beer, I watch the most incredible sunsets—vibrant hues of oranges, pinks and yellows mixing and mingling in the sky, until the golden circle of sun slips lower beneath the water that grows navy blue with the oncoming darkness. I can't believe that everyone else can sleep through this, but I'm not quite willing to share it, either.

Most nights, I simply sit and soak it up. Other times, I pull Francesco's card from my purse and stare at it. The card has become worn by now, the corners crumpled and soft. I imagine calling him, hearing him say, *"Bella,"* in that honeyed voice, hearing him tell me he misses me. But then I feel ashamed and I stash the card away again, wondering what it says about John and me that I keep thinking about some boy in Rome who can't even buy himself a proper scooter. I love John, I know I do, but sometimes I find myself wanting to be unattached and single. Wanting to find more Francescos and soap opera blondes. Yet at the same time, John is like family, and I can't imagine my life without him.

Toward the end of the sunset, *my* sunset as I've come to think of it, people start trickling out of their huts to get dinner. We usually sit with Johnny Red, Noel and Billy, and I've gotten used to the way they alternately compliment and rib me. Billy is especially sweet.

"You're burning a bit," he said one night, leaning toward me and running a finger over my shoulder. "Best to put something on that."

There are others at the Sunset that we've become friends with, too, and who usually join us for dinner. There's Gunther, a short Norwegian whose favorite English word is *wicked*. He applies it to everything—the beach, the drinks, the food, the bars, the women. And then there's the two Swedish girls, Lina and Jenu, both of whom appear stereotypically Swedish with blond hair, blue eyes and translucent ivory skin. They seem to gaze at me intently when I speak. Whether this is from their efforts to decipher my English or an actual interest in me, I can't say.

The rest of the guests at the Sunset are a mix of Europeans, Canadians, Aussies and a few Americans thrown in for good measure. A dizzying din of languages and accents rises during the dinner hour. Whenever we meet someone new, someone who doesn't speak English or can't understand my Italian, it's a challenge to converse, but we try, using gestures and stilted words. Kat is the best at it.

"I...am," I heard her saying one night in a loud, slow voice. She was standing by a table of German men, pointing toward herself, "from...Chicago." When the men responded with enamored but confused looks, she said, "You know the cliché—Chicago, bang bang," and pantomimed shooting a gun, Al Capone style.

"Ah!" the group cried, understanding. "Chicago, bang bang!"

The men love Kat, as they always do, and she seems bent on finding a new one each night. I wonder if I should buy her a box of condoms, but I don't want to piss her off by assuming she's sleeping with all of them, and I don't want to encourage her if she is. She's always been outgoing and certainly never shy about sex, yet Kat now appears to have a compulsive edge to her scamming. She still won't talk about the Hatter incident, and I still think it's messing her up. I watch her every night as she moves about the terrace, friendly to a fault, constantly talking or flirting.

Meanwhile, I find myself sticking to our usual table at the edge with Lina and Jenu, the Irish boys and Gunther. Each night, I watch them devouring plates of moussaka, Greek lasagna or souvlaki oozing with cucumber sauce. My mouth waters, and I imagine diving headfirst into the cheesy moussaka, but I hold myself to Greek salads, liking the feel of my body as some of the bar exam weight comes off.

After dinner, Spiros gathers the troops around midnight to give those who are ready to party a ride into town, where things are just beginning to hop. One night as I headed for the truck, I glanced around for Kat and Sin and found them talking by themselves at the bar, their heads inclined. Kat laughed, throwing her head back, putting her hand on Lindsey's forearm, and I missed them then, even though we were in the same room.

That night on the way to town, I slumped in the back of the pickup, gripping my head, attempting to save my hair from being wind-whipped into a beehive. When Spiros finally ground to a halt, I raised my face over the rim of the pickup, shocked at the sight. The sleepy village I'd seen on our way in from the ferry had been transformed with the dark sky, the air full of battling music from different bars, the main street glutted with strolling people and crawling cars. Lights were strung along telephone poles and across the tops of houses, making it seem as if the stars were hanging low, blocking out the real ones above.

That night, like every one since then, we followed our nightlife routine, which was set by the Irish guys, who apparently fancy themselves as our ambassadors to Ios. This routine dictates that we start at one of the small pubs in the village that line the winding stone sidewalks. The bars have dubious names such as Bar 69 and Orange Love, and they serve colorfully named drinks like the Nipple Lick, which is some Kahlua concoction, and Blue Balls, a purplish-neon drink with God-knows-what in it. Around two in the morning, most people make their way to one of the late nightspots, both of which sound Gaelic rather than Greek in persuasion. The Dubliner is a big sprawling club with indoor and outdoor dance floors. The favorite among the Sunset crew, though, is Sweet Irish Dreams. It's small compared to the Dubliner, but that doesn't stop them from letting in everyone who can pay the cover price. The place becomes so crammed with humanity that everyone stands or dances on any available surface—the tables, the benches, the chairs, even the bars.

On most nights when we arrive at Sweet Irish Dreams, the Irish boys will muscle out a spot for us. Lindsey scoots to Billy's side in the hopes that tonight will be the night. Kat prowls the place like a lion. I am one of the gawkers.

A few years ago, I wouldn't have blinked twice before climbing on one of the tables and shaking my thing. Now, though, I'm afraid that if I shake it too hard, I'll send people and glassware flying. Still, I know that I've lost some weight, and I'm not sure whether it's that or the charge I got from my night with Francesco, but somehow I must have plugged in the mental Vacancy sign on my forehead because I'm getting hit on by cute guys at an average of a few times an hour. I know this shouldn't flatter me. Sweet Irish Dreams is a breeding ground for one-night stands, a fact no one tries very hard to cover up. But I am pleased, my anemic self-esteem becoming healthier with all the attention it's being fed.

I play a game with myself, trying to guess the nationalities of these guys by the style of the come-on, and I'm getting good at it. The German guys stand and stare for at least an hour and only walk over when their friends push them away like eleven-year-old boys on a playground. In sharp contrast, the Italians don't have to think about it at all. Once they spot you and decide they want you, they just drop the lids of their eyes, lick their lips and sidle up to you without a word or a glance back at their group. The English blokes usually try the team approach with two or three guys at once, apparently trying to give everyone an equal shot.

It's the shy guys from the smaller countries that I like best, though, maybe because I can fool myself into thinking that they see something more in me than a reason to buy a condom. Lars is one of those guys. A tall, lanky Norwegian with curly, almost white hair, he strolls over to me one night as I come out of the bathroom. At least I think he's going for a stroll, although he moves like a guy whose body has just sprouted two feet and whose limbs feel foreign to him.

"Hello," he says, ducking his head down so he can reach my ear.

"Hi," I say. I consider just walking past him, like I might with one of the Italians, but his face is earnest and open.

"I am Lars." He nods when he's done with the sentence, as if pleased that he said it properly.

"Casey," I say, nodding back.

He smiles a little, his gray eyes moving over my face, from my lips to my eyes to my hair and back again, which is completely unlike the Italians, who generally go straight to my cleavage. "May I buy you a drink?" He smiles a little more widely, and I'm sure he and his buddies practiced this line on the plane.

I hold up my full beer and shake it a little to show him I don't need one. His smile fades. I can see him wondering what to say now that his good line has failed him.

"I have a boyfriend," I say, but he clearly doesn't understand. "Boyfriend," I say again, louder, but it's futile. I shrug and point to Noel and Johnny Red, who oblige by gesturing for me to hurry back.

Lars nods, giving me an endearing, sheepish little shrug, before he lopes away.

"What about us?" Noel says when I made my way back to our spot.

"What about you?" I say, slipping onto a vacant bar stool

between him and Johnny Red. Noel has tanned dark brown by now, the sun etching fine lines around his eyes. Johnny, meanwhile, just seems to multiply his freckles with each foray into the daylight, so that he's become spotted to the point where the freckles are almost joined together.

"Well, you don't seem to fancy any of these blokes—" Noel says.

"Not that you should," Johnny Red cuts in.

"No, no," Noel says. "Bunch of pansies, but maybe you should consider one of us."

Noel and Johnny begin modeling their muscles for me, curling their biceps and striking weight-lifter poses, grunting along with each one. I laugh and clap my hands, leaning back and looking from one to the other like I'm trying to decide between the two. We're yucking it up like that when Sin walks over.

"What are you guys doing?" she says, shaking her head at the spectacle Noel and Johnny Red are making.

"She's trying to pick which one of us she wants to shag tonight," Johnny Red says, striking another muscle-head pose, and he and Noel and I all crack up again.

I notice that it feels a little peculiar, though, a little embarrassing almost, to be laughing like this with the Irish boys instead of Sin.

One night, I meet an Australian girl named Nicky. We'd already bumped into each other at the bar and in the bathroom, so when she accidentally steps on my foot ten minutes later, we laugh and introduce ourselves.

"We're supposed to be friends, eh?" she says in her heavy, Aussie accent that I find endearing. She has spiky gold hair and a ripped, lean body.

"Looks like it," I say.

We talk for twenty minutes, giving abbreviated versions of our life stories. It isn't hard to shorten mine. There's little more to say than, "I went to college, I went to law school, and here I am." Nicky, though, has to condense years of travels and adventures. She's been away from Sydney for three years, during which time she's been to India, Morocco, South Africa, Europe, the U.S., and a handful of countries I've barely heard of.

"How can you stay away from home for so long?" I ask her.

She waves a hand. "Oh, it's no big deal, is it? That's what all me friends do. We run around the world for years and years, and then we go home and settle down."

"Wow," I say, fascinated by the concept. "It's like you're escaping everything. You just get to run away."

"Ah, no, darlin'. It's not like that, actually. This is all about finding, not escaping."

I scrunch up my face, unable to follow her.

"See, this trip," she says, "this living in hellholes half the time, never getting a hot shower, always being poor, it's not heaven on earth or anything, is it? It's one big learning curve. It's learning about other people, other countries, and most of all, about me." She keeps talking, describing the cesspool she lived in while in New Delhi and the job she took in Amsterdam that entailed selling space cakes in the Red Light District. She'd done all that, she tells me, to find out what she's made of, what she can take, what she wants to do with the rest of her life.

"Wow," I say again, struck by the elevated level of her thinking, so clearly miles and miles above my own. I briefly consider moving to Amsterdam and selling hash brownies instead of practicing law in Chicago, but I can't see how that would make me learn more about myself.

I lose Nicky when I make another bathroom run, but her spiky hair and her lean frame keep coming back to me. Nicky is a true traveler, I realize, while I am merely a tourist. During the six months I lived in Italy, I'd seen the difference.

I was a traveler back then, learning the language, seeking out places that weren't in the guidebooks, meeting people whose families had lived in the area for hundreds of years. But I'm back to tourist status now, going to all the places every other tourist goes, meeting more Italians, Irish and English than Greeks, scratching the surface of a place rather than really digging into it. Come to think of it, this is how I'd led my life lately. Even my relationship with John is only scratching at the surface these days.

Sometimes I imagine John here at Sweet Irish Dreams, standing in his button-down shirt, glancing around at all the craziness, shaking his head. He wouldn't be curious about all these people the way I am. He'd simply find it amusing. John sees the world as straightforward rather than something with odd facets, hidden paths or alternative journeys. He doesn't agonize, he makes choices. He doesn't whine and moan when something goes wrong, he moves on. His parents, Gary and Mary Sue Tanner, still live in Butterfield, Iowa, the same place they've been for the last thirty years, in their nice little house and their nice little community with very few curves in the road. The funny thing is that although John has moved on to the big city, he still sees his existence the very same way.

And maybe that's the big difference between us. John has already carved out his life, while I want more than I have now, more than I am now.

13

On our seventh full day in Ios, I decide to go into the village instead of lying on the beach. Ostensibly, I want to
change money and buy postcards. The truth is I'm sunburned
and sick of picking sand out of the various crevices of my
body, and I'm also tired of the underlying friction between
Kat and Sin and me.

I can't help but wonder if we truly will be friends forever,
the way we promised in college, and that's the thought that
rocks me, scares the shit out of me, really, because if I don't
have them, I'm lost. I need them more than John, maybe even
more than my parents. If my parents raised me into near
adulthood, Kat and Sin picked up where they left off. They
listened to me cry for days when I'd broken up with Todd,
my high school boyfriend, and they'd come to watch me try
out for the university debate team, taking me out for pizza
when I didn't even make the first cut. We'd done this for each
other—quizzing one another before tests, waking each other
up for exams, borrowing clothes and makeup and pick-up
lines. We went home for holidays together and took turns

making pans of birthday brownies. We relied on each other like newly assigned sisters until we seemed like family. But I still have so much left to do—*lots* of growing—and I don't want to do it without them.

I decide I'm being entirely too morose for a Greek vacation, and so during my egg whites and plain toast breakfast, I ask the group whether anyone wants to join me in town. The Irish boys immediately sign up, and once that's done Kat and Sin opt for the trip as well. I know Sin is motivated by Billy's presence, but I can't help but hope that the friendship tide is turning back in my direction.

The six of us hike the hill in the midday sun, our feet kicking up bursts of dust around our legs. By the time we reach the village, we're hot and sticky. We stop at a plaza with a long, thatched roof, housing five or six stores that sell refreshments, postcards and trinkets. I pick out a few postcards for John, my parents and my brother, Danny. On Danny's card there's a donkey dressed in a fringed bikini with the words *Dressed For Action In Ios* across the bottom. I'm not even sure what it means, and I hope it's not some thinly veiled reference to sex with animals, but I think Danny will find it funny. He's a weird kid. Last year, he painted his dorm room blood-red and hot-pink. When I asked him exactly what look he was going for, he replied, "French Bordello," as if that were the most obvious thing on the planet. All the rest of the postcards that I purchase show the blue skies, azure water and whitewashed walls of the village. It's the first time I can recall seeing postcards that accurately reflect the beauty of the place. On second thought, I buy a few more to keep for myself.

I find Noel and Johnny Red at another store, haggling with a leathery old man over some small hand-painted clay pots. When they talk the man down to a meager $4.00 a pot, I jump in and buy two for John. He likes authentic knicky-knacky things like that.

I carry my items to one of the picnic tables in the front of the plaza and sit down to write John's postcard. Thank God there's only about four inches of space to fill, because I can think of nothing to write other than, "I fooled around with someone else, someone amazing. I'm sorry."

I stare at the empty card. Finally, I jot, "Hi hon!" That seems cheerful and unlike an adulteress. Then I add, "We're on the island of Ios now." I get an urge to write a line from a Jimmy Buffet song that says, "The weather is here. I wish you were beautiful," but I don't think John would find it amusing. Instead I write, "Just sitting on the beach and drinking lots of beer." I only have a sentence or two of space left, because I'm writing big, loopy letters. I add, "We'll probably leave for another island in a few days. I'll let you know where I am."

Now for the closing. I know I should write the standard line John and I always put on cards or notes—"L.U.A.," our abbreviation for "Love You Always." But just thinking about it panics me. It seems too glib, too much of a promise. It also sends memories rushing back, making me remember all the wonderful things about John. The John who spent three hours helping me through my notes for my federal taxation final. The John who burns CDs for me, filling them with Miles Davis and Ramsey Lewis tunes, as long as the word *love* is in the title. The John who makes me feel safe and warm. He used to do that, anyway. Lately, he's been way too preoccupied with work or way too comfortable with me.

I remember a conversation I tried to start with him the week before I left. I was smoldering inside with horrifying thoughts about my new law firm and the potential of getting sucked into a corporate wormhole out of which I'd never be able to crawl. But John was working as a lawyer, after all, and he liked it. He'd reassure me that my fears were groundless.

"I'm scared of working for a living," I blurted out. I was sprawled on his couch, bathing in the central air-conditioning, which was lacking from my stifling apartment, while he was on his leather chair with the Sunday paper. "I know it's silly," I said, "but I don't want to turn into your average working stiff."

He curled down a corner of the sports section so that he could see me, and said, "You won't," then went back to the paper.

Did he think he knew me well enough to just dismiss my fear as idle nervousness, or was he avoiding an unpleasant topic, one that might make him reflect on his own life? Each time I started a conversation like that, I mistakenly hoped he'd say, "What a fascinating idea. What exactly makes you uncomfortable? How can you address that? You're such an amazing person, you will never be a failure." Maybe what I really wanted was a therapist.

I force my attention back to the postcard. I consider writing "I love you" at the end. Surely that's the thing to do, something he'll expect to see, but I can't bring myself to do it. I don't know if I mean it in the way I used to in the past.

"Love, Casey," is all I can manage.

I buy some colorful stamps, slap them on John's postcard and drop it in the mailbox before I can think about it anymore. After scribbling a few innocuous lines like, "Having a great time," I drop in the postcards for my parents and Danny, as well.

When I return to the table, I find the crowd nursing bloodies and screwdrivers. Kat is on the public phone set up outside one of the trinket stores, screaming with laughter as she speaks, most likely to Steve, her father. Similar to her relationship with her mom, Kat is more like a buddy with her dad than a daughter. They drink together, go to Cubs games together. I think they've even gotten stoned together. I used to think this all very hip and urban, compared to my more stereotypical suburban relationship with my parents, who wouldn't know a roach clip if it bit them, but now I feel sad for Kat. Who was ever there to mother her, to take care of her? Certainly not Patricia or the Hatter. Sin and I have been there for her, but it seems as if she doesn't want that of me anymore.

"You're up next, Casey," Billy says, pointing to the phone. "We've all had our turn."

"Oh. Great." I'm flattered that Billy's remembered me, but I'm not prepared to call anyone. I know I should phone John, but just writing the postcard had been hard enough. Surely, if he hears my voice, he'll sense my betrayal, and a phone call is not the place for that kind of conversation. I decide to call my mother instead. She isn't one of those parents who expect me to check in every twenty minutes, but she'll be pleased to be informed that I'm alive and well. Plus, I can use the high international rates as a way to head off a lengthy conversation.

"It's all yours," Kat says to me when she hangs up. I take the screwdriver Noel is offering and walk to the phone. I'd never thought of drinking vodka while talking to my mother, but it seems like an idea long overdue.

"Hello, hello!" I yell when she answers, not sure if she's able to hear me.

There's an awkward clicking sound on the phone, probably some intercontinental cash register ready to charge me fifty bucks for this call. I hear my mother bark, "Who is this?" in a gruff, scratchy voice, but maybe it's the connection.

"It's me, Mom. Casey."

"Oh, hi, sweetie." Her voice softens, and for a second I remember when she used to take care of me, listening to my woes and sagas, before it flip-flopped and became the other way around. "Where are you? How's your trip going?" she says, causing me to fall further into the memory, because she sounds as if she really wants to hear, and I need so badly to talk, even if I don't tell her everything.

I plow into an ecstatic retelling of my travels, minus Francesco and my hospital visit, going on and on about the boat to Greece, which I embellish to "a gorgeous cruise ship" and the Sunset, which I describe as "palatial."

It's only when I begin to slow the running of my mouth that I notice my mother is curiously quiet. Too quiet.

"Mom, are you there?" I ask, raising my voice.

"Yes. Yes, I'm here." I wait for the flow of words to follow. For the last year, I don't think I've asked my mother one question. She just *talks* about whatever happens to be in her head that day, whatever she did that day, launching into diatribes about the sales she hit at Bloomies and the latest product for hot flashes. Yet now I only get more of the annoying intercontinental clicking sounds.

"So, what's going on with you, Mom?"

"Well, let's see. What's going on with me?" she says, her voice taking on a shrill tone. "Let's see," she says again, as if she's really trying to remember. "Ah! I know what's going on. The dog died, and your father moved out."

I freeze. My eyes take in Noel handing out another round of screwdrivers to the crew, everyone laughing at something he's saying.

"Wait. What do you mean? What's wrong with Bailey?" Why am I asking about the goddamn dog?

"She was old, honey. She died in her sleep."

"And...and...what did you say about Dad?" I set my screwdriver on top of a garbage can and cover my eyes. All at once the sun seems blinding.

"He left. He's gone. We're getting a divorce." She sounds perky, yet emotionless, as if she's reading items off a grocery list.

I shake my head, trying to process her words. My mind feels a block behind the parade. They've been having problems, but according to my mother, they'd recently agreed to therapy. People who see a therapist stay together, right?

"Why, Mom?" It's the only question I can squeeze out of my throat, hoping she won't launch into her negligees-versus-sweatpants explanation again.

"Oh, honey, you've seen us." I hear the zing of the sliding door over the phone line, which means she's going out on the deck. The deck is where my mother always paces when she's on the phone, convinced that if she did it inside, she'd wear out the carpeting. In the summer, her bare feet pad across the wood planks. In the winter, her boots crunch over the snow, her blond hair bouncing around her face with each step.

"We've been miserable," she says, "and your father's decided he doesn't want to try anymore. He wants to throw in the towel." She spits out the last words.

"Where is he, Mom? Does he know about Bailey?" My dad adored our lazy golden retriever. Maybe that was what pushed him over the edge.

"He's at the condo," she says, referring to the one-bedroom condominium my parents kept in the city so they could stay downtown after dinner and a show. Danny and I used to call it "The Condom" and joke that it must be the only place they had sex, since there was certainly no evidence of coital relations on Orchard Lane.

"I left him a message about Bailey," my mother tells me.

"Is he okay?"

"I really wouldn't know," she says, a bitter scrape to her voice.

"I'm sorry, Mom. How are you doing?"

"I'm fine!" she chirps, clearly disingenuous.

"Seriously, how are you?"

"No, really. I'm fine!" My mother has always been able to do this. She can deftly switch from an outpouring of emotions straight into her Queen of Denial mode.

Before I can say anything else, she continues in her fake cheery voice, "Well, I've got to go, sweetie. I've got errands to do." As if her husband hadn't just left her. As if the fucking dog hadn't died from the trauma of it all.

"Mom!" I shout to stop her from hanging up without saying goodbye, an annoying habit of hers. "I'll come home. I'll get the first plane out of Athens."

"No! I do not want you to cut your trip short," she says, enunciating each word in the don't-fuck-with-me-voice I've heard only a few times before, like when she busted me at age sixteen filling up the gin bottle with water to cover up the loan I'd taken.

"I'm fine," she says, her voice mellowing a bit. "I don't need you here."

"Are you sure?" I ask, secretly relieved when she answers yes, because I'm not sure if I can deal with this right now. I am truly my mother's daughter, the Princess of Denial.

I consider calling my dad at the Condom, or maybe Danny, who's back at school, but there's a growing line for the phone. I also want to believe that if I don't talk to any more family members I won't have to face the reality of the situation. I'm like a child who covers her eyes and thinks you can't see her, just because she can't see you.

As I walk back to the picnic table to join everyone, I hold my screwdriver in one hand and pull my sunglasses from my purse, putting them on to hide my eyes. I'm not one of those women who look wistfully beautiful when they're about to cry. On the contrary, my eyes bulge, my skin splotches and my nose runs. Not pretty.

The ability to hide behind my glasses makes me want to cry even more. I know divorce happens every day, but my parents have been married for twenty-eight years. You don't just call it quits after nearly three decades.

"How are things at home?" Billy asks as I approach the table.

When I don't answer immediately, Kat and Lindsey glance

up at me. I stand there in the sun, in the protection of my shades, wanting desperately to break down and spill the whole ugly mess. But I feel so distant from them, as if my real family and my family of friends are all falling apart.

"Everything's okay," I say, polishing off my screwdriver in a few short swigs. "Everything's okay," I repeat to reassure myself.

14

That night at Sweet Irish Dreams, I inhale the drinks with a vengeance. Anything to stop the constant image of my mother sitting alone at the kitchen table, her head in her hands. After a heavy onslaught of beers, I stop being a gawker, and for the first time, I join the crowd dancing on the tables and chairs.

"Hey, look who's here," Kat says, as I climb up on the stone table next to her. "Welcome."

"Thanks."

It's a tight squeeze because of the slight Danish kid with doe eyes who's running his hands up and down her hips.

"Will you get me a beer?" she asks him sweetly. She has to repeat the question a few more times until they break the language barrier and he understands.

"Tuborg!" he suggests, his eyes lighting up at the thought of being able to provide a fine Danish beer to an American lass.

"Sure, sure, Tuborg is fine," she says, giving the kid a shove in his chest so that he almost topples from the table.

"What do we have here?" Kat asks, turning back to me, squeezing my arm a little.

"What do you mean?"

"You've been rather tame every night, hanging out with Noel and Johnny by the bar. What brings you up here?"

"Nothing," I say, surprised she noticed. I glance around the place, taking it in from this vantage point. It's jam-packed with people, the air thick with smoke. The music switches from a house mix with a thudding bass to a funked up reggae number, apparently a popular song around these parts, because everyone starts dancing faster, raising their arms until the space is a sea of waving hands.

The music gives me a little boost. I turn back to Kat and say, "I'm ready to turn it up a bit."

I feel powerful saying something like this, even though I don't know what the hell it means.

"Oh, you want to turn it up a bit, do you?" asks Kat, raising an eyebrow.

"Yep," I say with false bravado. To prove my point, I try to sway my hips and snap my fingers to the pulsing beat of the music. It's been so long since I've been dancing, though, that the movements feel disjointed, and I nearly sway my ass right off the table.

"Whoa!" Kat says, steadying me. "Try not to move your feet."

She illustrates by undulating her body and throwing her head back in a way that's fluid and sexy. I see male heads turning in our direction. I try to mimic Kat, tossing my hair around a little, but I'm as successful as a kid playing air guitar at an Aerosmith concert.

"You know, if you really want to cut loose, we're going to need some shots," Kat says, jumping with feline ease to the floor and pushing through the oncoming horde of would-be suitors.

I'm thrilled that Kat is making such an effort. I lumber

down after her, smiling politely at the men who've collected around the table. One of them is the Danish kid Kat had been dancing with. He strains his neck to look around me, proudly holding out two bottles of Tuborg beer.

"Where Kat?" he asks in broken English, his eyes widening with the growing realization that she's gone.

I could take him with me to meet Kat at the bar, but I want her to myself right now. Just two gals out on the town, tearin' it up.

I shrug. "I don't know," I say slowly, so he understands. I take off before he can protest.

But when I reach the bar, Kat is already on top of it, dancing with two eager-looking black guys with hulking muscles, both dressed in tight vests. She shrugs, giving me a look that says, "Who knew this would happen?" I did, but I smile and try not to look disappointed. For all my talk about "turning it up," I'd actually hoped that Kat and I would end up in the corner, talking like we used to.

I'm thinking about where to go and turn it up next when Kat crouches down and places a shot glass of cedar-brown liquid in my hand.

"What is it?" I call up at her.

"Whiskey," she says. "Here's to being single, sleeping double and seeing triple!"

With that toast, one of Kat's life mottos, she tosses back her shot. I follow suit, making a big show of plunking my glass on the bar as if to say, "Damn, that was refreshing." Inside, I fight valiantly not to grimace.

I look back at Kat, who's already engrossed, dancing with the black guys again. There isn't a spare inch between the sandwich they've made of her. They look like a giant human Oreo.

"I'm going to the bathroom," I say, cupping my hands around my mouth to be heard over the music.

"I'll be here," she mouths, and keeps grinding.

As I pick my way through the throng, I spot Lindsey engaged in what appears to be an animated conversation with Gunther. Her bobbed hair has grown a little long, and she's slicked it back with gel. Combined with her tiny frame and big brown eyes, it gives her a seductive look, a trait I wouldn't normally apply to Sin.

As I approach her, I can see that while acting like she's listening to Gunther, she keeps looking over his head, sweeping the room distractedly with her eyes. It reminds me of the way my father talks to my mom lately, pretending he's interested in her ramblings. No wonder she shifted them to me.

"What's up, you two?" I say when I reach them.

"Hey, Casey—wicked!" Gunther says, squeezing me around the waist with a fierce embrace. He's one of those huggy, affectionate teddy bear type guys who never seems like he's leering or hitting on you. I squeeze him back, feeling his soft beard on my cheek.

"How are you doing, Case?" Sin says, her eyes still searching the room. She doesn't seem to notice when I fail to respond.

Gunther fills the void by declaring, "I am going to find a drink!" He raises his right arm as if it holds a sword and he's declaring war. With another squeeze, he's off to fight the battle of the crowd.

"Who're you looking for?" I ask her, knowing damn well.

"Hmm?" She glances around once more before looking me square in the face for the first time.

"Who're you looking for?" I repeat.

"Oh, it's Billy. I haven't seen him in at least an hour."

"I thought you guys were hitting it off." Actually, I have no clue what, if anything, has gone on between those two.

She shrugs. "You never know."

"He's definitely hot," I say, hoping she'll open up to me, maybe tell me why she likes him. Maybe this will lead to a whole conversation, which is a novelty with us right now. Secretly, I'm glad that Billy is giving her a run for her money.

"Oh well." Lindsey gives a nonchalant shrug that isn't entirely convincing. "There are more fish in this ocean, right?"

"Sure," I say, refraining from asking whether she even remembers how to fish. Since she dumped Pete years ago, she's rarely dated.

Just then two guys walk up to us. They're both attractive, but dressed rather formally for this place in pressed khaki shorts and starched linen shirts.

"Good evening, ladies," one says in an upper crust British accent that makes me feel like I was raised on a pig farm. "It's our first night in town. Care to show us the ropes, so to speak?"

"Sure," Sin says, linking her tanned, smooth arm through mine. It feels good to have some connection with her again, even if it's this small, physical one. I smile at the guys, not interested in either, but excited that Sin is including me.

The two guys, it turns out, are a couple of preppy highbreds from London.

"Our fathers are members of Parliament," the light-haired one informs us, as if expecting us to genuflect. He reminds me of the Abbey Road version of the snooty frat boys on *Animal House.*

"Mmm," I say, not bothering to smile or feign interest.

But Lindsey had been a poli sci major before selling out and going into advertising. She quickly engages Biff, as I'd begun to call the blonde, in a rousing discussion about the Labour party and the Euro dollar. Meanwhile, Biff's friend, the other prepster, could not be less interested in Lindsey or me. Since the brief introduction, he's been gazing upward at a leggy redhead in a ridiculously short white dress.

I excuse myself, although neither Sin nor Biff seems to notice, and make my way toward the bar on the other side of the club, the one not occupied by Kat and the Oreo Brothers.

I order a vodka tonic with lemon, and I stay there with my elbow on the bar, ignoring the shoving of the crowd and the people behind me shouting for the bartender. As much as I've tried to forget about it tonight, I'm haunted by the thoughts of my mother, alone and lonely in our big stucco house.

I gulp the rest of the cocktail, then try to signal the French girl behind the bar for another. The male barkeep who helped me before has disappeared. I raise my eyebrows and hold out a hand, palm outstretched, but the bitch won't give me the time of day. She's leaning over, and just about out of her fitted denim shirt, as she pours an upside down margarita into the mouth of some joker who's lying over the bar.

"Scusi!" I call, thinking that maybe she's actually Italian and not French. "Excuse me! Hello! *Bonjour!*" At this point, I'm waving drachmas and struggling to keep the strident tone out of my voice. In my head, I see my father packing his favorite jeans and flannel shirts in a moving box. What do you have to do to get a goddamn drink around here?

The female bartender is down at my end of the bar now, grabbing a bottle of some green liquid and pouring it into a glass with that up-down, up-down arm motion bartenders do when they want you to think they're giving you a lot for your drachma. Yet still she ignores my calls for help.

Just as I'm about to launch myself over the bar and throttle her, an arm around my waist pulls me back.

"Need some assistance?" Billy asks in his quiet Irish brogue, an amused glint in his eye.

"Oh, hi. I want a drink. I'm just trying to get a vodka tonic, but I'm having a little trouble."

"Vodka tonic!" Billy calls to the saucy French wench, who immediately snaps to attention and into action.

"Here you go," Billy says, placing the cold, wet drink in my hand. He clicks the rim of his glass with mine. "And here's to you getting what you want."

"You know," I say to Billy after I've thanked him profusely for the alcohol, "Lindsey is looking for you."

He seems uneasy. "Yes...well," he says. "I'm not quite sure what to do about that."

"About what?"

"Well," Billy says, looking up at a woman who's dancing on the bar, as if she can give him the answer. "I think that Lindsey might, uh...might fancy me." He's practically shuffling his feet now and tugging at the neck of his T-shirt. "And I think Lindsey is a lovely girl, very sweet. It's just that I don't exactly fancy *her.*"

"I see." I wish I could muster up some malicious glee that Sin won't be getting what she wants this time, but the old best friend in me feels a twinge of disappointment for her.

"I mean, we've been talking," Billy says. "It's just that I fancy someone else." He looks at me and cringes, as if I might strike him, beat him into liking my girlfriend.

"Lindsey's tough. I'm sure she'll get over you."

"Right, right." He seems relieved. "Now back to my toast. To you getting what you want. Tell me what that is."

"That's quite a question. Do you mean what I want tonight or what I want out of life?" I attempt a nonchalant laugh, but it sounds like a donkey braying.

"Well, let's start out small. How about tonight?"

"Tonight I want to get drunk. I want to have a ridiculously good time and get stupid drunk." I try to make my words light, but they sound bitter, and I see the moving truck pulling down our driveway on Orchard Lane.

"I don't know about the getting pissed part," Billy says, eyeing my vodka tonic, which is nearly gone, while he's barely sipped his. "But I can help you with the good time. How about getting up there and giving it a whirl?" He gestures at the bar.

I pause, trying to come up with a feasible excuse, but then I think, why not? What the hell? Billy helps me onto the bar and stands behind me so that we both fit. I try once again to imitate Kat's gyrating, hair-flipping dance style, but I can tell from the quizzical looks I'm getting from the French bartender that it isn't working. I slow to a gentle swaying that I'm more comfortable with. I feel Billy's thighs graze the back of mine. He matches my movements, and I can't help but compare his confident, graceful ways to John's more standard step-clap, step-clap dance routine.

As the music turns to a slow but funky version of "Sexual Healing," a number of people around us start to cling to each other like a scene out of *Dirty Dancing*. I glance over my shoulder at Billy, surprised to find his face looming right behind me. I wonder if I'm having a drunken, side-mirror moment where everything looks closer than it appears, but then I notice his hand on my hip. It's that hand, holding too firm to my body, that makes me realize he meant *me* when he said he was interested in someone else. He squeezes my hip, and I get a *ping,* as Kat and Sin and I call them, those once-in-a-while feelings that travel straight from your stomach to your crotch, when you suddenly, inexplicably, find yourself turned on. I haven't pinged in an eternity, and while I'm happy and surprised to find that I still have them in me, this is the wrong time, the wrong place and the wrong guy.

"I have to use the bathroom," I say, and without waiting for Billy to answer, I bend down, place my hand on the bar and jump off.

I really don't need this, I think, as I push through the packs of groping couples. I'm flattered, of course. Unreasonably, fabulously, over-the-top flattered, but I haven't even sorted out Francesco and John. I don't need another one to worry about. Not to mention the fact that Lindsey has been after Billy, and our unspoken code of girlfriend ethics dictates that I stay away from any man that she or Kat are dating, were dating, are pursuing or are even thinking about pursuing. I don't need to give her another reason to hate me. I decide to lose Billy when I leave the bathroom.

Just as I reach the loo, I hear someone call out, "Casey!"

I turn around and see Billy a foot or two behind me. "I'll wait for you," he says. "I'll wait right outside."

I'd hoped to sort out my thoughts in the bathroom, but I've forgotten that the facilities at Sweet Irish Dreams, like many of the bars on the island, are coed. It's nearly impossible to banish thoughts of men from my mind while I jockey for mirror time with a long-haired Italian stud who's eight inches taller than I am. It's unbelievable how these guys have eyes only for themselves as they're staring in the glass, but the minute they step outside the confines of the W.C., they give you unveiled glances as they size you up for potential post-bar activities.

I apply lipstick in what I imagine is a sexy pout, trying to maneuver my head toward the bottom corner of the mirror so that the Italian stud has adequate room to finger-comb his hair, which happens to look much healthier and glossier than mine. I put on a little powder next, relieved that Billy hasn't followed me in here. I wanted to have a crazy, riotous time tonight without anything to complicate it. I wanted to drink until I forgot about my parents, and dance the thoughts of John away.

But Billy is standing outside the W.C. when I exit.

"Here you go," he says, looking altogether too cute as he hands me another vodka tonic.

"Thanks," I say, taking the drink. I sip it and search the

room, trying not to meet his 7-Up-bottle-green eyes. "Should we go find the gang?"

"I'm a bit tired of group activities," Billy says. "Care to try the deck for some fresh air?"

"I really should find the girls," I say, continuing to sip my drink, then stirring it with a pair of tiny straws. I don't add that the girls already gave me the barroom equivalent of the cold shoulder tonight, and they won't be missing me anytime soon.

"Well," I hear Billy say. "I don't know where Lindsey is, but I'd say that Kat has her hands full."

He points to the bar on the other side of the room, where a small crowd has gathered. The focal point of attention is Kat and the Oreo Brothers, who are still dancing erotically, running their hands over each other like something out of a bad hip-hop video. I debate whether to pull her off the bar by her ankles. I look around for Sin, to see if she's noticing this, too. Maybe she'll want me to take charge, like in the old days, to save Kat from herself. But Sin is in another corner of the bar, still locked in an apparently heated discourse with Biff. It strikes me that we're here in Greece together, yet we're on opposite sides of the room, the opposite sides of so many places these days.

"Look, Billy," I say, turning back to him. "I don't want to be presumptuous, but I have a boyfriend at home." He doesn't respond so I keep talking. "Lindsey is my girlfriend, and she has a thing for you, which means that nothing can happen with us."

A fat, ugly pause hovers between us, and I begin to feel a flush creeping up my neck and into my face. Maybe I've misread him. Maybe he didn't *fancy* me, after all, and now I've embarrassed us both.

"Well, that's quite a shame," Billy says then. "Quite a shame."

I exhale a massive breath of relief that I'm not as big of an ass as I'd feared.

"But I just want to spend a bit of time with you," he says. "Maybe just talk, aye?"

I glance back at Kat. The crowd has grown, and she shows no signs of stopping.

"I guess I could use some air," I say to Billy, and I turn toward the deck.

15

The small deck is cluttered with plastic tables and people engaged in either serious conversation or serious tongue wrestling. I glance at Billy, wondering which group he wants us to join.

I'm about to make an excuse and head back inside when he takes my hand and steers me toward a table that's opening up at the end of the deck, overlooking the street. Feeling his large, warm hand around mine, I can't do anything but follow him.

"Ah, this is good," Billy says, sinking into a chair. "It feels good to get some air, doesn't it?"

"Mmm," I agree, not trusting my voice. I sit down and make like I'm interested in the street scene below us. Not much of a scene, really—just two stumbling kids trying to shove gyros in their mouths but having most of it land on their shirtfronts.

"Actually, you seemed like you could have used some air all day," Billy says.

"What?" I give him a sharp look. "What do you mean?"

"Nothing, nothing," Billy says, holding his hands up in surrender. "It's just that ever since you phoned home this afternoon, you've been..." He makes a face like he can't find the words. "A bit wound up," he says at last.

"Wound up? I'm not wound up. I'm relaxed. I'm having a great time."

Billy nods. I notice him watching my hands. I look down and see that I'm fiddling with the clasp of my watch. I make myself stop, but I'm uncomfortable with the stillness of my body because it allows my mind to start churning again. I take a few sips of my drink and play with the straws, stabbing the lemon in my drink repeatedly. Billy watches me for another moment before placing his hand over mine, very slowly, very gently, in the manner of a cop who eases cautiously toward the crazy criminal and says, "Just give me the gun."

I don't pull my hand away immediately, like I know I should. When I raise my head, the concern in his eyes and all the alcohol in my system push a teariness to the surface. Embarrassed, I yank my hand from his and begin batting at my eyes, feeling like a complete fool.

"I'm sorry," I say, looking upward at the stars. I read in *Glamour* that you can stop yourself from crying if you stare straight up. It has yet to work for me, but I always give it a shot just in case.

"Don't be daft," Billy says. "Tell me what's making you sad."

"Nothing." I gulp the remainder of my drink and try to signal a passing waitress for another. She must be related to the French wench, because she ignores me completely. When I turn back to Billy, he's sitting patiently with an empathetic smile on his face.

"Okay?" he asks.

"Yeah, I'll be okay," I say. "If I can just get another drink." I'm fighting the urge to spill the saga in my head about my parents and John and my so-called law career, but who could care about this crap but me?

"Tell you what," Billy says. "I'll consider getting you another drink as long as you tell me what's got you so low." He looks at me matter-of-factly, and I wonder if he's pitying me. Or maybe this is one of those esoteric seduction tricks they teach guys in Ireland.

"That's very sweet, but you don't need to hear my problems."

"Please yourself then, but I'll make you a deal. I'll share my drink with you, and you tell me what's going on. Then I'll treat you to a drink if you still want one, yeah?"

I exhale, glad my tears are gone for the moment. "Fine," I say, giving what I hope is a casual wave. "It's no big thing. My parents are getting a divorce, but who cares, right? Lots of people get divorced. So that's it. I'm ready for that drink." I crane my neck to look for the waitress.

Billy pushes his glass toward me. "I'm sorry," he says. "That's tough. I've been through it."

"You have?" I perk up. Jesus, what a shit I am. I'm actually happy that his parents are divorced, as if this could make him understand me more.

"Yeah, sure," he says. "My mum and da split when I was seven."

"Oh, that must have been awful. I'm an adult, and I should be adult about this, but you were just a kid."

"Well, it wasn't fun. People don't split up much where I'm from, but as you said, I was a kid, and kids bounce back. I never knew what it was like to grow up with a whole family, so I never missed it. You're going to have a harder time, I'd guess, because you've had a real family."

I stare with dull eyes at the tabletop. I hadn't even thought of it like that. I mean, I hadn't thought about the whole family not being together for birthdays or the holidays or whatever. I always took that for granted. I think of the Christmas china my parents have collected over the years, white with a delicate forest-green tree painted in the center.

"When did you find out?" Billy says.

"Today. That's what the phone call was about. I called my mom, and she said it's over."

"Well, that smarts, doesn't it?" Billy pulls his mouth down, making a miserable face that still manages to be funny.

I laugh, and it feels good.

"I'm not even really sure what happened," I say. "I don't even know the one main reason why they're divorcing."

"Maybe they don't, either."

I think about this for a second. He could be right. I open my mouth and start talking about it, and before I know it, I've spoken for at least five minutes. It's a relief to get some of this out of my head, and amazingly, Billy doesn't look as if he wants to run.

"Did they fight a lot?" Billy asks.

"No. Never. I think maybe that's part of the problem."

"Maybe," he says. "My parents did nothing but yell, and that didn't work, either, did it? You have to at least talk to each other."

I nod, thinking of John and me having one of our many quiet evenings on his couch. We've grown more and more silent as we've become more comfortable with each other. If it keeps up like this, I'll forget the sound of his voice. I can see us in sixty years, gray and wrinkled, still on that couch or bumping into each other with our walkers. Maybe I'll be deaf by then and I won't mind the silence.

Billy and I, however, keep talking. He tells me about his job working for a footwear designer, and I nearly swoon. A man who understands the importance of shoes! I tell him about my own job, which I'm dreading like the plague. I even tell him about John, and it's both weird and comforting to speak of him here, thousands of miles away. I decide that Billy and I could be great friends if only he moved to Chicago and stopped being so goddamned cute. I try to ignore how adorable he is when he makes funny faces to illustrate a point. I try not to be flattered when he puts his hand over mine for a second or gives me a sultry smile.

When our conversation lulls for the first time, I notice that a lock of dark curly hair has fallen over one of his bottle-green eyes, and those eyes, I realize, are staring at my lips. I wonder briefly if the Bronze Coin lipstick I'd applied in the bathroom has survived the vodka tonic. Then the thought is gone, and Billy's face is moving closer, closer to mine. I find myself leaning in toward him slightly, our faces now only a fraction apart. Billy's eyes close as his lips press into mine. Slight pressure and then more, his tongue pushing my mouth open. I get a swell of desire right before it all screeches to a crashing halt.

"You bitch!" I hear.

I jerk my head away from Billy's in time to see Sin storm away. Kat stands there for a moment, a beseeching look on her face, before she follows her.

16

"Christ!" I say, hanging my head in my hands.

"Shall I go after them?" Billy asks, his hand on my shoulder.

"No, no. Just stay here, please." I plow my way through the mass of revelers, craning my neck to look for Lindsey and Kat. What have I done?

Some schmuck walks into my path. "Want to dance?" he slurs, his eyes on my chest.

I stiff-arm him, and he crumples to the ground. I ignore the irritated looks of patrons whose drinks he's spilled and push on.

As I near the door, I see Lindsey moving outside at a quick pace, with Kat in pursuit.

I call their names as I race down the stairs after them.

I push open the door and burst onto the street, nearly colliding with them. Sin stands with her feet wide, hands planted on her hips, shaking her head in disgust. Kat's arms are crossed, and she's looking around as if someone can save her from this situation.

"I cannot fucking believe you," Lindsey says. "There are a million guys on this fucking island, and you have to go after mine!"

"How is he yours?" I ask, trying to sound incredulous and failing.

"You know what I mean, Casey!"

"I know. I'm sorry. I didn't even mean for it to happen."

"I don't want to hear it," Lindsey snaps, and marches away.

I start to go after her, but Kat, who's been standing quietly and biting her lip, puts a hand on my arm. "Just let her go, Case."

"I swear," I say to Kat. "We were just talking. That's it. He'd kissed me for the first time when you guys walked in, and I barely had time to respond. Nothing else would have happened."

Kat doesn't look as pissed as Lindsey, but she doesn't look pleased, either. "I believe you, hon. Just give me an hour to cool her down, all right?"

I nod, not knowing what else to do. Even though Sin has been a bitch to me lately, I shouldn't have allowed this to happen. I'm terrified that it will sound the death knell on our friendship.

"I'll be there in exactly an hour," I say.

Kat nods and turns away.

I trudge back up the stairs of Sweet Irish Dreams, my mind splintered into a number of screaming headlines: Girl Kills Friendship by Kissing Pal's Scam! Respected Couple Divorces After 27 Years! International Sex Scandal—Boyfriend Says He Knew Nothing Of Overseas Trysts! The overload in my head has rendered me stone-cold sober. I can't even get drunk without fucking it up.

Billy leans against the door frame at the top of the stairs. His eyebrows shoot up as soon as he sees me. "Everything all right, then?"

"No. Everything is definitely not okay. Lindsey is furious. She won't even talk to me."

"But why? Does it have anything to do with me?" he says.

"Of course it does. It has everything to do with you," I say, my voice low, resigned. "Well, not everything." I shake my head. How can I explain?

"I'm sorry," Billy says, but there's a faint grin at the corner of his mouth.

"What are you smiling at?" I ask, exasperated.

He shrugs. "It's just that I think you're fantastic."

That stops me cold. I don't know why he would say that. I've done nothing but bitch and moan and call for the barkeep all night. Still, this makes me forget about Lindsey for a brief second.

"Thanks," I say. Then another thought dawns. "You're all smiles because you've got two women fighting over you." I poke him in the ribs.

"Little ol' me?" he says, his voice full of false modesty.

"You're loving this, aren't you?"

"I've had worse nights."

"Well, I'm glad someone's having fun." I try to put on my most annoyed tone, but he looks like a kid on Christmas morning.

"Shall I take you home so you can duke it out some more?"

"There won't be any catfights, if that's what you're looking for."

"Damn." He snaps his fingers.

"I can't go back just yet, anyway. I told them I'd wait an hour."

"Then we'll take the long way down the beach."

I consider this for a moment. I certainly don't want to stay here at the bar. There's no more fun to be had. I could slip and slide down the hill to the Sunset on my own, but then

I'd be right behind Kat and Sin, and I need to give Sin some time to calm down.

"We're just walking," I say to Billy. "Nothing else."

"Right," he says, with an emphatic nod of his head. "Nothing else. Got it."

Billy and I walk past the bars clanging with music and bodies, past the late-night souvlaki stands, to where the road dips over the side of the island. Instead of taking it down and to the left, the direct route toward the Sunset, we follow a worn, dirt path through vacant lots and a couple of campsites. The temperature has mercifully dropped from the blazing hundreds of the day into the still-warm eighties. For some reason, though, I'm chilly with a scary premonitory-type feeling. I hope I'm not becoming psychic, because it seems to me that my friendship with Kat and Sin, the one I've cherished most in the world, might have been dealt a near fatal blow.

Billy slips his hand in mine, and this time I hold it like I would a close friend's, taking some comfort from it. He stops and turns to face me when we reach the top of the hill that leads down to the beach. The moon is huge and orange and nearly full over the water, the soft lapping of the waves just barely audible.

He raises his eyebrows again and gives me a smile as if to say, "Come on. It's all right," and I can see he wants to kiss me again. While I should be annoyed, I actually stand a little taller, deciding that I love Greece for the men who come here. I haven't gotten this much male attention since one night years ago when my skirt got trapped in my underwear, and I walked around for thirty minutes showing my black panties to the crowd.

I shake my head. "It's just bad timing," I tell him. "I'm not getting along with my friends right now, or at least not like we used to, and now I go and kiss you. Or you kissed me.

Or whatever. The point is that I couldn't take it if I had to lose them. You know? It's just...it's just not going to happen."

He sighs. "Look at the water then," he says, turning me around to face the beach a couple hundred feet below us. "If you won't let me put my hands in your knickers, we can at least enjoy the scenery."

I laugh as he wraps his arms around me. His chin rests on top of my head, and I suddenly wish I could crystallize this man, this minute, the almost full moon reflecting off the sea. I could take it out later and look at it from all the different angles, without fretting that my closest friends in the world are through with me.

Eventually, we walk down the hill, skidding a little on the dusty path until we reach the beach. The sand is silvery under the moonlight, naked and cool without all the naked people lounging on it. A wisp of a breeze puffs off the water. It's so calm here compared to the bar. Billy pulls me down with a gentle tug until we sink into the sand about five feet away from the rolling waves. He sits behind me, his knees around me, in exactly the same way Francesco did that night in the Colosseum, but it's different now. Francesco had been all lust and fluid movements, and while there's no doubt that I'm severely attracted to Billy, it's more comfortable with him.

"Tell me about Ireland," I say, wanting to hear about him, about anyone other than myself for a change.

"What do you want to know?"

"My family is originally from Cork," I say. "Tell me about that."

"Ah, well that explains it," Billy says, giving me a squeeze. "All the brightest ladies are from Cork."

I smile. I can't help it. "Do you like Ireland?"

"It's like any other place, I suppose. It's got loads of problems, but it's home."

I keep asking questions, and he keeps talking, describing the land, the pubs, the customs, his family, his other friends.

It feels wonderful to be sitting in a man's arms, watching the waves and talking easily—the type of moment I'd been wanting from John for so long.

After about a half hour or so, I'm starting to feel tired, and I know it's time to get back to Lindsey and face the music. I stand and tug Billy's arm, but he won't get up. He just cocks his head, giving me those eyes again.

"You're relentless," I say, inwardly thrilled at his persistence. "I have to get back, so get off your ass."

"But it's your ass I want to get on."

I start giggling, knowing I should be stern—maybe act a little appalled—but I like Billy's lighthearted ways. After I finally pull him to his feet, we stroll down the beach toward the Sunset, swinging our arms. When we get to the stone stairs leading up to the hotel, Billy steps toward me and grabs me in a big hug.

"I had a lovely time with you tonight," he says. "And I'm sorry about causing problems with Lindsey and Kat."

"Sure you are."

"I'm not saying that I'm not a bit proud."

I smack him on the back, too hard, apparently, because he starts coughing.

"Honestly," he says. "I'm sorry."

"It's not your fault." My voice is muffled by his neck. Finally, I let go and face him.

"I'll see you tomorrow?" he asks.

"Of course," I say, but I don't really know what tomorrow will be like for Billy and me. Or for Kat and Sin and me, for that matter.

As I approach our hut, I see the lights blazing. Shit. I'd held out a tiny shred of hope that maybe the intensity of Sin's wrath would have exhausted her, causing her to fall into a dreamlike sleep that would last seven to ten days. I keep moving toward the hut, and I can hear voices, Sin's especially,

sounding spitting mad. The rest of the huts are dark and shuttered, with everyone either sleeping or still at the bars. Our
windows are open, though, and as I get closer, I can hear them
clearly.

"She's just not…" Sin is saying. "She's just not the person
she used to be."

Her words reach me like a sock in the gut. She may be
right or partly right, but it isn't easy to hear.

"Oh, it's not that bad," I hear Kat answer.

"I'm not only talking about this Billy thing. That's just the
tip of the iceberg. You know it as much as I do. She's totally
different. She's a shell of her former self."

I stand frozen by the open window, holding my sandals by
the straps, suddenly feeling so tired.

"She's had a rough time lately," Kat says, trying to stick up
for me again. "Cut her some slack. She just took the bar
exam, and it's obvious that she's not happy with John."

"So why doesn't she talk about it? Why aren't I hearing
this from her?"

I can imagine Sin doing her famous tapping routine, one
of her little legs jutted out, the foot tapping faster and faster
until she practically draws smoke from the floor.

"I mean, I could understand," Sin says, "if she just fucking
told me what's going on with her. I still can't believe that she
dissed us for that Franco dude."

"Francesco," Kat corrects, and I love her for it.

There's a pause, and I can just imagine the scorching look
Sin is sending Kat. She doesn't like to be interrupted when
she's on a roll.

"Whatever," Sin continues. "She totally blew us off, then
she comes to this big revelation that she's sorry, and she wants
it to be like it used to be, but nothing's changed. And now
this. This thing with Billy. She knew I was putting in union
dues all week, but that didn't stop her for one second."

"Sin. Be fair," Kat says. "You don't really know what hap-pened, and you haven't been exactly..." Kat halts, as if hunt-ing for the right word. "Friendly," she concludes. "Let's just talk to her."

This is my cue to burst in like a masked avenger and plead my case, but I don't know what my case is. I don't have a great excuse for why I kissed Billy except that I was feeling alien-ated from Kat and Sin, and he was there to talk to, and then suddenly we were kissing. I also don't know how to defend myself against the accusations that I'm a different person than I used to be, because it's true.

I remember a conversation I had with my brother earlier this summer. We were at a party for my aunt and uncle's an-niversary, sitting on a dark, grassy slope behind the house, watching the party though the windows. Danny offered me a joint, but I refused. I had to study when I got home. Danny took another hit, narrowing his eyes as he drew in his breath, then putting the joint out on the insole of his tennis shoe.

"You know why I like to get stoned?" he asked me.

"Because you're a deviant member of society who has no balls otherwise?"

He ignored me. "Because it gives me a sense of place." He went on to describe this "sense of place" as the time when he was unconcerned about yesterday or tomorrow or even an hour ahead. When he was high, he only cared about the current moment.

I told him that I knew what he meant, but that I could get that way without the pot. Actually, I was talking out of my ass. Those times, those "sense of place" times, had been episodic at best. Yet during this trip, I'd begun to feel a few of those moments. Visiting Italy, a country I felt at home in, and the time I spent with Francesco had helped bring me out of the shell Lindsey referred to. But then my friendship with her and Kat had stalled and sputtered, and my parents' divorce announcement had scared whatever moments of clarity I'd begun to muster back into the humid air.

So, instead of a grand entrance, I turn the doorknob quietly and push it open, until I stand facing the two people who used to know me best.

17

Their conversation halts. Sin is in midtap, still dressed in a black miniskirt and tight lavender shirt. Kat sits on her cot in men's boxers and a tank top, her back leaning against the wall, her knees drawn up. Sin glares. Kat just looks startled to see me.

Sin opens her mouth, but I hold my hand up, and I start talking before she can get a word in.

"I know you're upset about Billy, and I understand why, but what you saw on that deck was just a little kiss. It was the only one we had, and I didn't mean for it to happen."

"Ha!" Lindsey barks out a sharp, disbelieving laugh.

"Seriously. We'd just been talking and talking, and...it happened."

"Oh, this is too much." She throws her hands up and turns toward the wall.

I try to stay calm despite her sanctimonious bit of acting, but her attitude is pissing me off.

"I know it sounds lame," I say, keeping my voice even, "but it's true. I even told Billy that you were looking for him."

"And?"

I look down and scratch absently at my forehead. "And he said he wasn't interested."

Lindsey spins around, her eyes narrowed. "Don't even try to play this off like you were out there fighting for my best interests. You're damn right it sounds lame. And don't try to tell me that that kiss I saw was all that happened. What have you been doing for the last hour?"

"Oh, quit your holier than thou attitude. If you would have let me explain instead of stomping off, we could have handled this at the time."

"So it's my fault that you've been rolling around on the beach with him?"

How does she know we've been on the beach? Did they follow us? Kat points silently to the back of my shorts. I brush off the sand with a distracted hand.

"That's not what I'm saying. We weren't rolling around, for one thing." I hold myself back from telling her that I *could* have been rolling around. I certainly *wanted* to roll around. "What I'm trying to tell you, Sin, is that you never listen to me anymore."

"I don't listen?" She sounds surprised. "You don't talk anymore, Casey."

"And so I'm not myself anymore, right? I'm just a shell of my former self." I mimic her high voice.

For a second, she looks remorseful, then resigned. "I'm sorry you heard that, but it's true."

"Fuck you," I mutter, dropping my sandals on the floor. Their wood heels land with a thud.

"Fuck you?" Lindsey says. "What is going on with you? You've got a boyfriend at home, but you pick up that Italian dude and forget about us. Then you keep avoiding us this whole week. Kat and I came out on the deck to find you tonight because we were worried about you, and we find you with *another* guy, a guy you know I like, and now you come here accusing me of not listening to you?"

"I'm sorry about Billy. I really am," I say, my voice measured, as if I can turn down the volume on this whole argument. I slump onto the bed opposite Kat. "It really did just happen. I didn't intend it. You're right in the sense that it's not the type of thing I would normally let happen, because we're friends, and I know you had a thing for him, but to be honest, this hasn't felt like much of a friendship for a while."

"No kidding," she says with a sneer.

Sin and I go on and on like this. Kat stays on the bed with her back against the wall, biting a thumbnail, watching the whole thing like some kid whose parents are arguing.

Finally, I can't come up with any other explanations, not that Sin would hear them or discuss them, anyway. There's a lull that feels truly scary. "Tell me something, Sin," I say. "Why are you such a bitch lately?"

It's out of my mouth before I realize it was just a thought in my head, not something meant for public consumption. I lean back a little, ready for another tongue thrashing.

But then Lindsey does something I've rarely seen her do. She leans on the dresser and starts to cry.

My eyes dart to Kat. Her hand falls away from her mouth, and she looks at me with pleading eyes, as if to say, "Do something."

"Sin," I say, getting up and approaching her as I would a wounded but still dangerous animal.

She raises her head before I reach her. I freeze, and I can feel Kat doing the same thing.

"Did it ever occur to you," Sin says, her eyes red and raw already, the tears still streaming, "that I might be jealous?"

"Of what?"

She snorts in exasperation, which stems the tears for the time being. "You, you idiot."

I shoot a look at Kat. Her wide eyes tell me it's the first time she's heard this.

"Why?" I can't think of any other words to say. This doesn't even make sense.

"You've got everything," Sin says.

I look down at myself as if expecting to find that some other person has inhabited my body. Why would she be jealous of me?

"Like what?" I say.

"Like you were on law review, and you just graduated from one of the top schools in the country, and you've got this great new job." She leans over the dresser again.

"But, honey," Kat says, finally speaking up. "You're at one of the best ad agencies in the nation, and you're about to make vice president."

Sin mumbles something we can't hear.

"What's that?" Kat says.

Sin lifts her head up. "I already got it," she says in a too-loud voice.

"You got it? You're a VP?" I clap my hands, forgetting for a moment that I hate her.

Sin nods, her face miserable, crumpling into tears again.

"Congratulations!" I say.

"That's wonderful! Why didn't you tell us?" Kat jumps off the bed and crosses the room to hug Sin. I want to do the same, but I'm still afraid she might strike me. Just as well, because she shoos Kat away.

"What is it?" Kat asks. "Why aren't you happy about this?"

"Because nothing's changed!"

I'm stumped. "They didn't give you a new office?" I say, taking a stab.

Sin exhales loudly, as if she's been trying to explain logarithms to first-graders. "Nothing's different. I thought things would change when I made VP. I thought my life would be better, more magical or...or I don't know. I can't explain it."

But I know what she means now. "I thought the same thing when I got the job at Billings Sherman & Lott," I say. "I thought I was really on my way, that I would have a career, and my whole world would start sparkling, but I've been working there part-time, and I've got to tell you, nothing's sparkling yet."

"Really?" Sin says with a sniffle.

I nod.

"That sucks." Kat sinks back on her bed.

I keep nodding.

"But you have John," Sin says.

Now I'm stumped again. "You don't even like John," I point out.

"Oh, he's fine. It's not him."

I see Kat and Sin exchanging a look.

"What is it then?"

"He's sweet," says Kat in a noncommittal voice, "and I'm sure he loves you a lot...."

"But," I say, giving her a lead.

"But..." Kat starts biting a thumbnail again. She looks at Lindsey for assistance.

"You just don't shine when you're with him," Sin says.

I blink a few times, attempting to process this. It seems like they might be on to something, but I can't help feeling defensive on John's behalf. I can bitch and moan about him and fool around with other guys, but that doesn't mean anyone else can malign him, even if it is disguised as an insult to me.

"She's right," Kat says. "He is very sweet, but he's not as fun as you are, and I think he's rubbing off on you."

Sin nods.

Was that what it was? Had I begun to assume John's personality into mine, diluting it?

"Wait," I say to Sin. "If this is all true, then why would you be jealous of me and John?"

"Because you have someone who loves you, someone who cares if you come home at night." Her eyes start to well up again. "Then to top it off we go to Rome, and you find *someone else* who seems to really like you, and then Billy..."

"Ah," I say, understanding now how my life has looked through Sin's eyes. Funny how it's a load of uncontrollable crap to me, but to someone else it seems like a dream. "It's not so great for me, you know. This trip was supposed to be an escape from all the other shit I have to deal with when I get home."

"What other shit?" Lindsey says, cutting me off, exasperated with me again. "You're going to be coming back from a long vacation. You're done with school and the bar. You don't have anything to worry about."

"That's just it," I say, hearing the climbing shrill tone in my voice. "I'm done with school, I don't know if I passed the bar and I'm terrified of working for a living. To be honest, I don't know how to be a lawyer! Law school teaches you nothing practical. And then things aren't right with you guys, which I can't handle. To top it all off—my parents are getting divorced."

"Oh, for Christ's sake, they're having problems, Casey. Don't be so melodramatic," Sin says.

I honestly think about giving her an Erica Kane style slap across the face and asking her how she likes that for melodrama, but I just sit back on the bed and clench my hands. "When I called my mom today, she told me my dad's gone. He moved out. It's over. And there's more...." I start to sniffle. "Bailey died."

It's my turn to cry now, and I can hear Lindsey and Kat murmuring, moving toward me, hugging me awkwardly from both sides. Finally, I think, finally.

"I'm so sorry," I can hear Kat say. "I'm so sorry, Case. Why didn't you tell us sooner?"

"I didn't feel like you cared."

"What do you think it's been like for us?" Lindsey abruptly pulls her arms away from me. "You haven't seemed like you gave a damn about anything for a long time."

"I know," I say. "I know you're thinking the same about me, but we have to somehow rise above this."

"You have to open your mouth first to give us the opportunity to 'rise above it.'" Lindsey makes quotation signs with her hands as she pantomimes my words. I hate when people do that.

"I tried to talk to both of you tonight, but you weren't exactly receptive."

Kat holds me away from her slightly and gives me the raised eyebrow.

"It's true," I say. "I tried being with you tonight, but you were too busy entertaining the crowd. And within two minutes of finding you—" I point at Lindsey "—you were in a heated political debate with that British chump."

"He wasn't a chump, and that doesn't mean I wouldn't have dropped everything if you'd said that you needed to talk."

"Could've fooled me," I mumble.

Lindsey snorts and stomps over to her backpack on the floor. She takes off her shirt, rummaging in her pack for something to sleep in.

A moment of uncomfortable quiet passes before Kat asks, "So what do we do about this, you guys?"

I slump back onto my bed. What *can* we do? I'm so exhausted, I can barely speak. "Can we sleep on it?"

"Fine," Lindsey says, standing up from her backpack. "Fine," she says again, before walking to the bathroom and closing the door behind her.

I pull the sheet over myself and shut my eyes, not even bothering to take off my clothes.

"Night, Case," Kat says a few minutes later, turning off the lights. When I don't answer, she says, "It's going to be all right, you know."

I nod in the dark, although I doubt it.

18

Despite my fatigue, I sleep fitfully that night, shifting my legs every few minutes in search of cool spots on the sheets. I want desperately for everything to return to normal with Kat and Sin, but I'm tired of pretending things are all right when they aren't. I see now that I've done this too many times, in too many different situations. I've put on a happy face and acted as if all were fine and dandy, ignoring the fact that things were about as dandy as a root canal.

Take John, for instance. If I was honest with myself, I'd have to admit that the things about him that were beginning to gnaw at me, I knew all along. When I started dating him, we had healthy getting-to-know-you discussions, but in general, I saw that he wasn't much of a talker, that he wasn't going to spend long, candlelit nights with me chatting over a bottle of Beaujolais. Yet I had wanted a boyfriend so badly. I wanted a date for New Year's Eve and someone to watch movies with on Sunday afternoons. I wanted to be able to use the term "my boyfriend" in conversation. *My boyfriend* and I saw a fabulous play this weekend. *My boyfriend* sent me these flowers.

I have to meet *my boyfriend* for drinks. So I turned his quieter, more reticent personality into what I thought was a positive. I recall explaining to Kat in a bright voice, "It's great. He's not a big people person, but he doesn't care if I am, so I can make the rounds at a party, and he's okay to be left by himself." I remember her barely nodding, looking at me as if I'd just said that the war in Bosnia had been a good thing.

There were other things that bothered me about John, too, like his anal housekeeping, his insistence that all shampoo flip tops be securely closed after use to avoid accidental leakage, and his requirement that the toilet paper rolls be placed so that the paper pulls down, not up. I'd seen these things from the start, but I'd either ignored them or put an optimistic spin on them. "Isn't that adorable?" I gushed facetiously when my mother overheard him admonish me to put the mustard in the door of the fridge, *not* on the second shelf. My mother made a face as if to say, "To each his own." All these things had come back to haunt me and were taking on the quality of nails on a blackboard.

I don't want to let the same thing happen with Lindsey and Kat. There's something lacking in our friendship, some element of understanding and ability to be on the same page that we've always carried with us. The distance I've created since dating John could partly, but not completely, be to blame. That's why I can't gloss over it anymore and say, "You're right. Everything is fine. Let's go back to the way we used to be," as I had in Rome. Kat and Sin are too important to me.

I'm finally able to steal a few hours of sleep, but I'm awakened at ten in the morning by Sin, already dressed in khaki shorts and a white baby-doll T-shirt.

"Case," she says, nudging me roughly in the hip. "Wake up. I want to ask you something."

"What?" I say, rubbing my eyes, trying to free myself from the twisted sheets. "What is it?"

Sin is all-business this morning, standing with her hands on her hips. "I went to town and found out that we can take a boat to Mykonos at two o'clock today and get there by early evening. What do you think?"

"Leave Ios?" I ask, somewhat startled, thinking that I'm not quite ready to move on.

This has been happening to me for the last few years. I'll panic at any small change in my daily routine, taking comfort in always knowing what's around the corner, the ease of simplicity and repetition. Like here at the Sunset, for example. Although relations have been strained with Sin and Kat, I have my routine. I know what time the family serves meals. I know how to get an Amstel from the fridge and how many drachmas to leave on the counter. I know how to stumble my way home from the bars. What I don't know is whether I'm ready to give up the safety of that routine.

"You still have time to see Billy Boy if you want," Sin says.

"It's not that. I'm just trying to think. What does Kat want to do?" I look around the room for her.

"She's getting breakfast. She wants to go."

When I hesitate, Lindsey looks pissed off. "Look, in light of everything that's happened and our talk last night, I think we need to get out of here. Just the three of us."

I nod, trying to think this through.

"We have to make a decision," Lindsey says. "I need to get back to town and buy the tickets." She drops her head a little. "Casey, maybe this will help."

I feel a surge of hope. "Let's do it," I say. "Yeah…let's go."

"Great," she says, and she gives me a clumsy pat on the leg before she leaves.

After a shower, I go looking for Billy. I don't want to leave without at least saying goodbye. No one answers when I knock on the thin wood door of his hut. As I start to turn away, I hear a voice call from inside. I look back in time to see Billy stick his head out the door. His black curls are dripping wet and the only clothing he has on is a tired purple-and-yellow beach towel, slung low over his hips, a happy trail of dark hair leading from his lower abdomen to the towel.

"Hey!" he says, looking happy to see me, and I feel a ridiculous pride that I can cause such a reaction in him.

"Good morning." I give him a slow once-over, the pride, along with the knowledge that we're leaving, making me bold.

He smiles, somewhere between bashful and seductive. He glances down at the towel, but makes no effort to hike it up. "Want to come in?" he asks, raising his eyebrows like Groucho Marx.

I laugh. "I thought we'd have breakfast."

"Well, I thought I'd have you for breakfast."

Normally, this remark would send my eyes rolling, but Billy is sporting such a mischievous grin, I want to follow the happy trail and rip the towel from his hips. He reaches out and takes my forearm, his touch giving me another *ping*.

"So what about it?" Billy says, gesturing with his head toward the room, his fingers a soft presence on my skin.

"Where are Noel and Johnny?" I ask, stalling for time.

"Already at the beach. C'mon," he says, pulling me into his chest, which is still slightly wet and smells of soap. I want to rub my face against him.

"C'mon," Billy says again, holding me closer to him, leaning in to nuzzle my neck.

"I shouldn't," I say feebly, but like some swooning heroine in a hoopskirt I let him pull me inside.

Billy's hut looks about the same as our room, although his is littered with Amstel bottles and dirty clothes. We'd at least made some effort to keep ours presentable. His room makes me think of the one-too-many fraternity houses I'd spent nights in, fighting off lecherous advances. When I think back to how many close calls and scary situations I allowed myself to get drawn into, I feel like making the sign of the cross—a skill that has decidedly atrophied over the years—in thanks that I'd survived those situations relatively unscathed.

"I'm sorry about the mess," Billy says, seeing my expression. He begins dumping bottles in the trash, collecting errant garments hanging from doorknobs and the mirror. "I wasn't expecting company."

Billy isn't at all like the frat boys whose clutches I'd broken away from, but the reminder has brought me back to earth. I still have a boyfriend at home, a fact I've conveniently ignored for a while, and I still want to make things better with Kat and Sin. Bopping Billy in this hut is certainly not going to help either situation.

"Listen," I say, watching him scoop tubes of suntan lotion off a bed and into the garbage. "I really think I need to get some food to calm my stomach. Too much booze last night, you know? How about meeting me on the terrace when you're ready?"

"Wait a bit," Billy says, stopping his frenetic cleaning. "What's the matter, eh?"

"I just can't do this."

I start to try to explain, but Billy jumps in, "We're not doing anything, Casey. It's all right."

He moves closer to me, his towel swinging with the movement, and for a moment I both fear and hope that it's about to fall off. But at the same time, the room feels tiny and cramped.

"Just meet me for breakfast, okay?" I lean in and touch my lips to his cheek, a sort of a peace offering.

"Sure," Billy says, although he doesn't sound thrilled. "Be right there."

When I get to the terrace, I'm relieved to find Kat gone already. I don't want her to see me with Billy.

I walk to the bar, which is being manned by Spiros's daughter, Samantha.

"Hello, Casey!" she chirps, her bright eyes gleaming. Pencil in hand, she's ready to take my order. Ever since our journey to the hospital, she seems to favor me over the other guests, unfailingly cheerful and cute. "What you want for breakfast?"

I smile at her accent and her eagerness, wondering if I'd ever been that hopeful and motivated.

"Hmm..." I study the breakfast menu written on a blackboard above Samantha's head.

I know the menu by heart already, but I'm giving myself time to launch a full-scale food debate in my head—egg whites versus cheese, sliced tomato versus toast. My mouth waters at the thought of real scrambled eggs with feta cheese and thick slices of freshly toasted Greek bread laden with butter, but I'm liking my body better after having shed some poundage. Then I realize that the real reason I'm trying to stay away from the eggs and toast is the knowledge that Billy is on his way to meet me, and I don't want to eat like a pig in front of him. I give myself a mental smack for this idiotic line of thinking, as if Billy would actually think I was thinner if he didn't see me eat. Ridiculous! Hadn't I denied certain parts of myself for years because of John? No more tennis, no more late nights with the girls, no more live music.

"Scrambled eggs with feta and toast," I say to Samantha, "and extra butter."

* * *

Out of the corner of my eye, I spot Billy walking toward me. I turn and see he's wearing a huge smile and, unfortunately, clothing now. He has on wrinkled green shorts and a white ribbed T-shirt with three buttons undone, giving a glimpse of a tanned chest.

"Hey," he says to me as he bends down to give me a kiss. I'm not sure if he's shooting for my mouth or my cheek, so I wiggle around a bit, and it lands awkwardly on the right side of my nose.

Billy doesn't seem to notice. "Can I buy you breakfast?"

"Sure, big spender," I say. Breakfast is included in the room rate. "But I already ordered."

"I'll do the same. Be right back." Billy squeezes my shoulder and gives me another smile before striding off to the counter.

My feta eggs are delicious. I shovel them on my toast and wash them down with a big, cold bottle of Evian, not letting myself care what kind of image I'm presenting to Billy. His food arrives shortly after mine, and he eats with similar gusto. We must look like a couple of starved refugees.

I steal glances at him, wondering if I will ever see him, or for that matter, Francesco, again. Francesco had given me his address and phone number, and I assume Billy and I will exchange digits. My knee-jerk inclination is to try and keep in touch with both of them, but my sane mind tells me this would be a bad move for two reasons. The first, of course, is John. It had been betrayal enough without bringing it home with me. The second reason is my belief that vacation romances should be left on vacation. In the bright light of real life, it's impossible to escape the annoyances and incompatibilities that are glossed over when basking in the golden hue of a sunset or hiding in the dark of a hotel room.

I'd learned this lesson all too well when I met a nice boy from New Jersey while spending a weekend in Key West. We strolled the boardwalk and had a picnic in the sand. It was romantic and dreamy, but when he visited me a few months later, everything irritated me. I found his "Joy-Zee" accent gauche. He wore immense amounts of cheap cologne that lingered on my sheets. He spent an inordinate amount of time in front of the mirror parting and reparting his hair from side to side. And his clothes! I'd essentially seen him in bathing suits and T-shirts in Key West, but in Chicago, when I told him we were having dinner with some friends, he exited the bathroom in tightly pressed acid-washed jeans, black high-top Reeboks and a teal silk shirt. I claimed mysterious female difficulties to avoid introducing him to my friends or partaking in any physical contact that evening. I was relieved to drop him off at the airport the next day.

"So," Billy says when we're finished eating. "Everything all right with your friends, then?"

"Yes and no," I say. "Lindsey was pissed off and still is, but we talked about some things." I shrug, not wanting to rehash it or go into specifics.

"Then we'll spend a bit of time together today, yeah?"

I look at my watch and realize we have to leave in about an hour for the boat, and I still have to pack.

I shake my head. "We're taking off today. We're going to Mykonos."

"When was that decided?"

"This morning. Lindsey and Kat want to move on."

"You're going then," he says, a statement, not a question.

"Yeah, I'm going."

Billy is silent and actually looks sad. "How long do we have?"

I glance at my watch again. "I need to leave in about an hour, and I have to pack first."

"How about I help you?" he offers, giving me the Groucho Marx eyebrows again.

I laugh, imagining Billy sitting on my bed, holding my

backpack while I give him long kisses every time I place something in it. But then I imagine Lindsey walking in and going berserk.

"I don't think so," I tell Billy.

"I guess you're done with me," he says, standing from the table. "You've used me, and now you're casting me off."

I laugh and stand with him.

"It was a treat," he says, moving around the table to hug me.

I squeeze him back. "It was."

He turns and walks away, and I stand there like an idiot, a wistful smile on my face. It's only when I'm back in the room with the door shut that I realize Billy hadn't asked for my address or my phone number.

PART III
MYKONOS, GREECE

19

It's hard to leave the Sunset. A week and a half in a climate and culture so different than my own seemed much longer. Even though things with Kat and Sin had been strained, I'd become attached to all the other people at the Sunset, the slow-moving lifestyle.

I take one long look around before getting into Spiros's pickup, hoping to spy Billy rounding the corner, possibly professing his love, begging me to stay. Instead, I see Gunther on the terrace, his arms around the Swedish girls, who are waving and blowing kisses. But no Billy.

Spiros gives us big bear hugs when he drops us off at the ferry and yells warnings about watching our purses and backpacks. The air is stilted between Sin and Kat and me. You'd think I'd be used to it by now, but after almost ten years of friendship, a decade of spring breaks and happy hours and late-night crying sessions over boys whose names we can't remember now, there's no way that stilted is ever going to feel normal. We lumber awkwardly onto the boat, our packs strapped firmly to our backs, no one speaking. The ferry isn't as crowded as the one we took to Ios, and we're lucky enough to land a table in the bar area of the ship. Formica covers the entire room, while music blasts from the speakers—the stereotypical Greek music you'd expect to hear at Epcot Center in Disney World. In order to compensate for the climbing heat outside, they've cranked the air-conditioning to Everest-like temperatures.

We order hot teas, put our backpacks on the floor, our feet up on our packs, and lean back in our chairs. As I sip my tea, I steal quick glances at each of them, trying to read their moods, their thoughts, but they give nothing away.

Lindsey finally breaks the uncomfortable quiet. "So, did you say goodbye to Billy Boy?"

I glance at her to see whether she's being serious or throwing verbal darts at my head. Her face is bland, and she seems to be waiting for an answer.

I respond with a simple, "Yeah."

She nods, as if thinking this over, her face as serious as a doctor delivering bad news. "Will you talk to him again?" she asks.

"No," I say, in an "of course not" tone of voice, secretly wishing my answer was a hearty "yes."

"What about Francesco?" Lindsey asks, her expression a little amused now.

It's patently unfair that she can still read me so well after two weeks of barely speaking.

I shrug, wondering how to change the subject, and slurp away at my tea.

"Are you going to write love letters and drive up your phone bill?" She's leaning toward me now, looking sadistic.

I lean in, too. "Fuck off, Sin," I say, in a lowered, measured tone. "I've already apologized for Billy, and I'm sick of your crap."

I sit back in my chair, shaking my head, tired of the bickering and the chilly air. Why is she doing this? Because she let her guard down once and let us see that she isn't happy? Who is?

Lindsey's mouth opens immediately as if to retort, but Kat slaps a hand on her thigh to stop her. "She's right," Kat says in a firm tone. "Lay off, okay?"

Sin shuts her mouth and makes a face as if to say, "Fine. I don't care."

I let my shoulders relax a little. Kat just stood up for me, and minimal though that may have been, it's like a warm blanket thrown over my shoulders. It gets me off the defensive enough to see that I need to be direct. With the deteriorating condition of my parents' relationship and my questions about John, this friendship might be the one thing I can salvage.

"We've got to get over this, you guys," I say.

Sin is expressionless. There's a slight pause, but then Kat moves closer to the table.

The bar is completely full now, and the Disney music seems jauntier and louder than before. I pull my feet off my pack and scoot my chair in toward the table. I take a deep breath and, before I can talk myself out of it, I say, "I need you guys right now. I think we all need each other."

"What do you mean?" Kat says.

I think about how I should phrase this. "On one hand, I've lost some weight, I've met a couple of great guys and I've been in this tropical paradise, but at the same time, things are weird with you two." I point at them with my spoon. "I don't know what I feel about John, my parents are splitting up and I have to start work soon." I start tapping the spoon on the side of my hand. "Nothing seems to make sense right now."

"Well, what do you want us to do?" Lindsey asks, sounding sarcastic as usual. Ah, the comfort of good friends.

As if taking a drag of a cigarette, I suck in another deep breath, refusing to jump at her bait. "What I want is to have fun and relax, and I want to spend time with both of you, some serious girl time."

"We've already tried that," Sin says, but her voice is neutral now, as if she's waiting for me to continue, to tell her how it could be different this time.

"We *said* we were going to try it, but it seemed like you two kept meeting a lot of guys, and then I met some guys, and there goes our time together."

"Exactly what are you suggesting?" Sin asks. "A prohibition on all males?"

From the expression on her face, Kat is mortified at the thought.

I try not to laugh. "I'm not saying we can't meet people, whether they're male or female, but I'd like the three of us to stick together for a few days."

No one says anything for a moment and the tinny Disney music becomes overpowering.

"All I'm saying is that we should make an effort to spend some real time together," I say, raising my voice to be heard over the damned music.

Lindsey shrugs her shoulders.

"I can do that," Kat says, appearing to have calmed herself.

I look back at Sin.

A few seconds go by, then a few more.

"Sin?" I say.

"We can give it a whirl," she calls over the music.

Mykonos is the Greece that you see in movies. The cafés that sit in front of the bobbing boats of the port are much more charming than the more basic restaurants of the Ios docks. Here, huge flower boxes line the restaurants' perimeters, and there are crisp linens and real silver on the tables. White speckled streets the size of sidewalks weave away from the port, past the blue-painted doors of the white buildings, past an abundance of jewelry stores. Blue-domed rooftops dot the sky, standing tall above the rounded white homes, which seem to sparkle in the sun.

This time, there're no hostel or hotel workers to greet us at the port. Mykonos is full, we're told by the people at the information booth.

"I'm so glad we waited in line for forty-five minutes to hear that," Sin says.

Just then the ferry pulls away, and I feel a creeping panic. We're homeless! We're here without shelter or a plan!

"Fuck it," Kat says, pulling her hair into a ponytail. "We'll find someplace."

For two hours we pitch and stumble around the village with our packs, our faces shiny from the heat. We knock on countless doors and beg countless innkeepers to give us a room, a closet, *anything*. My panic rises again, and I'm seriously considering whether we should head back to the docks and wait for the next boat to anywhere when we come across a quaint inn called Hotel Carbonaki, which is situated at the outskirts of the village. The owners, an older couple, nod and tell us they have one room left. I nearly kiss them.

White stone steps lead up to our small but bright room, which overlooks a tiny pool surrounded by blue cloth beach chairs. After a dip, we shower and go in search of a place to eat. It's already nine o'clock, and the peaceful village we'd seen in the daylight has metamorphosed into an outdoor Studio 54.

"This is like South Beach on steroids," Kat says as we pass four model-type women. They're gaunt in tropical micro dresses, smoking at a table outside a restaurant, no food in sight. We see at least a hundred more of their brethren, both male and female, strolling as if on a catwalk. Many of the men are obviously gay, shirtless with leather pants, walking arm in arm with other boys. There's also a number of long-haired Guiseppe-type Italians dressed in their finest. I steal a glance at Kat and see that she's doing her best to control the Pavlovian drooling.

All the tavernas on the main drag are jammed, with at least an hour's wait for a table, so we keep walking until we find a small restaurant tucked away on a dead-end street. Square tables painted sea-green are set up in front of the storefront café. We spot the only empty one resting near a brick wall under a circle of streetlight.

"Welcome!" says an elderly woman with curly gray hair and a toothy grin. She gestures toward the open table. "Sit, sit! To drink?" she says.

"Vod-ka ton-ic," Kat answers, overenunciating and speaking loudly, as if the volume will help the woman to understand.

A flicker of amusement lights the woman's eyes as she nods, apparently understanding perfectly. She looks at Lindsey and me.

"Some red wine?" I ask Sin in a tentative voice. Red wine used to be our shared drink of choice, enjoyed over many opposite-sex advisory meetings and dinners with the girls, but it's been a long time since we've split a bottle.

There's a pause, but then she nods.

"What you have for dinner?" the old woman asks after bringing Kat her drink and pouring our cabernet into short glasses, setting the bottle on the table.

"Men-u?" Kat asks, confused.

"No menu, no menu," the woman says. "You come to kitchen." She gestures for us to follow her, and walks away.

In the kitchen are a few women wearing aprons, their black hair tied back, tending to two large stovetops. They give us shy nods when we enter, quickly returning to their stirring, chopping and cutting. The room is hot and smells of something spicy, something with tomatoes in it.

Our waitress waves a wrinkled hand toward a large wooden island that commands the majority of space in the kitchen. "What you have for dinner?" she repeats.

On the island they've arranged earthen platters filled with food. There are tomatoes as big as my head stuffed with rice and sausage, grape leaves encircling meat and vegetables, various cuts of tender white fish and huge portions of moussaka.

I glance around as Kat and Sin ask about the preparation of different dishes, thinking that John would love this kitchen with its huge pots hanging overhead and the racks upon racks of spices. I remember how he cooked dinner for me on our third date. It was just spaghetti and meatballs, but he had set the table with cloth place mats and napkins. I could tell that he'd bought them that day, because they were still creased from being folded, and the price tags were on the back. I thought it was the sweetest thing in the world. When he brought me my plate, I saw that he'd carefully arranged the meatballs and the sauce, sprinkling freshly grated Parmesan on the top just so. He smiled when he placed it before me.

"What do you think?" he said, and I knew that he meant more than the spaghetti.

"It's perfect," I told him.

The thought of this makes my heart sink. As much as this trip has made me wonder about John, about our relationship, I simply can't imagine what my life would be like without him.

"Casey," Kat calls, pulling me away from my thoughts. "What are you having?"

I move toward the food, suppressing a powerful urge to request the entire inviting tray of moussaka. Instead, I select a piece of white fish with some rice on the side. Kat, of course, asks for two helpings of the moussaka.

Sin and I have just begun to make our way through the mellow red wine when our dinners are delivered.

The old woman hesitates by our table as we begin our meals. "Good?" she says. "You like?"

"Mmm," we all say through mouthfuls of food. The fish has completely surpassed my expectations. It's so fresh, it tastes like it was caught thirty seconds ago.

"You enjoy Mykonos," she says, still standing by our table, nodding at each of us. "Mykonos good for you girls."

"Sure, thanks." I'm not certain what she means or how else to respond.

She stays there for a moment longer, before she finally heads back to the kitchen.

"She reminds me of Belle," Lindsey says when she's gone, and we all crack up.

Belle was our housemother at the sorority. Her real name was Marilyn, but she was so crazy that we called her Bellevue, Belle for short. Belle seemed to never sleep and was forever lurking around. On many a night we'd raid the kitchen about 4:00 a.m. after coming home from the bars. We'd stuff our faces with the mashed potatoes that always seemed to be left over in the fridge, yelling our conversation as only the drunk and the truly tone deaf can do, and suddenly Belle would appear out of the pantry. How long she'd been in there, we'd never know, since there was no other entrance.

"Hello, girls," she'd say in her dramatic, smoky voice, throwing one of her colored feather boas over her shoulder. She always wore them after 8:00 p.m., when it was too late for someone from the Panhellenic Council to stop by.

"Did the boys molest you?" she'd ask with a lecherous grin. She wanted all the gory details, but only a few brave souls would actually confide in her. Yet even when you told her nothing, Belle was always around when you got home, always staring and nodding knowingly, as if she knew that you'd lost your underwear somewhere in that hovel your boyfriend called an apartment and that you'd neglected, again, to make him wear a condom.

I had thought Belle nuts at the time, but now I'm struck by the fact that I could actually end up like her. I mean, if I can't be satisfied with a nice guy like John, maybe I'll never be happy with anyone. I pour myself a healthy refill of wine to drown the thoughts.

The first bottle relaxes and mellows us, and when Kat decides to switch to vino, we order a second. The mention of Belle, in addition to terrifying me about the prospects of a lonely life, has brought on memories of college. We tell and retell all our stories, which are full-blown novellas by now as the exaggeration and fictitious details grow with each version.

"Why, exactly, did I spend six months with that Jimmy Tate character?" Kat asks, wrinkling her nose in distaste. "What did I ever see in that guy?"

Since Jimmy Tate represented Kat's longest relationship to date, Sin and I remember it in detail.

"A very large penis," Sin reminds her. "That's what you saw in him, or should I say, in you."

We talk of raucous football weekends and booze-filled road trips. We shriek with laughter as we remember the cruel joke we'd played on Troy Tellers, who after sleeping with Kat and secretly videotaping the encounter, was uncouth enough to show the video at a Monday night meeting with a hundred of his closest fraternity brothers. Three weeks later, when he'd forgotten about Kat and moved on to other victims, Troy received a phone call from the student health clinic informing him that he'd been listed as a sexual partner for one of their patients, who'd contracted a nasty case of the worst type of herpes.

"Now listen, son," Lindsey says, mimicking the matronly voice she'd used to call Troy. "You'll have to tell everyone you come in physical contact with that you might have this."

We'd learned from Troy's roommate that for three days

after that call, Troy refused to attend class or even leave his room, choosing instead to spend his time inspecting his privates with a handheld mirror. Luckily for Troy, that nice woman from the health clinic called back to report that it was a mistake, and that she was terribly sorry for any inconvenience, but not before Troy had informed his roommate and at least one woman of this possible affliction. After that, rumors that Troy had numerous communicable diseases spread rapidly, and Troy rarely had any films to show his frat buddies anymore.

As for Kat, she'd acted as if it wasn't so bad that a videotape depicting her superior oral abilities was loose on campus. At the time, I believed her relative nonchalance, but now I wonder, and I almost bring it up. I find I can't, though, because it feels so good to reminisce, to remind ourselves how close we were, how close we might be again. I can't bring myself to break the happy spell that's settled over the three of us.

Unfortunately, someone else breaks it for me. Two someones to be exact—two tanned, well-dressed men who could be related to the Kennedys. They amble up to our table, both about six feet tall, wearing expensive-looking slacks and pastel golf shirts.

Jesus, they're dressed alike, I think, before I glance around our table and realize that Lindsey and Kat and I are all wearing various forms of the little flowered dress, Kat's much littler, by the way.

"You look like you're enjoying yourselves," says one of the Kennedys. He has straight brown hair and eyes so blue they must be colored contacts. His friend, who looks like a Ken doll with his blond hair and jutting, square jaw, nods at us.

"My God—Americans!" Kat says, giving her highest voltage smile. "I'd begun to forget what my mother tongue sounded like!"

The Ken doll beams back at her, matching her watt for watt. "We don't want to interrupt your dinner," he says, "but we're heading to the Scandinavian Bar, and we thought you might want to join us."

I feel like saying, "What, exactly, made you think that?" but I keep quiet.

"Scandinavian Bar?" Lindsey says in a wry tone. "I thought we were in Greece."

The Ken doll introduces himself as Trent and his friend as David, then explains that the Scandinavian Bar is *the* place to go until 2:00 a.m.

Here we go again, I think. Just when we're having fun, just us, we have to meet these two, and you know damned well they'll be around for a while, buying drinks for Lindsey and Kat—and for me, too, of course, since it would be rude not to—but the whole time they'll be secretly hoping that I'll find my own man so they can be left alone.

I wonder why I'm assuming that neither Trent nor David would be interested in me. I am, after all, the one who got Billy's attention—not Lindsey. But the doubting part of myself feels that had been a fluke, a coincidence, or possibly a mistake on Billy's part. Well then, was Francesco a mistake, too? This self-defeating circle jerk gets me nowhere, so I tune back in to the conversation.

"It sounds like a blast. What do you think?" Kat says, and I can tell she's excited. I want her to be happy, I really do, so I smile back.

"Want to go?" she says when I don't answer right away.

"Sure," I say, trying to sound game, and some part of me thinks it does sound like fun to check out the island nightlife. Mykonos *is* supposed to be one of the most happening places in Europe. But some other part of me, some large part, wishes that instead of Mykonos, we'd gone to some secluded slip of land where it was just the three of us.

★ ★ ★

The Scandinavian Bar is the sole business occupant of a tiny plaza surrounded by whitewashed houses with arched doorways. The bar itself is a small, unimposing, oak-lined pub that could never accommodate the crowd it attracts. Instead, the patrons spill out of the place and fill every inch of the plaza, its doorsteps and stairways. Greece, apparently, doesn't have any of those pesky, you-can't-drink-in-a-public-thoroughfare laws.

We stand at the entrance to the plaza looking for a waitress and talking. Kat and Lindsey both listen to the Kennedy boys, who explain that they're traders in Manhattan, but neither of my friends appears to be overtly flirting or turning up the volume. I'm pleasantly surprised. It seems that they're following through, in a way, with our little pact to spend more time with the girls and less with the boys.

It's clear that we'll never find a waitress standing where we are, but luckily, Trent and David spot a pack of English people they know who've managed to corner a large chunk of real estate just outside the bar. It takes us at least fifteen minutes to travel there because the crowd is nearly impenetrable, and no one is particularly interested in making room for anyone else. Muttering "excuse me" and "sorry" about a thousand times, we slip and squeeze past women with moviestar good looks and a few drag queens who are even prettier, past the Italian stallions and the rest of the beautiful people. Finally, we all congregate with the English crew, packed tight like we're in the front row of a concert, and the introductions are made.

"This crowd is unbelievable," Kat says, glancing around at the slim and ridiculously well dressed hordes of people.

"It's enough to make you feel like a fat arse, isn't it?" responds Jenny, a stout English girl with mischievous green eyes and a sprinkling of freckles over her nose.

I like her immediately. In fact, I like most of the group. The Kennedy boys are less preppie and predictable than I'd thought, and the Brits are loud and friendly.

Sin uses her miniature frame to her advantage, sneaking to the bar and back, arriving with a tray of cold, dripping bottles of Tuborg. Our little gang cheers for her, and I see a genuine smile light up Sin's face. I take one of the bottles and relax, letting myself enjoy the company and the people-watching from our prime vantage point. It's hard not to compare myself to the stylish women with stick-straight hair and bodies, four-inch heels and perfect makeup, but I'm in a particularly good mood, and I'm able to wrench myself out of that mind rut easier than usual.

An hour flies by, with various members of our group leaving to get beers or make bathroom runs, then pushing their way back in, their faces flushed, their arms filled with bottles for everyone. At one point, I let myself get jostled to the edge of the group. I take a deep breath and look up at the star-filled sky, thinking how lucky I am to be here, far away from home. Home. The thought of it brings in the image of my father's packed suitcases lining the hallway, and my stomach falls. The feeling is like the one I had at my grandfather's funeral a year ago. I'd been talking with my cousin Trish, and we began to laugh about the monstrous Halloween costumes we'd designed when we were eight years old. Suddenly, in the middle of throwing my head back with laughter, I remembered why we were together—my grandfather's death—and I felt as if I'd been socked in the gut. It seemed that my mind would let me forget the awful realities for a sweet, short time, before they slammed back, lest I think they were gone.

"What's up, Case?" Kat asks, as she reaches me by squeezing past two of the English guys who are tossing back vile-looking shots. "Bad beer?"

I give a slight smile at her attempt of humor. "Sorry. I was thinking about my parents."

"Don't," Kat says. "Don't apologize for feeling shitty that they're splitting up."

She pauses for a second, as if thinking about something then asks, "Do you want to get out of here? We could go some place more laid back, some place where we can chat."

"Oh no," I say, so surprised by her kind gesture, that I immediately reject it. "I'll get over it. It's no big deal." I'm sure that Sin and Kat would rather stay here and party than listen to me mope, and I like this place, too. I'll shake off the thoughts of my parents. Princess Denial to the rescue.

"It is a big deal, and hey—we've got a whole week here. I'm sure we'll be able to follow the trail of beer bottles and find this place again." Kat gulps the rest of her Tuborg and signals for Lindsey.

"We're thinking of going," Kat tells Sin once she's picked her way over to us. "Some place a little quieter where we can talk."

"Fine with me," Lindsey says. She nods, her face open, and I realize that she means it.

"We don't have to go," I protest one more time, but I'm secretly thrilled.

"No arguments," Kat says. "We're out of here."

20

We find a half-filled taverna by the waterfront with a good view of the cruise ships and their strings of white lights, the sound of jazz music tinkling across the water. It's the type of magical setting I dreamt of during the tedium of my bar exam classes.

Lindsey orders another bottle of cabernet for us.

I've taken only two sips before it happens.

"Look," she says, talking fast, rearranging her wineglass, the napkins on the table. "I want to tell you something."

I'm not sure if she's talking to Kat or me, so I take another swallow of my wine.

"I want to say that I'm sorry." She puts down her wineglass as she says this, and the glass makes a knock on the table that gives her statement a sense of finality.

I blink a few times, still unsure what we're talking about, who we're talking to, when she looks me square in the eye.

"I'm sorry," she says again.

I put down my own glass, blinking furiously as if this might help me process her words. I don't think she's ever apologized to me, and it sounds so foreign coming from her mouth. I skid my eyes over to Kat, who looks as surprised as I do.

"I was way too harsh on you," Sin says. "I had reasons to be mad at you, don't get me wrong, but I let my envy take over. I hated myself for feeling that way, and that made me act even more like a bitch."

Kat reaches over and squeezes my hand, which I recognize as her way of apologizing.

"I'm sorry, too," I say. "I'm sorry I came in late that night...."

"It wasn't even during the night. You came home in the *morning,*" Sin says, but then she claps a hand over her mouth. "Sorry," she manages to say through her fingers. "That just slipped out. Keep going. If you want to, I mean."

The rebuke takes away a little of my desire to flagellate myself, but I do keep going. I have to.

"I'm sorry about Billy, too," I say. "Hearing that my parents were officially over just threw me. I needed someone to talk to, and he was there, and then all of a sudden he was kissing me. You saw everything that happened between us. I shouldn't have let it get that far, but nothing else happened. I promise."

"I believe you," Sin says. "What can I say? The main thing is that I've been jealous of you, of you and John and what you have together."

I shake my head. "There hasn't been much to be envious of lately. He's never around anymore. We hardly spend any time together."

"But you just took the bar exam," Kat says. "Now that you're done, it should free up some time."

I scoff. "My new job will probably keep me busier than the damn bar. Plus John works like crazy, and I can't see that changing anytime soon." I give Sin a little smile. "So you see, there's nothing much to be jealous of. Besides, you could have a serious relationship if you want."

"Yeah, Sin," Kat says. "You could have had it with Pete, but you dumped him."

Sin ducks her head, her hands playing with the napkin, pulling on its edges. "I need to tell you guys something." Her voice is grave.

There's a horrible pause at the table. A million possibilities float through my head—she has cancer, she's converted to Scientology, she's a lesbian.

"Pete dumped me," Sin says.

This is almost more shocking than the others.

"*He* dumped *you?*" Kat says.

Sin nods, her face miserable.

"Why?" I say.

"He said I was too uptight, too controlling. I realized that it's a pattern. I do it to every guy I date. I get regimented, wanting everything my way, refusing to take no for an answer. I tried to change, but it was too late. I'd already made him crazy." For the second time this trip, Sin starts to cry. Kat and I coo over her, rubbing her shoulders, pushing her wineglass in front of her.

After getting the entire story, we hash out the Pete scenario, going over and over what she could have done differently, whether she can change her ways, whether there's still a chance with him.

"I'll have to think about it," Sin says, her brown eyes redrimmed now. "I don't know if I still want Pete. He could be married by now, he could have a kid. For all I know he's living in Alaska."

"Give yourself some time," I say. "Bat it around for a while."

"You know," Kat says, "you two wouldn't have these problems if you were like me. All fun, no attachments."

She says this in a funny tone, like she expects us to crack

up, but neither Sin nor I say anything. Lately, Kat's man-eating just isn't as amusing as it used to be.

"What?" Kat says, laughing at her own comment, even if we won't join her. "What is it?"

Sin turns to me, and she gives me that look, that look that says *Take over, please!* That look I've been waiting for this whole trip.

"Why do you think you're like that?" I ask Kat. "You know, the whole relationship ban?"

"I don't know." She sounds annoyed. "I've always been like this."

True, but she hasn't always been so compulsive. "What about lately, like this summer?" I say.

She shrugs. "What do you mean?"

"Has it changed at all? Have you changed?"

"No." She snorts.

"What about after the Hatter incident?" There, I've said it.

Kat's jaw tenses. "One has nothing to do with the other."

We're all quiet. "Look," Kat says, "the Hatter attack only told me what I knew all along."

"And what's that?" Sin says.

"That men just want me for sex." Sin and I don't say anything, and Kat rolls her eyes. "Oh, don't think 'poor Kat,' because that's fine with me. I love sex."

"Hey, who doesn't?" I say.

"Well, exactly." Kat throws her hair over her shoulder. "And that's all I want from them. That's it. I like the attention, and it makes me feel good."

"Does it?" I say. "Does it make you feel good all the time?"

Another silence, a very long silence that I make myself stay out of completely. "Well, maybe not so much lately," Kat says at last. "Lately it's more like a habit. Something I just do."

"Why?" Sin asks.

"Because..." Kat throws a hand in the air. "Because it proves something to me."

"What?" Sin says.

"That—that..." Kat bites her thumbnail, gazing toward the table. "I guess it makes me feel special."

And there it is. Kat has stumbled on her own pattern, her own reasons for it.

We keep talking, taking turns pouring the wine for each other, and while it may be true that my family as I know it is disintegrating, I feel the wheels of the family I have with Sin and Kat clicking back into place.

The next day, Kat, Sin and I walk to the village center, a little square overrun by strolling vacationers, scooter rental stands and shops selling postcards and sarongs. This village "center" is actually on the fringes of town, and it's nowhere as picturesque as the rest. The only reason it flourishes is because the buses that run to Paradise Beach, the main beach, line up here, and, therefore, so does everyone else on the island.

The buses, it seems, were built roughly around 1920 and last cleaned about five years after that. They're decrepit, filled with sand and old beer bottles, and even the smell is like a not-quite-empty keg left out overnight in hot weather.

Sin, who has overly sensitive olfactory powers, almost swoons as she steps inside.

"Sit by the window," I tell her.

She does, hanging her head out like a dog looking for air as the bus chugs into action and crawls out of the village. Soon, though, she's forced to pull her head inside because the vehicle clearly has no shocks, and it bumps and lurches down the dirt road. The driver steps on the gas, clouds of dust rising around us, and as we race over a hill, it seems like we're airborne.

Sin lets out a little yelp and covers her mouth, while Kat gives a holler, raising her arms like she's on a roller coaster.

With a crash, the driver lands the bus and shifts into a higher gear, shooting down the steep decline past lonely little houses that look as if they're made of clay. We swerve around a corner, veering into the opposite lane, and the sea comes into view—icy blue with glittering diamonds of reflected sunlight.

Sin gasps. "Christ, it's beautiful," she says.

The driver screeches to a halt once he's reached the edge of the beach. We see tawny sand strewn with thatched-umbrella-covered tables and thousands of seminaked or, in some cases, downright naked sunbathers. Just like everywhere else in Mykonos, the crowd is gorgeous. Whippet-thin, topless women lay frozen in mute rows, their faces turned up toward the sun. A pack of guys plays volleyball, flexing their bronze muscles with each thump of the ball.

We walk toward the far end of the beach because Sin says the clanging house music pouring from the bars is too loud for this time of the day. I agree and lead them farther and farther down the sand because I'm ready to try the topless thing, and I want as few people around me as possible. The problem is, there's no secluded corner of this beach, so when I finally spot a small, vacant plot of sand, I grab it.

As I arrange my towel next to a woman I'm sure is a supermodel I saw on E!, I thank the gods that I've lost weight during this trip. I slather SPF 30 on every reachable surface of my body, and when I can't put it off any longer, I sneak an arm around my back, ready to unhook my top and flop over on my stomach. But my damned bikini won't unclasp. I wrestle with it, feeling like an eighth-grade boy in the back of a movie theater working on his girlfriend's bra. I hunch over, stretching my other hand around like an octopus, my fingers scrabbling at the hook.

"Need some help?" I freeze, then turn my head. Kat and Sin, both already topless, are standing with their hands on their hips, amused expressions on their faces, watching me struggle.

"Maybe," I say.

Neither comments on my choice to bare my breasts today. Kat just walks over and, with one flick of a hand, unhooks me.

I straighten up and look down at myself. "Jesus, they're white, huh?"

Kat and Sin try not to laugh, but I don't need confirmation on this one. While the rest of my body has achieved a mellow, golden sort of tan, my boobs were hibernating. Now they look like headlights on a black car.

"You better get some sunscreen on those girls," Sin says.

I glance down at myself again. "I have to put it on my boobs?"

"Well, I'm not going to do it for you," she says.

"It's a little like public masturbation, but you'll get used to it." Kat says as she applies sunscreen to her own "girls." When she's done, she twists her hair up into a knot and promptly plops back on her towel and into a deep slumber.

"Damn, that girl can sleep." Sin pulls a book from her bag. "That's something else I'm jealous about. I could never crash in this heat."

I put a big dollop of sunscreen in my hand, rub both of my hands together and take a deep breath. Now or never, I say to myself. And then I commence public breast rubbing, massaging the lotion into my even whiter breasts. As I do this, I notice that the supermodel's boobs are small and nut-brown, natural looking, while mine seem obscene, especially in my own hands in front of thousands of people. When I'm sure the "girls" are properly protected, I turn over on my stomach. They've gotten enough exposure for today.

I gaze absently at a ridiculous article in my magazine called "Top 10 Stipulations for Better Oral Manipulations." "Number Ten," it says. "No teeth." Hard-hitting journalism there.

"You know what time it is?" Sin says about an hour later. She puts her book down and drops her head, peeking at me over her sunglasses.

Her words thrill and terrify me at the same time.

You know what time it is? This is the phrase Sin uses on Kat and me whenever she wants to call us out on something. "You know what time it is?" she'd said to Kat during our senior year. "Time for you to get serious about poor Jimmy Tate or let him down easy." And the same year, she'd told me, "It's time for you to get your applications in. Law school isn't just going to come to you."

The thrilling part of hearing the question is the fact that it's been over a year since the last time, and it means that she still cares about me, that we're still tight, still best friends. The scary part, though, is that Sin is rarely wrong about these things. I'm not sure I want to hear what time it is.

I put my head down on my arms. "What?" I say, my voice muffled.

"Time to call John," she says. When I don't respond, she says, "You know I'm right."

I squeeze my eyes closed and run through the scenario in my head. If I call him now, it's probably around 4:00 a.m. in Chicago, which means that he's fast asleep. John always turns off his ringer when he goes to bed, so I could call and get his machine and simply leave a message without having to speak to him. I clamp my eyes shut tighter when it strikes me that I'm a complete shit. I haven't spoken to my boyfriend in eons, and yet I'm trying to devise ways to steer clear of him. Denial and avoidance at its finest.

"I'll do it now," I announce to Lindsey, conveniently failing to remind her what time it is back home. "I saw a pay phone by the bar."

I throw a T-shirt over my head, and before it gets any later in Chicago, I walk toward the public phones.

"Good luck!" Sin calls behind me.

21

As John's phone rings, a tinny, distant sound, I bite the arm of my sunglasses, waiting for the mechanical voice of his answering machine. I've already scripted a short but cheery message to leave him, telling him that I'm safe and sound, that I miss him and will call him later. The pay phone is bolted to the plywood side of a bar called Cortica's, which consists of three wooden walls and a twig roof, the open side facing the beach. The tables in front of the bar are mobbed. The couple sitting closest to me is leaning toward each other over uneaten plates of tuna salad, their faces menacing, spitting words at each other that I can't understand, but I can tell they're not nice.

The phone rings for the third time. One more ring until the machine picks up. I take a deep breath, readying myself for my speech.

Instead, I hear John's sleep-filled, "Yeah...hello?"

Stunned, I don't respond immediately.

"Hello?" he repeats.

"Johnny?" I manage to squeak out.

"Hey, baby, is that you?" he says, sounding much more awake now.

"It's me." I stop then, caught wordless without my rehearsed message.

The voices of the bickering couple escalate. No one seems to notice but me. At the table next to them are four pasty-white guys who must have just gotten off the plane. They chug their beers, slapping each other on the back, making a pyramid out of the cans.

"How are you?" John says.

"Uh...great," I stammer. "Great. How 'bout you?"

"Well, I'm glad to hear from you. I left the phone on all night for the last week. I was worried."

"Nothing to worry about here. We're having a blast." I chirp.

"I've missed you," John says, sending a stab of guilt through me.

"Yeah, me, too." I find I'm telling the truth. I haven't been pining away for him, but now that I hear his earnest voice I remember how much he loves me, how good he is to me. Like Sin and Kat, John has become a family member.

"How's your trip, babe? Having fun?"

"Rome was amazing," I say, relieved to find a safe topic. "You know how much I love Rome. I got to go to all my favorite places—the Pantheon and the Colosseum." But suddenly I can feel the rocks of the Colosseum floor against my back as Francesco's fingers brush my breasts. I cough.

"Sounds nice," John says.

If only he knew.

"Then we went to Ios," I continue. "That's in Greece."

"Of course." He sounds a little miffed.

"Oh, I'm sorry. Of course you know that." If there's one thing John despises it's being condescended to, which is never my intention. "Well, anyway, Ios was wonderful. The beach was fabulous." As was Billy, I think, before I shut down that locomotive of a thought.

In front of me, the couple have pushed their plates aside, and it looks as if they might come to blows. The beer tower created by the pasty-white boys climbs higher on their table, the site of an imminent crash. I tell John about the Sunset, Spiros and his family, and the craziness at the bars.

"Um-hmm," he says. I can almost see him nodding, his brow pulled down. Listening, when he decides he wants to do it, is one of John's best attributes, a skill polished from years of practicing law, focusing on his opposing counsel, preparing himself to nitpick over every word. This wavering of his, though, from complete disinterest to intense concentration, makes me crazy. It's hard to have a light conversation with the guy. And it makes me nervous when he's um-hmming in his listening mode. It means he senses something is off.

I speed up my words, telling him that we're now on the island of Mykonos, staying at a little place called Hotel Carbonaki.

"I'm glad it's going so well." John pauses, and I know it's coming—some question about what he's picked up on his radar. "You sound strange, though. Are you sure everything is all right?"

"It's probably just the connection, because all is right with the world." I cringe at the Shirley Temple tone of my voice.

"You're sure?" John sounds unconvinced.

"I'm positive, and I have to go because there's a huge line for the phone." I look back at the empty stretch of sand running along the plywood wall behind me.

"Okay, hon. I love you." His last phrase hangs there.

"I miss you, too," I say, but I get a horrible, sick feeling in my stomach. Why didn't I say it back?

"I love you, too!" I say, trying again, but he's already hung up.

As I place the phone on the receiver I notice that the fighting couple is gone, and flies are buzzing around their tuna salad.

I pick my way back across the sand, the hot grains burning my feet, making me lift my feet high with each step. I maneuver over the sprawled, tanned limbs, careful not to stare at the occasional flash of pubic hair on the nude sunbathers. A pungent coconut aroma rises around me, reminding me of Florida vacations, notably my mother lubed up with Hawaiian Tropic.

Kat and Sin are sitting cross-legged on their towels, Kat pointing to a pair of shoes in her magazine, handing it to Sin.

They both look up with expectant faces when my body forms a shadow over them.

"How'd it go?" Sin asks, plopping the magazine on her lap.

"He knew something was off." I sink onto my towel. It's covered with sand now from people who've walked by, and the grit sticks to the back of my thighs. "He could tell."

"What did you say? You didn't tell him about Francesco, did you?" Kat says.

"No. Of course not." I roll onto one hip, trying to rub off the film of sand and sunscreen from my legs. "If it meant something, I'd tell him, but it doesn't."

I look up at Sin and Kat, both of them uncharacteristically quiet. "What?" I say. "It was just a fling. Not even a fling, really. It was a—what's the word? A mash, a make out, a roll around. It won't affect anything."

Neither of them speaks, and their silence says volumes. I growl and flop back on my towel, an arm over my head.

A few hours later, the Kennedy boys stop by our towels. Trent looks even more like Barbie's boyfriend with his perfectly tanned abs, blond hair and perfectly pressed blue trunks, which I'm sure he bought special for the trip.

"Want to go with us to Super Paradise Island?" David says, looking a little more relaxed in long surfer shorts.

"And what might that be?" asks Kat as she stands to face them, dusting sand off her arms, unperturbed by the fact that she's topless. I hastily tie my bikini top around my neck. I'd finally mustered the courage to sun my breasts, lying on my back in clear view of hundreds of strangers, but now, seeing these guys whom I've actually shaken hands with, I feel the need to scramble for cover.

"Super Paradise?" Sin says. "It sounds like a Japanese game show."

"It's just a little piece of rock about ten minutes away by boat. Everyone heads there for happy hour."

Sin looks at me. "What do you think?"

I'm not even sure what they're talking about—a little piece of rock?—and I'd been anticipating a shower and a nap, but what the hell. I nod.

We board a dilapidated fishing boat for a few hundred drachmas and jockey for position with the other passengers. Perspiring, sun-baked bodies shove forward, clambering for a seat or a spot along the edge. Now I know what it must be like to be an illegal alien from Cuba, attempting to smuggle into American waters on a tiny boat with too many other people. I lose Kat and Sin in the push, finally lodging between the side of the boat and a huge guy with a sweating bare chest. I angle myself around until I'm facing out toward the water.

Once the craft is packed to the point where we will surely sink, it starts with a long whine and putts slowly out of the bay, turning left. We stay near the rugged coastline, a move that I'm sure is designed to allow us to swim to safety if need be. A few white villas dot the rocky shore until eventually there's nothing, just an expanse of brown craggy land, a sight my father would call breathing room.

My dad drove me to high school for three years, until my

mother convinced him that I wouldn't be a flight risk with
my own car. Every morning, we'd pull out of our once-
trendy neighborhood just outside Chicago, where the paint
jobs were starting to show signs of flake, the paved driveways
cracking and turning gray. Neither my father nor I would
speak. I was an insufferable bitch in high school, and I re-
garded talking before nine in the morning on the same scale
as nuclear war. My dad had learned early that he couldn't
change this. He drank his coffee from a plastic mug with a
travel lid that reminded me of a baby's sippy cup, and he kept
quiet until we passed an empty field that had turned harvest-
gold in the autumn or a park with snow-capped trees in the
winter.

"Breathing room," he'd say when he saw the field or the
park, hitting the power controls so that, rain or shine, blizzard or tornado, the front windows would roll down, whipping my hair-spray coated bangs about my forehead.

"Take a deep breath, kid," he'd say, his voice hearty. "Get
some good clean air in those lungs."

My part of the ritual was not to fight him on this. He
wasn't making me talk, after all, so I could throw him a bone.
We'd both suck in great chestfuls of air and let it out slowly,
repeating the action a few times over. Then he'd close the
windows, and blissful silence would reign again.

Now as the boat lists around huge rocks rising out of the
sea, I grip the side wondering where my father is today.
Probably at the Condom or the office. I decide to call him
when we get back to town, assuming the boat is able to make
the reverse journey. I've put it off long enough.

The other call I need to make is to Gordon Baker Brickton, Jr., the new master of my universe. Gordy, as he's called
at the firm, is a well-known defense litigator specializing in
products liability. He's defended everything from faulty axles
that sent cars careening off the road to hazardous toys that
broke into small parts and were swallowed by children. Gordy

had approved my request for a month off after the bar exam, but he'd asked that I call one week before I came back.

The boat hits a wave and everyone grabs everyone else, trying to stay upright. I get a queasy, headachy feeling, but I don't think it's seasickness. It's the realization that my career as a lawyer will begin in a mere eight days. It seems inconceivable given the sea air whipping my hair, the greasy, half-naked bodies surrounding me, but it's true.

The boat rounds the coastline and immediately, the thump of bass mixed with human voices rises above the sputter of the boat's engine.

Trent hadn't been kidding when he called Super Paradise a piece of rock. It's literally that, maybe a half mile in diameter, and why someone has decided to build a bar on one side of it escapes me.

I see two thatched roofs housing the actual bar areas, about five hundred yards between them. Every inch is packed with the young and the restless—beautiful patrons clothed minimally in bathing suits, dancing their asses off under the blue sky. I wish I'd worn cuter shorts. I snatch my lipstick out of my bag and apply it, hoping to jazz up my appearance.

After climbing off the boat and onto a treacherous little dock, we hike up the rock path to the action.

"Unbelievable," Lindsey says, taking it all in.

The music is earsplitting, and people are dancing on every possible surface, including around the pool area, where they tumble in after losing their balance. I begin counting the potential liabilities for which this place could get sued—the people being allowed to dance on tables from which they will surely fall and break ankles, the slippery surface of the rock floor causing drunks to stumble, the throwing of revelers into the pool directly on top of others dancing in the water. If this place was located in the litigious confines of the United States it'd be out of business already.

"Hello, darlings!" It's Jenny, looking like a plump Daisy

Duke in a pink-and-white gingham bikini. "I'm on my way to get a pint, c'mon."

She links an arm through mine, pulling me toward one of the bars. After securing bottles of lukewarm beer, Jenny, doing some sort of backward samba, pulls me into the crowd. The rest of the group joins us, and we begin dancing in a big, awkward circle like people do at weddings, waiting for some idiot to jump in the middle and break into a flailing version of Ricky Martin.

Kat, as unselfconscious as ever, launches right into a sexy dance with a flirtatious swirl of her hips. Immediately, guys from every country, like representatives of the United Nations, join our circle, surrounding her. She playfully faces one and then another and another, but to my surprise, she doesn't select one as her partner and drag him off behind a bush. Instead, she jumps back into place in the circle, slows the shaking of her hips, and waits for someone else to take the spotlight for once. Sin catches my eye, and we both smile.

A few minutes later, Jenny jumps in front of me, sambaing forward now, making me move back as I dance with her. She puts one arm on my shoulder, continuing to guide me in a backward dance. I'm trying to match her shaking shoulders, swinging my butt around dangerously, when I feel the arm on my shoulder give a little push, and in a flash, I find myself stumbling into space. The cool wet of the swimming pool smacks my side, and I sink to the bottom.

"You!" I say, pointing to Jenny when I come up sputtering.

She laughs and mouths "Sorry," with a fake, sheepish grin.

The rest of the group is laughing. I try to act furious, but the water is blessedly cool, so I take my time getting out. I'm shaking myself dry like a dog, standing at the side of the pool, when I feel a dull poke in my back. Turning around, I see a man whose massive shoulders make his short body look more square than tall. Coarse brown hair covers his arms, his hands, creeping up his back to curl around his neck.

"Yes?" I tug my shirt away from my body so I don't look like I'm in a wet T-shirt contest.

He licks his lips and lets a lewd, moist grin take over his face, running a hand over his wiry, muddy-brown hair.

"You want my cucumber?" the man says in German-accented English.

"Excuse me?" I'm leaning in, thinking I misheard him, when I feel the dull poke again, this time against my hip.

I look down. The man's hand is holding something in his shorts. A cucumber, I realize. He has stuck a large green cucumber in the fly of his shorts, brandishing it like a huge erection. When I look up, he gives me a lascivious stare, expecting me, I realize, to yelp like a schoolgirl and run so he can chase me around with this vulgar vegetable. I swallow down a lump of disgust that rises in my throat, and push away the inclination to do the five-hundred-yard dash, as he thinks I will.

"Yes, I do want it," I say.

A flicker of doubt crosses his face. "You want my cucumber?" he repeats again, shaking the thing now, a scary grin taking form on his shiny, wet lips.

"Oh yeah, I really do."

Reaching down, I yank the slimy, spoiled piece of produce out of his shorts. I take a chomp out of the end that wasn't in his pants, and a salty, gagging taste fills my mouth. I spit it out then, and with a fierce swing of my arm, I throw the rest into the pool. The man's face crumples now that his toy is gone.

Behind me I hear clapping and cheering. I turn around to find Kat and Sin clutching themselves, shaking with laughter.

"Good job!" Sin yells, and in a way I feel more proud than I did when I graduated law school.

★ ★ ★

When we arrive back at the Carbonaki, I tell Kat and Sin I'll meet them in the room after I call my dad and my new boss.

It's ten o'clock in the morning Chicago time, which means that both Gordy and my father should be at work. Gordy's will be the easier call. I try him first.

His secretary, the bitter Mrs. Tolden, answers with a clipped, "Mr. Brickton's office."

According to office rumor, Mrs. Tolden's husband had stolen away in the middle of the night fifteen or so years ago. Apparently, she had not been a happy woman before he left, but she'd become even more miserable after that. Despite the fact that she has no social graces to speak of, she's worked with Gordy for almost twenty years because she's one of those exceptional legal secretaries who can essentially practice law. Rumor has it that Gordy will tell her to write a Motion for Summary Judgment or a trial brief on a given case, and Mrs. Tolden will do it and do it well.

"Hi, Mrs. Tolden!" I call into the phone. "This is Casey Evers."

"Casey," Mrs. Tolden says in a stern tone. "The connection is terrible. Please phone back."

"No, no, no!" I yell before she can hang up. "I'm calling from Greece, so the connection won't be good."

"Well, why didn't you say so? I assume you're having a nice time." Before I can respond, Mrs. Tolden adds, "And I assume you want to speak to Mr. Brickton." She promptly puts me on hold.

"Casey!" Gordy's voice booms into the phone. "How's my newest legal star?"

All of Gordy's previous associates had been elected to partner in record time due to Gordy's high ranking in the firm's executive committee. Therefore, it's assumed that I'll be next on that list. This should make the corporate climber in me happy, but instead it gives me a sinking feeling. It seems that once I start working for Gordy, my life will be mapped out for me. I'll work my ass off, giving up much of my life for seven to nine years, at which time, assuming I'm not a complete incompetent, I'll be elected to junior partner status. My hours will then be reduced somewhat, but each day will be the same. I'll talk to clients, take depositions and make occasional court appearances when I can't get an associate to do it for me. At the end of the day, I'll head home on the same train I always take to some cookie cutter suburb lined with strip malls.

I gulp, attempting to shake off the image. "I'm doing great, Gordy. I'm calling from Mykonos."

"Excellent, excellent. Are you stirring up some clients for our international department?"

"Actually, if we were plaintiff's attorneys, we could probably sue the pants off a bunch of people out here." I tell him about the potential personal injury cases I'd seen at Super Paradise Island.

"Don't even think about it," Gordy says with false fierceness. Some attorneys can switch back and forth, representing plaintiffs, then defendants, and back again without a thought, but Gordy isn't one of those types. He's a defense attorney to the core.

"How's everything going there?" I ask, not really giving a damn.

Gordy fills me in on some office gossip—two senior associates are leaving to start their own firm, one of the top female partners is pregnant, the corporate group just landed a big client, etc., etc.

"So," he says as he finishes his summation, "when will we have the pleasure of your presence?"

"September third, the day after Labor Day, just as we planned." It's only about a week away. A week until my life grinds to a halt and hangs on autopilot for the next forty years.

"We certainly have the work waiting for you," Gordy says, sounding exceptionally excited. "We just got in a whole slew of cases dealing with defective bike helmets."

"Really?" I ask, feigning interest.

"There'll be a lot for you to do. And guess what?" He sounds truly keyed up now. "I've volunteered you to help Karen on a trial that's coming up in a few months."

"Is that so?" I fall into a chair by the phone and hit the back of my head repeatedly against the wall. Karen Bemmers is Gordy's previous associate who'd just made partner this year. She bears a strong resemblance, both in personality and physical appearance, to Cruella DeVille. I am scared shitless of her. There's no denying her legal prowess, but there's also no way that working hand in hand with her will be a good time.

"It'll be a great learning experience," Gordy says. "Absolutely tops!"

"Now I have something to look forward to," I say, hoping to hide the snide tone. "I better be going, Gordy."

"Sure, sure! Just enjoy yourself, and we'll be ready and rarin' to go when you get back."

"I can't wait."

As I hang up the phone I try to console myself. *It won't be that bad. Sure, you'll work hard, but you'll be making money finally, and you'll probably end up enjoying it.*

It doesn't help. I can't shake the sense of impending doom.

To make matters worse, I have to call my father now. Dad is a vice president at Chicago One Bank. His private line rings and rings until a bored-sounding receptionist informs me that he must be out of the office. Do I want to leave a message on his voice mail?

"No," I say. "Please page him." Unlike my call to John, I

don't have a pat message that I'm prepared to deliver. I'm not quite sure what I want to say.

The receptionist exhales audibly, as if this is causing her extreme trauma. "Hold on," she says, placing me on hold for a good three minutes, which I figure will probably cost me about twenty bucks.

Finally she picks up again. "I *told* you he was out of the office. You want his voice mail or what?"

"Yes." *You little bitch.*

"Hi!" my dad's cheerful voice calls into the phone, making me homesick. "You've reached Richard Evers. I'm out of the office or on the other line, but I'll get back to you as soon as I can. If you need immediate assistance, please press zero and ask for my executive assistant, Ellen Hamlin."

"Uh...hi, Dad," I say, struggling to put my thoughts together in a recognizable form. "It's Casey. I'm calling you from Mykonos, Greece. I hope you can hear me all right. Um...everything's good here. Having a really good time, but I talked to Mom and she said things aren't so good with you two. I was calling to see what's going on and how you were doing. Dad, I..."

My eyes start to mist, and I miss him. I miss both my parents, and the concept of them together as a couple.

"I'm sorry...." I say, my voice somewhat muffled. "It's just that I don't understand. I'd really like to talk to you. But listen, don't worry about me. I'll try you back again. Hope you're all right. I love you." I hang up the phone.

As I trudge up the stairs, something nags at me about my dad's voice-mail message. Something about the end of the message. He'd said, "My executive assistant, Ellen Hamlin." For the last four years, my father had referred to his thirty-something secretary as Ms. Hamlin, never Ellen. And what was an executive assistant? As far as I knew, all Ellen did was sit at a desk outside his office, typing his mail. Had she received some kind of promotion? I recall my mother's comments over the last few years about how my dad, who'd always been a staunch nine-to-fiver, was sometimes working late. Now that I think about it, hadn't he mentioned "Ms. Hamlin" a number of times in the last year or so? "Ms. Hamlin and I have been working on a big trust account." "Ms. Hamlin just returned from San Francisco and really enjoyed it." I hadn't noticed at the time, but weren't all the references a little much?

I stop on the landing of the stairs. It's muggy and airless in this little corner, but I'm frozen by a particularly horrific thought. Could it be that my father—my nice, suburban, cotton-Dockers dad—is schtupping his secretary? Maybe it's part of a full-blown midlife crisis. Next he'll buy a red convertible, start dying his hair and trade in his blue pinstripes for Armani suits with art deco cuff links. He might even marry this woman, this Ellen Hamlin who is so young she could have been a few years ahead of me at school. I sink onto the nearest step, and I sit there until this thought and the lack of oxygen start to suffocate me.

22

That night, we're eating Greek salads and warm crusty bread at a café in one of the bigger hotels when our waiter brings over a bottle of champagne.

"Compliments of the table in the corner," he says, pointing over my head, dipping at the waist in a formal sort of a bow.

I swivel around and see a table of dark-haired, olive-skinned men sitting below a leafy tree that's so green they look like stage actors in front of a backdrop. They appear to be in their thirties, most of them wearing expensive-looking watches, flashing us their white teeth as they smile and raise their glasses to us in a toast.

Kat and Sin and I lift our wineglasses back at them while the waiter sets out flutes for the champagne.

"Do we need to go over there and thank them?" I say. "Is that the proper protocol or something?" I can't remember the last time I was sent a drink, and back then it was most likely a plastic cup of keg beer.

"Fuck protocol," Sin says in a funny little voice. "They just want to screw us, anyway." She lets out a peal of laughter and sloshes more merlot in our glasses while the waiter pours the champagne.

Lindsey, I realize, is decidedly tipsy. The merlot seems to have brought back her old bristling attitude toward men. The one that's more humorous, more guys-suck-but-I'm-sure-I'll-find-one-I-like-someday kind of attitude.

Kat isn't jumping out of her chair to rush toward the table, either. "Very nice of them," she says, sipping her bubbly, "but I don't think a personal appearance is required."

Lindsey grabs her wineglass in one hand, a champagne flute in the other, and raises them both above her head. "A toast!" she says.

Kat and I lift both our glasses, too, waiting for her to continue, but Sin just sits there, her glasses listing side to side above her sleek, dark hair. I'm sure she's about to douse herself any minute.

"Go, Sin. What are we toasting to?" I say.

"Didn't I tell you?" She smiles widely, as if she's got a secret. "I'm calling Pete when I get home." She puts the glasses back on the table, some of the wine splashing onto the tablecloth.

"You are?" Kat leans in and clinks Sin's glasses.

"Yes." She says the word with a punch, then repeats it. "Yes."

"Well, then I'm going to take a big-girl step, too," Kat says.

"Uh-oh," I say. "Do we want to hear this? Does it involve petroleum jelly?"

"No." She makes a tutting sound and smacks me on the arm. "It involves my mom." Her chin drops a little. "I'm going to tell her about the Hatter."

Sin and I pat her on the back, murmuring "Good for you" and "You're right to do this."

"I mean, she's got to know, doesn't she?" Kat says.

Sin and I nod.

"If he hit on me, he could be having an affair."

I nod again, seeing the perfect segue, and I spit it out. "I think my dad's having an affair."

"What?" Kat says. "No! He wouldn't!"

Both Kat and Sin are big fans of my father. Everyone is, really. He's one of those happy-go-lucky guys who will cut the neighbor's lawn just because he happens to have the mower out.

I fill them in on my mom's comments about his working late, about his message and Ms. Hamlin's apparent promotion.

"You're jumping to conclusions on the basis of a voice-mail greeting?" Sin says, rolling her eyes in an exaggerated fashion, losing her balance in the process and nearly falling out of the chair. I move her wine away from her.

"She's right. You've got to chill," Kat says.

"What else could it be?" I say. "They've been married for twenty-eight years. There has got to be more going on for them to just throw in the towel like that."

"You're going to kill yourself with all this speculation." Lindsey rips off a hunk of bread, waving at the waiter with it. "More wine?" she says.

Later, it's the Scandinavian Bar again with the Kennedy boys, Jenny and the English crew. It's a night that rushes in on itself, a blur of bar stools and beer bottles and too-loud music until it's three o'clock in the morning, when Sin, acting like the Pied Piper of Mykonos, leads the staggering group back to our hotel and down the narrow stone corridor. Once outside, she points to the pool, her head raised proudly, as if she'd dug and filled it herself. Nearly everyone piles into the water, some fully dressed, others, like Sin, in their underwear. I stand on the edge, laughing at Jenny's story about some guy who'd tried to pick her up that night by sending her a plate of gyros.

Sin and Kat climb out of the pool at one point, both of them dripping in bra and panties, and move forward in an exaggerated tiptoe, as if they're sneaking up on me.

"No," I say, holding out my hands, backing up. "Not again! I've been thrown in one pool already today."

"Oh yes!" says Sin.

They grab me, Kat's hand firm around my arm, her eyes crazy and laughing, Sin's tiny hands pushing me, her mouth opening in a triumphant scream. And as I lift my feet, letting them pull me toward the surreal blue of the pool, I remember what it's like to have best friends.

The next morning, when we make our way downstairs, Sin clutching her head as if she needs to hold it on her shoulders, we're chastised by Mr. and Mrs. Gianopolous, the hotel owners, for bringing guests home so late—not to mention into the pool.

"No more swim at night," Mrs. Gianopolous says, wringing her hands on the gray cotton skirt of her dress. "No more naked."

We smile and apologize, not wanting to get kicked out and have to wander the village again. When she walks back to the kitchen, Mr. Gianopolous, a man of about seventy with approximately six black hairs shooting out of the top of his head, gives us a mischievous smile.

"Naked okay," he says, raising a finger to his lips. "You be more quiet next time."

That day at the beach, we rent Jet Skis. Sin and I stick to the shoreline in case she has to throw up all the wine she drank last night, while Kat heads straight out to the open water to "catch some air." Afterward, we have lunch at one of the thatched-umbrella tables, then lounge on the beach for a few hours.

I borrow the British version of *Cosmo* from Jenny and get embarrassingly engrossed in an article entitled "Be Your Own

Private Dick: How To Tell if He's Straying." Unfortunately, the article only offers suggestions like studying tire marks and odometer readings to see if your man has gone geographically astray; nothing to tell me whether my dad is shacked up with the young Ms. Hamlin.

I close the magazine and turn over on my back, feeling a little less self-conscious than yesterday about the warmth of the sun on my headlight breasts, thinking that even if my father were having an affair, what would it mean? That he'd wanted something different in his life, something new? I get a spark of anger on my mother's behalf before it's replaced with a slow, creeping disgrace. Isn't that why I'd rolled around with Francesco in the Colosseum and smooched with Billy on the deck—because I'd wanted something new? That I could be so cavalier with John's devotion scares me. What if I'm a serial cheater? I try to make myself regret Francesco and Billy. *Shame,* I think to myself. *Shame on you!* But I can't muster up the requisite remorse. Being the object of lust and affection had given my limping ego a sorely needed kick in the ass, one I wasn't getting from John, one I should have been able to give myself.

At five o'clock, everyone peels themselves off their towels and shakes away the sand that's collected on everything, getting ready to board the fishing boat from hell to Super Paradise again, but I take a pass. I want to walk around the village and buy presents for my family. Unlike the time in Ios when I tried to separate myself from the group by going to town, I don't feel alienated and sullen now. Rather, the feeling is wonderfully close to the way it used to be with Kat and Sin when we didn't have to be joined at the hip, wearing the same clothes or sporting the same haircut in order to be good friends. We could do our own thing, at our own pace, and still not lose that feeling that we'd talked only seconds ago.

We decide to meet back at the hotel in a few hours. Ten minutes later, I catch a bus to the village. I wander the stone streets, peering in jewelry cases lined with green velvet and making small talk—very small, given the language barrier—with store owners. At one shop, I purchase a rust-and-black-patterned cloth to wear as a sarong over my bathing suit, the way I've seen the supermodels do. But when I try it on by winding it around my waist and over my shorts, it looks more like a diaper than sleek European beachwear.

Seeing my confusion, the young woman manning the store rushes over. "No, no!" she says, shaking her head, smiling a bemused smile. She commands me to take off the shorts, then instructs me slowly, as one would a child, on three different ways to tie the sarong, her brown arms wrapping around me, swaddling me with the sarong in a way that's foreign yet soothing.

"Efcharisto," I say, thanking her, modeling the version I like best in the mirror. The sarong hangs to my ankles and is tied low on one hip. I feel very chic as I study it from various angles.

"Here, here!" the woman says, holding a rough straw bag to my side. It's entirely too much money for me to drop on a beach bag—nearly forty dollars—but the rust color matches my sarong perfectly. I can't resist.

I leave the store wearing my sarong, the rest of my junk shoved into my new bag, feeling like I belong on this island. I stroll the streets for what must be an hour, although I've lost track of time. I buy brightly painted wooden mugs for my father and a chunky silver necklace for my mom.

I stop and sit at a wooden table in front of an aqua-painted taverna and order a glass of white wine. After it arrives, I watch the crowd whiz by—gay men in short shorts laughing and shoving each other playfully; miniskirted women with Chanel handbags slinking by in gargantuan sunglasses; even a few backpackers stumbling around, apparently looking for a hostel. Normally, I'd be embarrassed to sit at a restaurant alone, making sure to have a book or a magazine close by, a pseudo friend. Today, though, I'm comfortable by myself, more comfortable than I've been in a long, long time. I've come out of my shell over the last few weeks, and I'm determined to burn the map that shows me how to get back.

I treat myself to one more glass of the tart wine and buy a bottle to bring back to Lindsey and Kat. The sun begins to set as I head toward the hotel, giving the village a pink-or-ange glow. The tiny Mykonos streets are mazelike, twisting and turning, leading past whitewashed houses and jewelry stores that all look the same after a while. I let myself mean-der, enjoying the cooler night air that's starting to wind through town.

Finally I locate the street I need, and I'm reaching into my new bag for the key to our room when I hear, "Casey!" The voice sounds strangely familiar. I glance up to see where it came from.

The bottle of wine slips from my hand, shattering on the cobblestones, soaking the hem of my sarong, yet I stand frozen.

At last I find my voice. "John?"

23

I remember vividly the night that John first told me he loved me. It came at a time when I never expected it. We'd been out to dinner, a long dinner like we used to have. We split a bottle of champagne and lingered over glasses of dessert wine and a plate of flourless chocolate cake. Four months had gone by since we started dating, and everything had a shiny, rosy tinge to it. I could just think of John and get a rush of happiness. We decided to walk home, hoping to shed some of the thousands of calories we'd ingested, and we walked along Clark Street, swinging our hands, feeling warm despite the bitter cold.

We saw him at the same time, a man stumbling toward us, mumbling under his breath. He wore layers and layers of clothes, as if he was ready to be outside all night. Both John and I got quiet as the man moved closer. John gripped my hand tight. The man passed by us without incident, though, and John loosened his grip. I was about to say something, something about dinner or the cake or something inane, when I felt a great shove against my back.

"What?" I yelled, starting to turn around, and then I felt a pull on the purse strap I held in my other hand. It took me a moment to realize that the man had come back. He and I yanked at opposite ends of my purse like two kids in a tug-of-war, me screaming obscenities. John just stood there for a second, as if his body hadn't caught up to what his mind was seeing, but then he charged. I mean literally *charged* into the guy like a bull, his head down, his arms back, and the man flew away from me, landing on the pavement with a thud.

"Oh my God," I said. "We have to get the police."

Police was apparently the magic word, because the man scrambled to his feet and took off in a sprint.

John grabbed me, hugging me so tight to his chest that I couldn't get any air in my lungs.

"I love you," he said, each word a definitive statement. "I love you so much."

"Me, too," I said, although my words were garbled by his coat.

That was the first time I realized that John didn't wait for the typical moment to say something profound or make a meaningful gesture. For all the strictness and daily consistency he applied to his life, he had a way of surprising me. It was something I liked about him, something that I'd missed lately. But he'd gotten me again this time.

John struggles to stand from his seat on his tan leather suitcase. It was one of the first things that impressed me about him—he had a full set of matching leather luggage, something I found incredibly adult, and therefore alluring, since I had been chasing adulthood down a long, endless street. He looks completely out of place now in this laid-back Grecian village full of sun. He's pasty-white in his navy-blue pants—the good ones he saves for casual Fridays when he's going out after work—and his white, button-down shirt. Little spots of red dot his cheeks, which I know from experience could either mean that he's very worked up about something or just very hot.

"Hi, babe," John says, his voice full of an uncertainty that I'm not used to. I realize that the spots might mean a third thing—that he's nervous. "Surprised?"

"Yes! My God." I rush toward him, then stop a few feet away, unable to find any other words, unclear what my body is supposed to do now.

He looks me up and down. "Wow...you look different...beautiful."

I ignore the backhanded compliment, unable to get past the shock of seeing him in the midst of this cozy vacation existence I'd created for myself, one that doesn't include him. He represents reality, the outside world, and the sight of him splinters my carefully crafted enclave. I struggle to rearrange the pieces, even as I take a step back and collect the shards of glass from the wine bottle. But it doesn't work.

"What are you doing here?" I ask, dumping the glass in a nearby trash can.

As John leans over to help me with the last few pieces of glass, I see him flinch at my question, his expression pained. "You sounded strange on the phone. I thought something might be wrong, and you're always telling me I'm not spontaneous anymore." He stands and brushes off his hands. "I bought a ticket for three thousand dollars and got on the next plane, and here I am." He shrugs, his face full of hope that I'll be happy to see him.

I know how hard it is for John to do something so expensive. While he was growing up, the Tanner family never had money for the crazy or the unnecessary, and despite his current six-figure salary, John has never lost that spendthrift outlook, subscribing to a rainy-day theory of finance. To my mind it's much more likely that you'll get hit by a bus before ever reaching that stormy afternoon when you decide to pull your money out of the bank, but that's me. And maybe that's John now, too. Maybe people can change.

"I'm sorry," I say, taking a few steps forward, crossing to him. I put my lips to his, but it feels foreign, unlike the kisses I shared with Francesco and Billy. He envelops me in a hug, which I return tentatively at first, then fiercely. I do think the world of John. I *love* him. How could I have betrayed him so casually? I squeeze him harder, pushing my face into the cotton of his shirt. He smells of aftershave, something he normally doesn't wear. Another change? I wonder. Or something he splashed on to cover the airplane smell?

John pulls back finally, gazing at me, his expression filled with relief. "I've missed you, babe," he says.

I nod and hug him again.

"Holy shit," I hear, and John releases me.

Kat and Sin are back from the beach, looking sun-kissed and as shocked to see John as I am.

"Hey, guys," John says, nodding casually in their direction, as if we were back in Chicago, standing at a local pub.

"He came to surprise me," I explain, trying not to notice their looks that say *Are you fucking kidding me?*

"Well," Kat says, shifting her see-through beach bag that's chock-full of crap to the other shoulder. "Welcome to Greece." Her tone isn't exactly open arms, and she seems to realize this. "When did you get here?" she adds.

"I got to Athens early this morning, and then I caught another flight here a couple of hours ago." Light banter, easy words, as if he didn't just surprise attack me on my vacation. My mood swings to and fro between surprise and irritation and flattery and hope.

"How did you find the hotel?" Lindsey asks cooly, as if trying to decide how to handle John's arrival.

John has never said anything bad about Sin, or about any of my friends or family for that matter, but I've always gotten the feeling that he isn't that thrilled with her. It's the way he clams up when she's around, his eyes watching her, studying her as if trying to make some sense of her often harsh words, her inability to stand around and make bullshit chatter.

But now he says in a pleasant voice, "Casey told me the name of the hotel when she called, so when I got off the plane, I went from one taxi to another until I found a driver who could understand me." He smiles and throws his arms up, and I can't help but smile with him. Good old boring John doesn't seem quite so boring anymore.

"Hmm," Sin says, like, *Isn't that interesting.* Then she turns to me. "We're meeting the group for dinner in an hour. You are going." It's more of a directive than a question.

"Of course," I say, because I'm not willing to give up my vacation the way I planned it. More importantly, the thought of being alone with John suddenly terrifies me. Would he see that I'd been unfaithful? If not, would I—should I—tell him?

I turn to John. "We've been running around with these people here. You'll like them."

"Okay," he says, running his hand through his fine brown hair. He'd probably envisioned dinner with just the two of us, because he'd just flown thousands of miles to see me. I can't blame him, but I can't change our plans, either. A dinner alone could lead to time alone in the room, which could lead to sex. On one hand, the possibility excites me. I've been feeling so saucy since my Francesco encounter, but if I fooled around with John because another man had made me horny, wouldn't I be cheating all over again? This sexual riddle only adds more confusion to the churning emotions in my head.

"Do you need help carrying your stuff to the room?" I ask John, wanting something to say. It'll be a cozy fit with the four of us in one room, John and I sharing a twin bed, but the island is full.

"No," John says, "but…" He pauses for a second. "I thought we could get our own room."

"We're going up," Sin says, probably sensing an issue.

"Right," Kat says. "We'll see you soon...or later...or whatever." John's arrival seems to have left everyone a little stunned.

I nod at them.

"Our own room, huh?" I say to John.

"Yeah." He sidles toward me, his hands on my hips, pulling me to him. He leans down and nibbles my neck. "We're a little overdue, don't you think?"

"Um-hmm," I say, in a noncommittal tone. It's been a while since he's been so hot and bothered for me. I wonder if it's because I've lost weight, or maybe it's the absence-makes-the-heart-grow-fonder theory. Still, I don't think I'm ready, for some reason. If we have sex, I might lose myself in it the way I used to, and then I might wake up in the same place I was before this trip, in the same emotional rut. I don't want to lose myself anymore. I want to be here for every minute, and yet I don't know if I can make love to John like that. It's been so long.

I'm about to explain the overcrowding on the island, when I remember that yesterday I'd heard Mr. Gianopolous turn down some backpackers, telling them he was full.

"Sure," I say to John, secure in the knowledge that Hotel Carbonaki is booked. "Let's go ask for a room."

We knock on the door that leads from the lobby into the Gianopolous's accommodations.

"Mr. Gianopolous," I say, when he comes to the door, wearing a tank top, wiping his mouth with a red cloth. "This is my boyfriend." I almost stall on "boyfriend." It seems awkward. "He just came from Chicago." He and John shake hands. "You wouldn't happen to have any rooms to let, would you?"

"Oh yes!" says the old man, clearly pleased to be helpful. "One lady just leave. Room 9."

He steps into the lobby, and reaching behind the desk, he hands us the key.

"Great," I say, trying to infuse my voice with something resembling enthusiasm. "Perfect."

24

"What is he doing here?" Lindsey says after I drop John in the new room and go to retrieve some clothes. Kat is in the shower.

"I don't know." I gather my makeup, scooping up a black cotton dress to throw on.

"You're moving into his room?" Her voice is incredulous. She sinks onto the bed, her face flashing with anger before it skids into disappointment. Her shoulders slump, and she shakes her head. Somehow this resignation I see in her is worse than the bitchy attitude she wore like a hood earlier in the trip.

I stop searching for my other black sandal and face her. "I don't know what's going on right now, so please, please, please cut me some slack. I have to stay with him, Sin. He's my boyfriend." There, I've said it again, and it feels a little more natural. "He just dropped a couple thousand dollars and flew to Greece to see me. I didn't tell him to come, but he's here."

Lindsey sighs. "I'm sorry, but this is supposed to be a girls vacation, after all."

"I know that. It's not exactly what we planned."

"Not exactly."

I shoot her a look, and she has the decency to appear sheepish.

"Sorry," she says.

I return to my search for the missing sandal, peering under the beds and Kat's pile of clothes. "I just can't believe he did this. It's so unlike him."

"Why did he say he came?" Kat asks, exiting the bathroom, naked and looking for a towel.

I find my tan sandals under a beach towel, but not the missing black one. "He said I sounded different on the phone. He wanted to make sure I was okay."

"Ooh, he sensed something," Kat says, toweling her hair.

"Ah!" I find my sandal wedged between a bed and the wall, but then Kat's words sink in. "What did you say?"

"Nothing," Sin says, giving Kat an exasperated stare.

"Well, he did, didn't he?" Kat says. "He knew something was wrong. He might have a feeling that you've been with someone else."

"Kat!" Sin tosses a pillow at her.

"Oh God, I hope not," I say. "I don't know if I can have that talk with him right now." Now I'm pissed off that John is here. This is *my* vacation, my escape.

"Don't focus on that now," Sin says. "It may not come up, or you may want to tell him, or something different might happen altogether. But I have to ask you—is he with us for the rest of the trip? Will he go to Athens with us?"

"I have no idea."

"Well—"

I cut Sin off. "Look, I need you guys to give me some time to sort this out."

"There's less than a week left," Sin points out. "Only a few days, really. How much time do you need?"

"I can't say. I just have to see what happens, what his plans are. Can you guys be patient with me?" I stand in the doorway with my makeup bag, sandals and clothes gathered in my arms.

"Sure," says Kat.

Sin waits a second before she finally nods.

"How's everything at home?" I ask John as we get ready for dinner. I take the towel off my head and as I do, my arm hits his shoulder. "Sorry," I mumble.

We used to be able to maneuver around each other effortlessly in the bathroom. I'd lean into the mirror, applying my mascara, while he brushed his teeth behind me. He'd shave while I sat on the toilet, rubbing lotion into my legs. But now we seem to have lost our rhythm, our sense of direction. We keep banging into each other, and each time I'm startled all over again to see him here.

"Work is crazy as usual," John says as he shaves his jaw, leaving a strip of skin in the white cream. "No one could believe I was going to Greece."

"I bet. I can hardly believe it myself."

God, why did he have to choose *now* to be spontaneous and crazy? I would have been ready to go home and face him at the end of this week, to try and improve things significantly between us, but here? I can't wrap my head around the fact that he's suddenly in Mykonos, in the middle of my girls trip.

John finishes shaving and turns away from the mirror to face me. "Do we have time for a little R and R?" He flicks the towel away from his waist. His nakedness embarrasses me somehow, and I nearly jump away in surprise.

"Oh! No. I mean, we've got to meet Kat and Sin downstairs in a few minutes."

He growls and pats me on the rear. "Then distract me. Tell me more about what you've done so far." He picks through his bag and extracts a tightly rolled pair of boxer briefs.

"Geez, there's been so much." I launch into a generic list of all the sights we'd seen in Rome.

"Have you met many people?" His question alarms me. It's unlike him to be interested in the small details. Is he searching for information? Has he discerned my infidelity, like Kat said?

"Well, let's see." I turn on the hair dryer so I have to shout above it. "There's Trent and David and Jenny." Conveniently, I skip over the description of any *acquaintances* made in Rome or Ios. I yell above the dryer's buzz, going on and on about the people we've encountered here in Mykonos. When I'm done, I dash into the room and pull my black dress over my head, stepping into my sandals as if I'm in a race, when what I want to do is close off John's people-you've-met line of questioning.

"Ready?" I ask, grabbing my purse and opening the door.

He nods, but I'm not so sure I am.

Dinner is a study in contrasts. The Kennedy boys, as well as Jenny and her friends, are friendly, rambunctious. They have the wait staff eating out of the palms of their hands and the manager buying ouzo shots for the table within the first hour. John, meanwhile, sits stiffly at my side, looking distinctly uncomfortable with all the boozing and yelling.

"Are you all right?" I whisper to him.

"Culture shock," he says. "Or something like that. I've spent too much time in the office lately, I guess."

But I know what's really going on. Every once in a while, when John gets in a social situation where he senses he's being judged or scrutinized, he gets flustered, the Iowa boy in him deciding he's not good enough, doesn't know enough.

Normally at these times, I'll talk a lot to cover up for his sudden lack of conversational skills. The first time my parents met him we were at an exclusive restaurant in the Loop.

In the bathroom, my mother said to me, "He's not a mute is he, honey?" When I said no, of course not, she replied, "So why not let him talk?"

I'd tried, but at such times, the gaps of silence screamed at me. I couldn't help but feel sorry for him, this high-powered lawyer, all tongue-tied and shy.

Yet now I see that my aiding John that way doesn't help either of us, just as his brief assurances that I'll be fine as a lawyer, without discussing the issue, doesn't help me. So I refuse my inclination to engage in mini conversations with him that would exclude the others, and I refuse to answer for him as I so often had. And there he sits, seeming more and more miserable by the minute.

"How long are you going to be here, John?" Jenny asks, refusing to give up.

"Not sure," he says with a bland smile, before he returns his gaze to the stuffed grape leaves he's rotating in a clockwise fashion around his plate.

Jenny plows on. "How do you like Mykonos so far?"

"Great. Really great." His eyes shift back to the stray piece of meat he's trying to return to the constellation on his plate.

Sin catches my eye and cocks her head in John's direction, mouthing, "Nice manners." She's right, but I still want to cuff her in his defense.

John and I are sitting at the end of the table, and I keep noticing a canvas that hangs on the wall above his head. It's a large oil painting of a man and a woman sitting in two chairs by the sea. The man has his arm around the woman's back, a cigarette in the hand that dangles from her chair. Smoke pours out of the man's mouth as he leans toward the woman, forming a screen between them. I keep staring at it, my eyes lifting past the white collar of John's shirt, past his concerned green eyes and thinning hair, until he becomes irritated.

"What are you looking at?" he says, twisting his neck around in a quick awkward movement.

"It's that painting...." I say, letting my words fall away. I can't stop staring at it.

"What about it?"

"Nothing," I say, making myself lower my eyes, forcing myself to focus on his mouth, which has kissed me a million times. What I don't say is that the painting strikes me as a metaphor of sorts, representing two people with something vague and intangible between them—two people like us.

When the manager returns to the table an hour later with another round of ouzo and the bill, John tugs my sleeve.

"Can we get out of here?" he whispers.

Kat hears him and raises an eyebrow at me.

I feel like barking, "No! This is my vacation. We're doing it my way," but I hold my tongue and take a deep breath, thinking that John has made an effort—a gargantuan, if misguided, one—by hauling himself all the way across the Atlantic to find me. I need to make an effort here, too.

I nod at him, and he throws a pile of drachmas on the table that would easily cover the entire check as well as the tab of the table next to us. I retrieve a few of the drachmas. "We'll see you guys later," I say. "Where will you be?"

"Scandinavian Bar as usual," Jenny says cheerfully.

"Will we *really* see you?" Lindsey asks, pushing her full ouzo glass away.

"Yes." I look at her as if to say *please.* I flash a fake smile at the rest of the crew.

"Where do you want to go?" I ask John as we leave the restaurant, turning a corner onto one of Mykonos's many snaking streets. I look around, trying to figure out if we're heading toward the docks or the heart of the village.

"Let's go someplace where we can talk."

That stops me dead. I've been craving those words for the

last six months. Lately, I'd have given *anything*—my apartment, my beat-up Mercury Tracer, my favorite Michigan sweatshirt—if he'd told me he wanted to talk. Instead, I was forever chasing him to give me anything resembling a conversation, while he just wanted to get back to the files he'd brought home, back to work. And he wants to talk now, in Greece. Murphy's Law.

"You want to talk?" I try to sound nonchalant. "Uh...about what?"

"Us. You and me." His words are confident and definitive now.

"You and me," I repeat stupidly, trying to give my brain some time to catch up with my mouth. I wish I could postpone this conversation until I could sort through the slush of feelings in my head. I nod for a second or two and finally look up to meet John's eyes. He flashes me his crooked smile, the one I can't resist.

"Let's go down to the dock," I say.

25

Once we're at the port, I spot an open table at an outdoor restaurant, but John wants to sit on one of the piers, a deserted strip of wood away from the action, and this makes me even more nervous.

We walk to the very end and take a seat, hanging our legs over the edge. A few bobbing fishing boats surround us, as does the quiet. Back home, our periods of silence had the ability to be comfortable if I wasn't pouting about them, yet now it feels lonely. I miss him, or rather I miss the time when we were carefree and easy. Maybe we could save what we had, though. He came all this way to see me, and now he wants to talk. As scary as it is, this has to signal something, some desire or ability to change.

"So..." I say, breaking the quiet when I can't take it anymore. "What exactly did you want to talk about?"

John looks down and plays with his watch, a gold Maurice Lacroix tank watch that I'd spent way too much money on last Christmas. When he finally looks up at me, I notice an uncharacteristic longing in his eyes. Not a sexual hunger like I saw in the hotel room, but a passionate, love-filled longing. I have the sense that this is one of those expressions that I've cherished whenever it's come my way, but now I feel removed.

"I don't want to lose you," he blurts out.

With that comment, all the things that I love about him come rushing back—his lopsided smile, the methodical way he reads the Sunday paper, the way he kisses me on the forehead before he leaves for work.

"Why would you say that?" I ask, my voice soft.

He keeps tugging at the band of his watch. "You've changed. Something's different. I can tell."

"What do you mean?"

He pauses for a long time. "You weren't the same all summer. You seemed far away and depressed. It made me sad." He shifts his eyes to me as he says this.

I'm shocked that he'd noticed. Not wanting to break the flow of his words, I only nod encouragement and wait.

"I wanted to help you, but I thought it was just the bar exam," he continues. "I thought you had to ride it out. I was being tough on you because I thought you needed to be tough with yourself."

Behind us there's a crash of breaking glasses from one of the restaurants. We both turn our heads toward the noise, seeing a waiter bending down to retrieve the remnants. When I turn back, I realize John is looking at me already, waiting for me to say something.

I wonder, briefly, if this is the time to tell him everything I've been thinking, everything that's happened, but I can't bring myself to admit my guilt. "It's true," I say finally. "I haven't been truly happy for a while. It had a lot to do with the bar exam, with my family, and you weren't helping much, but I'm better now. A lot better. I feel great, actually." It dawns on me that I do feel worlds different from the person who left Chicago a few weeks ago, and John, who's arguably the most important person in my life, had nothing to do with it. Nothing at all.

"I can tell you're not as down—" John searches my face with his eyes "—but you're still different, and I have a bad feeling about it. I mean, I'm glad you're happy, but..." He trails off, shaking his head.

We sit in silence again. I look down at my sandal-clad feet swinging back and forth above the dark, softly lapping water. My head is a jumble. I feel elated by John's attempt at our relationship, panicked that he somehow knows about Francesco or Billy, and fearful that he will push me to a big decision about our relationship. The thought of ending things with John has flickered in and out of my head during this vacation, but I really can't picture my life without him. Despite his flaws, I do love him. How could that part of my world be excised?

"I'm not kidding, Case." John grabs my hands and turns to face me. "I don't want to lose you. I love you."

"I love you, too," I say, meaning it.

John hugs me to him so tight it's almost painful. "I love you. I love you," he repeats in my ear over and over, enunciating each of his words, the same way he did that night in Chicago, that first time.

Tears spring to my eyes, and I clutch him in return.

"Let's go back to the room." John pulls away and looks at me. He seems relieved to see my tears, as if they're a watershed, an indication of the tide turning.

I'm about to agree when I remember my promise to meet Lindsey and Kat at the Scandinavian Bar.

"I can't," I say. "I told those guys we'd meet them."

"Tomorrow night." John kisses my eyelids, the tiny birthmark on my cheekbone that no one else ever notices. "Let's be alone tonight."

"I can't. I have to meet them."

"Casey." He sits back from me. "We haven't seen each other in three weeks."

"I realize that, but we weren't supposed to see each other for *another* week. I'm not going to blow off my friends for a guy. I've done that enough already."

It's out of my mouth before I can rein it in. I'm referring to Francesco, of course, and to Billy somewhat. I freeze and look straight ahead, hoping desperately John hasn't picked up on it. When I finally steal a glance at him, he's nodding as if he understands, probably recalling my grumblings this summer about how I didn't see my friends enough.

"All right," he says at last. "Let's go."

He puts on a cheery face, which, albeit fake, means he's trying with all his might to make things right with us. And it breaks my goddamn heart.

Our conversation by the dock has had a definite impact on John's mood. Maybe he feels like he got something off his chest or maybe it's his talk about losing me. Whatever the reason, he shakes off the withdrawn-Iowa-farm-boy temperament. The minute we reach the Scandinavian Bar, he buys a round of drinks for the crew. Then, after kissing me on the cheek and saying, "Go talk to your friends," he strikes up a conversation with Jenny. Unbelievable. I haven't seen such an effort in months. He keeps stealing side glances at me, as if to make sure I'm taking note of his initiative. I nod and smile, unable to decide what to make of it. It's so odd to see him in this setting, which I'd grown accustomed to without him.

"How's it going?" Kat asks when she makes her way back from the bathroom, looking stunning as usual. At least ten pairs of hungry male eyes had followed her walk across the room, and yet she seems oblivious. The diamond earrings, I notice, are nowhere in sight. In fact, they haven't made an appearance since we left Ios.

"It's all right, I guess." I can't stop watching John. "It's just a bit overwhelming. He charges over here, he's all sullen at dinner, then he tells me he doesn't want to lose me, that he loves me, and now..." I gesture across the room, where he's talking enthusiastically to Jenny.

"Wow," Kat says, her eyebrow raising.

"Yeah, wow."

"You made it," Lindsey says, coming up to us, a big grin stretching across her diminutive face. She touches me on the hand, and I can tell she's making an effort to be patient as I asked her to.

"I told you I would be here," I say.

"Yes, you did." She hands me her glass, and I take a sip of her water. "So what's the scoop?" she says.

I fill her and Kat in on John's declarations of love by the water. "I don't know what to think, you guys. I wondered over these last few weeks whether our relationship had run its course, but now this. I really think he's giving it his all—he flew here, he's really trying to talk to me like we used to." I can't seem to stop shrugging.

"It's like he sensed it," Kat says again.

This time I don't protest. We all nod in silence.

"But does it really change everything?" Lindsey asks. "He flies here and he tells you he loves you, but does that do it? Does that solve your problems?"

"No," I answer after a moment, "but it helps. I do love him, and if he keeps up this kind of effort, maybe it could all turn around. Maybe it could feel like we did when we first started, and I wouldn't lose myself again."

"Maybe..." Lindsey says.

A bit later, John kisses me on the forehead before he heads into the bar to buy another round of beers. Jenny walks over to me.

"Nice chap," she says in her lilting British accent. "How

long have you been together?" She's wearing a yellow miniskirt and a white shirt that shows off her freckles.

"Almost two years."

"I take it you didn't know he was going to show up?"

"No. It was a shock, to say the least."

"But a good one, eh?" Jenny asks, cocking her head to one side.

"It's good and bad, I think. This is supposed to be just a friends' vacation, so he's intruding on that, but it was a sweet gesture. It means a lot to me."

"So is he 'the one' then?"

I shrug for the thirty-fifth time that evening. "I don't know...maybe."

"Maybe?" Jenny says. "What do you mean, *maybe?*"

I laugh at her tone. "Well, I can't say right now. I love the guy, but we've had our problems."

"Listen," Jenny says, taking an authoritative pose, one finger pointed at me. "If he's the one—the man for you—you'd know. No ifs, ands or buts."

"I disagree. I don't believe in that lightning-bolt, love-at-first-sight thing."

Jenny looks at me with sincere eyes. "I'm not talking about love at first sight. I'm just telling you that you'll know in your gut and in your heart when it's right."

I gulp and pull at the sleeve of my dress, distinctly uneasy with this conversation, but unable to tear myself away or change the subject. "I think it's more of a leap of faith," I say. "If you love someone and you get along all right, you just have to decide if you're going to go for it or not."

Jenny shakes her head as I speak. "I know what I'm talking about," she says. "I've been there."

"Been where?" I laugh, trying to lighten the discussion, uncomfortable that it's clouding the already muddy waters of my thoughts about John.

She pauses and then says, "I've been married." A shadow

crosses her eyes, and she looks down at her drink. I think it's the first time that I've seen Jenny in a mood that's anything less than ebullient.

"You're married?" I ask, surprised.

"Not anymore. He died."

"Oh my God." I put a hand to my mouth. I can't even bring myself to imagine John's death. It sends a rush of terror through me. The poor girl. "When? What happened to him?"

Jenny stares vacantly at her drink as if remembering. She takes a deep breath. "It doesn't matter. What I'm telling you is that when I was with him, I knew without a doubt that he was the one I wanted to be with forever."

"But how can you know for sure?" I say, hoping she can give me some kind of authoritative, unmistakable sign.

"You just know. Absolutely. When you look at him, you know this is it."

"Maybe not everyone gets that." It would be just my luck to be the small percent of the planet's population that has to take a running leap of faith rather than get the calm, gut-based assurance Jenny is talking about.

"Perhaps," she says, taking a sip of her drink, but she doesn't sound like she believes it.

Possibly it's her English accent, for I tend to think everyone with such an accent is smarter than I, but Jenny's words about knowing ring true to me.

Just then, John is at my side. I look at him with a feeble smile, and all I know for sure is that I'm more confused than ever.

By one in the morning, John's eyes are drooping from traveling. Since I'm used to late nights by now, I'm nowhere near ready to leave, and even more importantly, I'm anxious about going back to the room. The thought of fooling around with him still seems alien. My Princess Denial mode kicks in again, making me want to push away the situation a little longer, yet I don't feel I can send him off on his own after he's just arrived. Surely he'll be too tired to want any action.

I'm dead wrong.

The minute we arrive at the room, John's eyes snap open again.

"God," he says, running his hands up and down my sides. "You feel so good."

He kisses me passionately, and I respond at first out of sheer habit more than anything else. I notice, like I'm observing it all from above, how odd his tongue feels, as if he were the stranger, rather than Francesco or Billy, whose mouths had fit on mine with precision. When he begins to walk me backward toward the bed, his hands caressing my breasts, I stiffen inadvertently.

"What's wrong?" he says, pulling back, his eyes full of worry.

"Nothing. It just seems too fast."

"Too fast? We haven't slept together in weeks." Irritation creeps into his voice, and I can't blame him.

"I know. That's what I mean. It's just been such a long time...." I trail off, realizing how lame my excuse is. It's not even an excuse, really. "And you need your sleep," I add.

"I need *you*," he says with conviction.

I give him a weak smile. I can't fight the feeling that if I have sex with John, I'll misplace the self-contentedness I've recently found and I'll slip back to my old ways. I consider going through the motions and fantasizing about Francesco, but that would be cheating on John more than I already have.

"In the morning." I take a step back and my legs bang into the wood frame of the bed. "Ouch," I say, bending down to rub the spot. "It will be better when we both get some sleep."

"How will it be better?" His eyes flash with anger. "What's with you?"

"Nothing. I'm exhausted, and I'm still surprised you're

here. Just give me a little time, all right?" I move away from him, unable to look at his face for fear he'll read my mind and understand my reluctance. Neither of us says anything for a while. A heavy silence hangs in the air as I walk into the bathroom and begin to wash my face.

After a minute, John comes up behind me in the mirror, putting his hands lightly on my hips. I meet his gaze in the glass, and I'm struck by the disparity I see there. My too-blond hair, bleached by the sun, and the golden tan of my face seem a sharp contrast to the pale of John's skin, the washed-out green of his eyes. We don't look like a couple, I think. We don't look anything like two people who've spent two years together.

"Are we okay?" he asks quietly.

Tell him, I think. *Tell him. Get it off your chest.* Jenny's words ring in my head. *"You just know."* But I don't know anything, and besides, I don't have to decide right now. This is no place to tell him I've betrayed him, no place to have a discussion about our future. We have years to make these decisions if we want.

"Casey," John says, his eyes pleading with me.

"Yeah. We're okay."

His eyes are still concerned, but he gives a grudging nod.

A few minutes later, when I'm curled in the crook of his arm, I'm amazed to find how safe he makes me feel. The soft, familiar skin of his chest, his just-scrubbed-clean scent—it's like a haven. I banish the questions about him, about us, to some far corner of my brain, and I will myself to sleep.

26

In the morning, John sleeps soundly, not surprising after an international flight. I try to move as little as possible, though, and practically hold my breath. I'm still not ready to have sex with him. At about 10:30, Kat pounds on the door. I know it's her because I hear the clatter of junk spilling on the tile floor and her voice whispering an obscenity.

When I open the door, she's stooping down, collecting sunscreen and sunglasses and ponytail holders. She has on low-slung shorts, a minuscule aqua bikini top and a towel over one shoulder.

"We gotta get Johnny some sun," she says, standing and shoving a magazine in her bag.

I smile at her, appreciating the attempt to include John.

I've escaped the sex issue again, and within thirty minutes, the four of us are on the packed bus heading to Paradise Beach.

John gazes out the window as the bus twists through the narrow, dusty streets, passing locals leading donkeys or zipping around dangerously on scooters.

"This is great," he says, turning on the ripped leather seat to look at me.

"Isn't it?" I nod, pleased that he's happy.

"John, look," Sin calls from the seat in front of us. She points to the immense stretch of beach and water playing out below us as the bus clears the hill and begins its trek down to the other side of the island. I love her for those two simple words.

Once we're at the beach, John watches warily as Kat and Lindsey reach behind themselves and unfasten their bikinis. As their tops are flung off, his eyes dart to my face, his eyes a little big. I try not to laugh at his stunned expression. I decide to leave my top on today to ease his discomfort. It seems the least I can do.

Kat and Lindsey commence public breast rubbing with sunscreen, and like a chameleon, John's pasty face turns deep crimson.

"Are they going to be like this all day?" he asks, leaning over to me and whispering.

"Like what?"

He scoffs. "You know what I'm talking about."

"Probably. Look around you, John. Most of the women here are topless."

"But I *know* them," he says before he flops back on his towel, his face turned firmly away from Kat and Lindsey.

John stays supine for no more than fifteen minutes before he trots off to the bar for iced teas. When he returns, he applies and reapplies sunscreen, then asks if anyone needs anything else to eat or drink. Kat requests a Diet Coke, and I ask for a piece of fruit. I watch him as he walks across the sand again, his white legs stepping through the labyrinth of bodies with determination. Normally, I would love him waiting on me like this, but it irks me now. I realize that he has no relaxation skills. They seemed to have trickled out of his head and body as he worked harder and harder, climbing more furiously up the partnership ladder. He might spend two hours on Sunday morning reading the paper, and he'll have beers with his buddies once every week or so, but that's it. He just can't seem to take it easy anymore.

When he comes back the second time, John sits, his body turned purposefully away from Kat and Sin, and begins brushing each speck of sand off his sandals with fastidious flicks of his hands.

"Want to take a walk?" I ask. Although I probably should be forcing him to keep his body still for half a second, I can tell by his shifting eyes and pursing mouth that he's antsy to the point of bursting. When you've been with someone day and night for two years, it's nearly impossible to hide a mood, and I'm creating an activity for him the same way you would a toddler.

John jumps at the opportunity, practically leaping from his towel.

We stroll at the water's edge so that our feet get splashed by a wave every few seconds. I don't attempt to fill the conversational void between us with tidbits or ramblings as I normally would. Perhaps sensing something, John stops and pulls me into a crushing hug.

"I love you," he says, for what must be the fiftieth time in two days.

I nod, smiling slightly. "Me, too." That much I know for sure.

He stands, squinting through the sun and into my eyes. "But..." he says, as if providing me the opportunity to disclose something unsaid. He hasn't been this perceptive lately, yet there are too many things unsaid already. I wouldn't know where to start.

"But what?" Lame, I know, yet nothing else comes to mind, and for once, I want John to do the work.

"Look," he says finally. "I'm not an idiot. I know something's wrong."

I pause. "It's not that anything's wrong exactly," I say at last. I'm terrified of this conversation and yet excited that we might have a meaningful exchange. "It's just that things are different now."

"Like what?" he asks, his brow furrowed. "What's different?"

"Lots of things." I pause again, wondering how to begin. How to tell him that I'm a different person than I was when I left Chicago a few weeks ago. "For one thing, I'm close with Kat and Lindsey again, and I won't give that up."

"I wouldn't want you to." He loosens his grip from around my waist, taking a slight step back as if affronted.

"I know you wouldn't." To his credit, John has never once tried to keep me away from my friends. I did that all by myself.

John nods and rubs my forearm a little. "Is that it?"

"No. For another thing, my parents are divorcing, and I don't know yet how that'll affect me, but I'll need you to support me."

"Of course." Then a startled expression crosses his face. "Wait a minute. When did you find this out?"

"Last week. I called home and my mom told me."

"God, I'm so sorry, babe." He gives me another hug.

"Thanks," I say, loving the comfort. I snivel a little. "My dad's not even living at home anymore. I tried to call him at work, but he wasn't there. I think he might be having an affair."

John leans back, his eyes wide, his mouth open a little. "No. Don't even think it, not until you know for sure." He runs a hand through my hair, cupping my face.

I plunge on, thrilled by his response. "I knew there were problems, you know, but to actually split? It doesn't seem real. Everything's changing and...I'm scared."

"Of course you are. Of course." He pats my back, and I

let a few tears sneak out. It's so good to be standing with him like this.

I suddenly know for certain that I want to give it a shot with him, and in order to do that I have to be honest. I have to put Princess Denial in the dungeon.

"I have to tell you something else," I say, turning my head to the side, resting it on his chest so I don't have to look him in the face. Instead, I see the sapphire water and a few Jet Skiers, a calm seascape compared to the warring emotions in my head.

"What is it?"

"I—I..." I stutter to a stop. How do you tell someone something like this? "I was with someone else."

"What?" He shoves me away from him, anger making his face spot with red.

I stumble back a foot or two, holding up a hand as if I can stop the progression of his thoughts. "Listen to me. I didn't sleep with anyone."

"What does *that* mean?"

I move with cautious footsteps closer to him, giving him an abbreviated version of my night with Francesco, keeping the specifics and the details out of it. But John keeps backing away from me, shaking his head and running his hands through his hair.

"And that was it?" he says, his eyes moving all over, from me to the water to the sand and back again. "Just that one night?"

"Yes. I saw him the next day, but we didn't do anything." I think about Francesco kissing me outside the hotel when he dropped me off for the last time. "Not really."

"And then *that* was it, though, right?"

"Well..."

"Well, what?" He cuts me off.

"I kissed someone in Ios, too." It sounds so horrible to my

own ears, so freakishly, soap-opera-y horrible. "It was a peck. Nothing else. And that's it, I swear."

"Jesus, Casey, I can't fucking believe you." For a moment I think he's going to cry—something I've never seen him do. His pale green eyes well up.

"I know. I'm sorry I hurt you." I try to touch him, but he yanks away, batting at his eyes with the back of his hand.

Then he goes still, his eyes narrowing, and I know he's picked up on something, those attack-dog lawyer skills homing in on some off-kilter detail. I review my words. There's nothing, I think, nothing. Because I've finally been honest.

"You're sorry you hurt me?" he says, repeating my words.

"Yes, of course."

He nods, as if he gets it now. "But you're not sorry it happened, are you?"

I stand mute. I can't lie to him. Not now.

"I'm right, aren't I? You're not sorry it happened," he says, still nodding.

"Only because it…I don't know." I rub a hand over my eyes. "Because it made me feel like I used to, but I am so, so, so sorry. I want to make it up to you. I want us to try to make things better between us."

"I *am* trying, Casey. I flew here to be with you. I'm trying to make sense of this new you." He spits out the last two words. "I'm trying to talk to you. I'm trying…" He trails off, his last words lingering in the air.

I glance down at my bare feet, unable to find any words that will comfort him. When I look up, his eyes are raw, his lips and jaw making small tense movements.

After another painful, quiet moment, he turns and stalks away.

"What happened?" Kat says when I make my way back to the towels a few minutes later. "John just grabbed his stuff and left."

She and Sin are sitting up, their faces worried. They've even put their tops on.

"It's such a mess," I say, drooping onto the sand, rubbing at my forehead. "Why did he have to come here? It's forcing everything to a head, and I didn't want to deal with this yet." My voice comes out like a wail.

"What do you mean, forcing it?" Sin says. She and Kat draw closer.

"I told him. I had to."

"About Francesco?" Kat says.

I nod, rubbing harder at my head, as if I can erase the scene.

"And Billy?"

I nod again.

"Shit," I hear Sin say. "How'd he take it?"

"Obviously not well!" My voice rises, and Sin reaches forward, patting me on the back. "I think I really hurt him, you guys. It killed me."

"What are you going to do?" Kat asks.

"I have to find him."

John isn't waiting in the room as I expected. I set off, walking the village streets in my bathing suit and sarong, my flip-flops making slapping sounds with each step. The place is quiet, since most people are at the beach, which makes my search a little easier, but I don't see him anywhere. I look in each taverna, expecting to find him getting quietly blotto. I look in the stores, in the cafés. I even stop people who look like they might speak English, asking them if they've seen a nice pale boy with light brown hair and washed-out green eyes. No one gives me any clues.

Finally, after wandering for hours like a lost mutt, I decide to take one more look at the bars by the pier. If he's not there, I'll wait in the room. He has to come back for his clothes eventually. He'll never leave without his best blue pants.

As I turn the corner onto the street that leads to the docks,

I see him, head down, walking quickly. After a few seconds, he raises his eyes and spots me. I search his face for some hint as to his mood, his thoughts, but he gives nothing away. When he reaches me, he wordlessly takes my hand, leading me to the pier where we'd talked last night. We sit side by side again, legs dangling over the water. John raises a hand and brushes a lock of hair from my eyes. He opens his mouth as if to say something, and then, as if thinking better of it, closes it with a short shake of his head.

He turns his whole body to face me, fumbling in his pocket. He pulls something out, but it's hidden in his hands. He brushes it lightly like he's dusting it off, and I see that it's a small, blue velvet box.

He opens it. At the same time, he opens his mouth and says simply, "Marry me."

27

My mouth now hangs open, but I'm mute with shock. I can't take my eyes off the brilliant square diamond resting elegantly on a thin wisp of platinum. Inside my head, pieces jangle loose and bat themselves around. My first coherent thought is that I'm ridiculously flattered. John wants to *marry* me?

John and I had spoken only briefly about marriage, and then only in the most general sense. He'd said that he wanted to be married eventually, but not yet, and I'd agreed, telling him that it wasn't one of my main goals to wear the white, at least not until I'd established myself and proven that I could be completely independent. We never specifically included each other in that general talk. But now here he is, his face brimming with hope.

"John," I say finally, wrenching myself back to the present, to the image of him offering up this olive branch in the form of a diamond on a bed of blue. "We have problems. I don't know if this is the solution."

The expectation in his eyes flickers and dims, but he pulls

himself up straighter. "I'll do anything for you. Anything. I'll talk to you whenever you want. I'll support you through your parents' divorce. I want you to have all the time you need with your friends. I'll go to counseling if you think we need that."

"I don't know——" I start to say, but he puts a finger to my lips, and pulls at my arms, turning me, until we're both cross-legged, facing each other. It dawns on me that during the few times I did consider marriage, this is not how I thought I'd get engaged—sweating under the sun, wearing no makeup and sitting like kids at camp.

"I love you more than anything in the world," John says, and he grips one of my hands tightly. "I've only truly realized that since you left. I'll do whatever it takes to make you happy. I want you to be my wife."

The words *my wife* send a shock through me. They sound possessive rather than comforting. Yet maybe this is the break-through I've been waiting for with him. Perhaps now his passion will fill in around his professional drive. Perhaps this commitment would mean warm, knowing looks and long talks late into the night. Maybe this *was* the solution. Maybe it did signal John's ability to change.

"Try it," he says, holding out the open blue box. He has a small smile on his face like a kid who knows he's about to get that birthday present he's waited for all year.

I pull the ring from its velvety perch, and it sparkles in the sun, reminding me of the way the sea glittered when I first saw it from the bus. I place it on the ring finger of my left hand. It fits perfectly. I hold it out, angling it this way and that, vaguely aware of John's growing smile as he watches me. But suddenly I feel a constriction, as if the ring is growing tighter, and there's a tightness in my chest as well.

I see myself then, in years to come, still unsatisfied, bitch-ing and complaining to the friends I have left or to some strangers in an identity-free support group for co-depen-dents, whatever that means. I see that John is willing to give me everything—everything he can muster. The counseling, the time with friends, the talks. Yet John's everything will never satisfy me. He is not *the one* that Jenny was talking about. I see that clearly now, where I'd only caught glimpses of it before.

I tug the ring off my hand and push it back into the box. "I can't, John. It's not right."

I'm struck by the fact that this gesture might have done the trick only a short time ago. It could have been enough. But after the last few weeks, I find myself unable to settle. What's the old adage? You don't marry who's right for you, you marry who's right for you at the time. Well, I want the person who's really right for me, even if I have to wait forever.

"Casey, please," John says, the smile plummeting off his face, his eyes pained again.

I despise myself for causing that look, that pain, but I can't do anything different.

"Please," he says again. "I'll do whatever you need."

"I know you will, but..." I pause for a moment, searching for the proper words. Turning my head, I see a cruise ship leaving its mooring. "We're not meant for each other," I say at last. "I'm not the one for you."

"Bullshit," he says. "You're the only one for me."

"John, what about everything I said to you? I just told you that I was unfaithful."

A spark of anger briefly interrupts the anguish in his face. "I'm willing to get past it."

I'm not, I respond silently.

My eyes cloud with tears. How did it come to this? I wonder. How can I hurt him like this?

"Don't do this, Casey," he says. "Don't do this. Just give it time."

"Time won't help." Then finally I say it. "It's over."

"No, no," he says, talking over my words. "We'll go to

counseling. I won't bring up marriage again. I'll give you all the time you want."

The urge to accept this time is so strong. It would salve his hurt, which shines from his eyes, but I see with clarity that procrastination would only be prolonging the inevitable.

"I'm so sorry." I pull him to me. His weight sags against my chest. He doesn't return the embrace.

I watch helplessly as John packs T-shirts, a bathing suit and his white button-down in the stiff tan suitcase. Normally, he's a meticulous packer, making small, wrinkle-free rolls of his T-shirts, separating his underwear from his toiletries. But now he throws in a pair of shorts with a haphazard arm, dumping running shoes and a can of shaving cream on top of that.

I panic momentarily, wanting to tell him to take the ring out and ask me again, but I can't get my mouth open to say the words. I try to convince myself that leaving John will be something like graduating from college. I'd loved University of Michigan, but I'd outgrown it. As painful as it was to leave Ann Arbor, I knew it was time to move on. Logically, this analogy works, but it trivializes John, comparing him to a campus where I was personally responsible for increasing the sale of Budweiser.

"Can I help?" I ask as he stomps around the room, gathering his travel alarm clock off the nightstand, snatching a shirt from the chair.

He throws me a stony glance, but his look softens after a second, and he shakes his head. I wish I could do something to alter that wounded expression, but it's time to face the music instead of ignoring the steady beat that's been thumping in the background like a neighbor's bass.

"Why don't you just stay the night?" I ask.

"I can't stay now. You don't want me, and I have to go."

"That's not true." And it isn't. Because when John left, it would be official. Over.

"The boat to Athens leaves at ten tonight. I'll just wait at the dock," he says.

"It's only seven o'clock. Let's get something to eat first." It's all unraveling too rapidly. I've been on this lazy vacation, growing accustomed to island time, and now John is here, and within twenty-four hours a two-year relationship has crumbled.

"I can't," John says, zipping the suitcase. "I have to go."

"I'll walk you to the dock." I move closer to him, desperate for a little more time.

"No..." He starts to say something else, but my shrill voice drowns out his words.

"I'm coming with you to the dock!" I say, snatching his bag off the bed and carrying it to the door, as if by doing this I can lessen his emotional load, as well.

John sighs and follows me.

The pier for the Athens liner is deserted. No noisy backpackers to divert our attention, no innkeepers hawking their establishments. It's eerily quiet, but for the water slapping against the dock. A well of emotions rushes up inside me— fear of being alone, guilt for causing his pain, relief that there has been some conclusion, some decision. Most of all, I feel sadness at the loss of him because even though it's the correct decision, he'll leave a definite gap in my life.

"I'll wait with you," I tell John, gazing out at the water, clutching the handle of his bag to stop my hands from trembling.

"No." He grabs his suitcase and drops it with a thud. "Just go."

"I'll wait," I say, as if I hadn't heard him.

"Casey. Leave," he says in a harsh tone.

I flinch, then slowly I touch his arm, his elbow and finally his shoulder, until he turns toward me. When his head finally follows and he looks at me, his eyes are brimming with tears.

"I wish you understood," he says.

"I do." I pull him to me. "It's just—"

"Don't explain any more." He leans his forehead against mine. "I can't take it."

At the sound of the tired resignation in his voice, my own tears rush out again. All I can do is hold him as tightly as possible. Seconds go by, then minutes.

At last, John pulls back, wiping at the tears with one swipe of his hand. "I'll be okay, Case. Don't worry about me."

"I'll call you when I get home. We'll go to lunch, or dinner, or—"

"You'd better go now," he interrupts, but he says this softly. When I hesitate, he whispers, "Please."

"You're sure?" I ask, wondering what else I can do to help him, help me. I feel completely out of control. This is it. This is it.

John nods, squeezing my hand.

"Okay," I say.

I stand for one last moment gazing at the person who'd been a family member, a friend and a lover for most of my short adult life. And now he would be none of those things. Just like that.

28

I walk aimlessly for an hour or so, the sharp whites and blues of the town taking on a warm orange glow as the sun sets west of the village. I'm not really sure where I'm going or what I'm going to do. I just know that I'm afraid to slow down.

It's over, I keep telling myself. It's done. I no longer have a boyfriend, a significant other, a lover. John is no longer a part of my life. I'm stunned by the speed of the events. I can't stop seeing his face, the tears spilling from his eyes.

At some point I concede defeat to the blisters forming on my feet, and find my way back to the Carbonaki. By the time I get there, Kat and Sin are getting ready to go out for the night, music blaring from my CD player.

"What happened to you?" Sin asks, looking alarmed at my tear-stained face and puffy red eyes. She crosses the room and turns off the music.

I slump on my bed and lie back. "I broke up with John."

"Whoa!" I hear Kat say. "What happened?"

I sit up again and look at them. "He proposed first, and then we broke up."

"Jesus," Sin says.

Kat sinks on the bed across from me. "You've got to be kidding."

I shake my head. "He had this beautiful ring. I don't know if he brought it with him or bought it here, but he said he wanted to get married, and he promised he would change. He looked so hopeful, holding out this box." I stop for a breath.

"What did you do? What did you say?" Kat asks.

"I actually thought about it. I thought maybe things could change, maybe I could be happy with John for the rest of my life. Then I realized I wasn't in love with him the way you should be when you get engaged."

"Did you tell him that?" Sin says.

"I just told him we weren't right together, and nothing was going to change that."

"How did he take it?"

"He's crushed, and I'm crushed that I did it to him."

"So where is he?" Kat looks around, as if John might walk in the door at any minute.

"He's down at the dock waiting for the boat to Athens. He won't stay the night, and he won't let me wait with him."

"Wow." Sin shakes her head, gazing at me as if she can't tear her eyes away. "How do you feel?"

"Terrible," I say. "Terrible that I had to make him so sad, and terrible because I'm going to miss him so much. But..." I flop back on the bed again, my mind reeling.

"But what?" Kat says.

"It's just that I knew it had to happen. I knew it was right to break up."

"Well, that's the most important thing," Kat says. "You have to be sure."

"I'm sure, but if you could have seen his face—" I start crying again. "It just killed me."

They fuss over me, and I give them the *War and Peace* version of John's proposal. We discuss the issue from every possible angle and the conclusion is always the same: You did the right thing.

"So, girlfriend," Sin says after the thirtieth rehashing. "What do you want to do tonight? What will make you feel better?" She tousles my hair.

"I can't go to the bars. I'm not in the mood."

"Well, then how about I get a bottle of wine, and we'll sit by the pool?" Kat says.

"That sounds perfect, but I have to make a call first."

It's the crack of dawn in Chicago, yet my father answers the phone with a chipper, "Rich Evers!"

"Dad," I say. "It's me, Casey."

"Casey, honey. Are you still in Europe? Is anything wrong?"

"Nothing's wrong," I say, arranging myself on a hard wooden chair in the lobby of the Carbonaki. "I'm sorry to bother you."

"You're not bothering me, sweetie," he says, and then adds, after a moment, "I was worried when I got your message."

"Are you having an affair?" I blurt out. I just have to know. A young couple that is passing by me looks alarmed as I say this, and they stick to the other side of the hall.

"An affair?" he says, sounding amused. "Of course not. Who would I have an affair with?"

"Little Miss What's-Her-Bucket. Your assistant."

"Ms. Hamlin?" He sounds entertained at the thought. "No, Casey. I'm not having an affair. Not with Ms. Hamlin or anyone else."

"Then why are you and Mom getting a divorce?"

I hear him exhale loudly, as if buying himself some time to compose an answer. "Your mother and I haven't had much of a relationship for years. Nothing could make it better, and I decided that life is too short to live like that."

"A bit selfish, isn't it?" I ask, thinking of my mother by herself in the big rambling house.

"Well, yes. I suppose it is selfish, but Casey, I don't know that you can understand what it's like to be in your fifties and realize that the majority of your life has passed you by, and you barely noticed it."

"What are you talking about? You have a great job, great family, lots of friends."

"Yes." He paused. "But there are so many other things I wanted for my life, too."

"Like what?" I ask, surprised by his words. He's always seemed like the content suburban family man. Or perhaps I never really looked past that.

"Well, did you know that I wanted to be a musician?"

"I know you played guitar in college." In my mind, I see a black-and-white photo of my dad at a university party, guitar in hand, a group of coeds in front of him.

"I did play back then, and I always wanted to be in a real band and to write music. Then I got the job at the bank, and I married your mother, and we had kids. I kept thinking I would get back to it, that I would pick it up again, but the years flew by, and I never seemed to have the time."

"I didn't know you were so unhappy," I say, the bitterness creeping back into my voice.

"Not unhappy. Just maybe unfulfilled." He exhales loudly again. "Listen, I know you're not asking for any words of wisdom from your old man, but if I could give you any advice it would be this—make all your minutes count, every last one of them. And start now because, honey, while the possibilities may seem endless, the time sure isn't."

"Geez, Dad, I didn't know you were such a poet," I joke, unaccustomed to his tone. He doesn't respond. "Guess what?" I say then, feeling the urge to confide. "There's another breakup to report."

"What do you mean?"

"I broke up with John tonight."

"Tonight? I thought you were on that trip with your girl-friends."

I explain about John's arrival, as well as his subsequent proposal and departure.

"So," I say, when I've finished the tale, "maybe we could start hitting the bars on Rush Street together."

My father laughs, sounding relieved to hear my attempt at humor, but it stops abruptly. "Are you all right, hon?"

"I'm going to be fine. It had to happen."

"Yes," my father says. "I know what you mean."

The hall phone starts to make clicking noises and a Greek woman's voice comes on, telling me, I assume, to deposit more money.

"I gotta go, Dad," I say.

"Okay, sweetie. Call me when you get home. And Casey, please know that I will always take care of your mother."

"I know you will."

"And you make sure you take care of you." He sounds a little choked up, but it could be the connection.

Kat, Lindsey and I sit at the edge of the hotel's pool, drinking wine out of the bottle.

"My dad says he's not having an affair," I tell them.

"Do you believe him?" Sin says.

I think about this for a moment. "I do. I think I was looking for a reason for their split, something concrete and obvious, but it turns out it's not that simple."

"What do you mean?" Kat takes a sip of the red wine, her chestnut hair falling over her shoulders as she does so. "If it's not an affair, then why?"

"He said they haven't had a good relationship for a long

time, which is true. He didn't see it getting any better, and wants more out of life than that."

"Sort of like you and John," Kat says.

Her words startle me. I'm not like my parents. Yet she's right. I want more from a relationship than I could ever get from John.

We spend the rest of the night talking, talking and talking, about everything and nothing. We decide to leave for Athens the next morning and spend our last few days there, seeing the Acropolis and the rest of the sights.

Later, despite the infusion of wine, I'm unable to sleep. My mind whirs over the last few weeks and spins on to those upcoming. Soon I'll be practicing law, living a nine-to-five existence, like you're suppose to when you grow up. It's not the hours that bother me, though. It's the drudgery of the law. A science of semantics, of crossing t's and dotting i's, built one case on top of another. But maybe it will be more than that, I tell myself. Surely it will be more exciting, more fulfilling.

I want to sleep, but I keep hearing the note of regret in my father's voice as he described hopes lost. *Don't let that happen to me,* I pray to whatever God might be tuning in, *please don't let that happen to me.*

29

Sin shakes me awake. "The boat leaves in two hours, Case.
Let's go so we can get tickets and a good seat."

I struggle to sit up, groggy from the few hours of sleep I
was able to muster. I finish packing, but when I'm done I realize that I've left a book and my black dress in the room John
and I stayed in. I let myself in with quiet, cautious footsteps,
as if something of John might have lingered there. The room
is barren, the air stuffy with the windows closed. I collect my
dress and book, and I stand staring at the bed, feeling the
smoothness of John's skin as he held me the last night. I'll
never feel that again—at least not with John.

"Case!" I hear Kat calling from down the hall. "Let's go!"

I move to the doorway, but I can't seem to get any farther
than that, nor can I tear my eyes away from the bed, seeing
John and me in sweet embraces over the years.

"Casey!" I hear again. "We have to go." I finally turn, and
slowly I shut the door.

* * *

"You okay?" Kat and Lindsey keep asking me as we walk to the dock, joining a parade of other travelers lugging suitcases and backpacks.

"Just thinking," I tell them, but I stay silent.

I feel like a prisoner being led to execution. Sure, Athens will be fun, but it's merely the beginning of the end. The end of this vacation, the end of my life as I know it. My future looms bleak. I glance down at my cotton shorts and fitted T-shirt, a vacation uniform of sorts, soon to be replaced with navy suits, pearls and tasteful pumps.

You're just scared to work for a living, I try to convince myself. *Everything will be fine.*

But I know that I'm lying to myself, as I've done so often before. I'm not afraid of working for a living. I'm terrified of working as a lawyer, because I have no passion for it. There will be nothing to get me up in the morning except the promise of a paycheck and the threat of the unemployment line.

We stop at a travel agency to purchase ferry tickets.

"Three to Athens, please," Lindsey tells the attractive young woman behind the counter.

"Certainly," she says.

I watch her turn and move to a table behind her, picking up three blue ferry vouchers. She writes the time of departure and the price on the first one, the second one. And just as she's about to start with the third, I say loudly, "No. Just two tickets."

"What are you doing?" Sin says, sounding irritated. "We've got to get to the boat and save seats."

"I'm not going to Athens," I say, sounding more sure than I feel.

"*What* are you talking about?" Kat asks, plopping her backpack on the linoleum floor.

"Excuse me," I say to the woman behind the counter. "We'll be one minute."

I pull Kat and Sin to the front corner of the store. "Look, I'm going to stay here or maybe go to another island for a while. I don't know. I just need to figure out what I'm going to do with myself."

"What you're going to do with yourself?" Sin says. "You're going to Athens with us and then home to start your job."

"That's just it. I'm not going to practice law. At least not right now."

"Are you crazy?" Sin says, her eyes wide.

Kat gives me a conspiratorial grin. "What do you have up your sleeve?"

"Absolutely nothing." I tell the truth. "I just know I don't want to be a lawyer."

"You could've thought of that three years ago, before you started law school," Sin says.

Remembering my dad's words, I tell her, "Better late than never."

Epilogue

I'm sitting on my balcony at the Astras Villas in Santorini. I'd considered staying at the youth hostel in the island's main village of Fira, but I opted instead for this secluded spot at one of the highest points on the island. It's more expensive, but my credit cards aren't maxed out yet.

I know I'm an idiot for spending this kind of money, which comes with an eighteen-point-five-percent interest rate, but it can't overshadow the absolute giddiness I feel when I look around my room. It's sparse but cleanly furnished with a double bed, a tiny refrigerator like I had in the college dorm, and a pine dressing table with a red brocade stool. The room is always filled with light from the French doors that open to this balcony. Below my porch a kidney-shaped pool sits surrounded by lime-green tiles, and much farther below that is the Aegean Sea. Only the occasional cruise ship and a tall, jagged chunk of rock, a remnant of a long-ago volcano, interrupt my view. Fuck the credit cards.

I cut a slice of the cheese I bought today in Fira, lifting my legs up onto the empty chair opposite me. The sun is only beginning to start its descent. I take another sip of crisp white wine, remembering my friends' reaction to my announcement that I wasn't returning to the U.S. just yet, nor did I plan to begin my job at Billings Sherman & Lott. Kat was thrilled, telling me she'd join me if she didn't like her job at the hospital so much. Lindsey was characteristically leery at first, interrogating me until she realized that I was set in my decision. I wasn't. I was terrified, but I held my ground. For once in my life I was going against the path that seemed the logical, proper route, and instead following what my gut told me was the right road.

Sin had finally broken into a cautious but warm smile and hugged me close. "Be careful," she said, "and get your ass home so you can tell us all the details."

"I love you guys," I'd said more than once as they prepared to board the Athens ferry. I'd promised never to let anyone or anything come between our friendship again. They waved frantically from the top tier of the ferry, like two passengers on the *Love Boat*.

Gordy Brickton had not taken my news nearly as well as they did. "This is akin to professional suicide," he'd said when I called, his voice rising. "You will never work at Billings Sherman & Lott, and after this gets out, you may never get a job in the Chicago legal community."

The Miss-Can't-Be-Wrong in my head jumped up and down, yelling, *"Tell him you'll be starting in a week. Don't throw this away!"* If Gordy was accurate, the law wouldn't be something to fall back on. There'd be no safety net at all. The new me gave a sharp jab, though, and said, *"Stick to your guns, girl."* I remembered the words of Nicky, the Aussie girl I'd met in Ios, telling me that travel and time alone wasn't about escape but about the learning curve, finding out what you're made of, finding yourself. That's how I intend to use this time.

So I'd taken a deep breath and spoken into the phone as calmly as possible, telling Gordy, "I'll cross that bridge when, and if, I decide I want to go there. Thank you for everything, Gordy." And I hung up. Just like that.

Surprisingly, my parents were both calm, my dad elated even, each telling me to take all the time I needed to straighten my head out (my mother's words). My mom even told me that she's started reconnecting with her own friends lately, that she'd forgotten how wonderful friends could be. It's a lesson we both had to learn, I guess.

There are times that I can convince myself that I'm like Julia Roberts at the end of *Pretty Woman,* when she has her shit together and is off to a better life. Then reality hits three minutes later, along with the reminder that I have no money, no job and I am a total lunatic. This lunacy is freedom, though, the first I've ever had. I know that I'm as messed up as I always was. It's just that I feel better about it all.

As for what I'll do, I haven't yet decided. I might stay on this gracious island for a while, possibly tend bar. I've always thought female bartenders were a higher echelon of cool, with the notable exception of the French bar wench from Ios. When I return home, I'll have to do something to support myself. I might start taking interior design classes, my profession of choice a long time ago, before I'd forgotten my passion for it, before I'd convinced myself that lawyering would be more profitable, more secure.

I will certainly have to face the music, or should I say cacophony, of my parents' rift. I can't imagine what it will be like to have them living in two different places and to have to take care of them, when I'm not so well off myself. It feels like a hand closing over my heart to think that something once so stable is now disintegrating, the same way John had been a stable and integral part of my life until Francesco and

Billy had inadvertently shown me passion, and I'd faced up to the doubts that had haunted me. Nothing will ever be the same, but at least I've had a semblance of a normal family life for twenty-six years. And I have a collection of friends who round out my family and whom I will never let out of my grasp again.

Fear puts me to bed and wakes me up in the morning, but in between I smile a lot. I am alone, jobless and without a man. Yet I have myself, or at least more of myself than I've ever had before. I have found a piece of home within my own skin.

The only plan I have set in stone at this very moment is to enjoy this wine and cheese and this sunset beginning to burn a rust-red. I might spend the night by myself sitting on the terrace or writing in my journal. I might go into Fira to the Orinos Café along the water to visit the waiter I met today while shopping for wine. Or I might not.

That's one well-dressed lineup....

Pick one up at your local bookseller!

Check out reddressink.com for
interviews, excerpts and more....

Now on sale from Red Dress Ink...

Loose Screws

Karen Templeton

Think *you've* had a rough week?
Meet Ginger Petrocelli. Left at the altar,
evicted from her apartment and freshly
unemployed now that her boss's embezzlement
is part of legal record, this thirty-year-old has a
few things to work out this summer. Like figure
out who she is, and more important, who she
wants to be. Fortunately for her, she has
a lot of time on her hands now....

RED DRESS INK
™

RDI0902R-TR

Strapless

Leigh Riker

Australia or Bust!

Darcie Baxter is given a once-in-a-lifetime chance to open a new lingerie shop in Sydney. So she packs up and moves to Australia, leaving New York City, her grandmother and her possessed cat behind. A whirlwind affair with an Australian sheep rancher sends her into panic mode, fleeing Australia with a bad case of the noncommittals. Who wants to be barefoot and pregnant in the Outback? But don't worry— she won't get away that easily!